BODY
and
SOUL

BODY
and
SOUL

JADE
WILLIAMS

Kensington Publishing Corp.
http://www.kensingtonbooks.com

DAFINA BOOKS are published by

Kensington Publishing Corp.
119 West 40th Street
New York, NY 10018

All Kensington Titles, Imprints, and Distributed Lines are available at special quantity discounts for bulk purchases for sales promotions, premiums, fund-raising, and educational or institutional use. Special book excerpts or customized printings can also be created to fit specific needs. For details, write or phone the office of the Kensington special sales manager: Kensington Publishing Corp., 119 West 40th Street, New York, NY 10018, attn: Special Sales Department, Phone: 1-800-221-2647.

Dafina and the Dafina logo Reg. U.S. Pat. & TM Off.

ISBN-13: 978-0-7582-1454-6
ISBN-10: 0-7582-1454-5
First Kensington Trade Paperback Edition: August 2006
First Kensington Mass Market Edition: September 2016

10 9 8 7 6 5 4 3 2 1

Printed in the United States of America

Chapter One

"Don't worry about avoiding temptation—at your age it will avoid you!" That was my sister Nicola's idea of a humorous birthday card. Laugh? I could have slit her wrists. Nicola's degree wasn't in Tact and Sensitivity. The truth is you know you're getting older when people send you those would-be-funny cards because they're too embarrassed to address the real issues: your advancing years and retreating sex appeal.

I looked at my face this morning. I mean I *really* looked at it for the first time in a year. My special thirtieth birthday gift to myself. Usually I can avoid it if I just concentrate on one feature at a time rather than looking at the whole picture. Unless I'm putting on makeup, that is. And I do that increasingly rarely these days. That way, I get an extra ten minutes in bed, and sleep is so much more important than anything else I can think of. I can't believe I just said that. Just goes to show how seriously sad my life is. Anyway, my birthday's like an annual pilgrimage. I journey to that unexplored region that is my body and I check that every element is where it belongs and is still recognizable for what it is. I was actually quite relieved that it didn't look used up. That's probably because it doesn't get put to a lot of use.

I've been thinking about sex a lot today. Don't get me wrong—I'm not addicted and I'm not sex-starved and, once or twice, I've come *this* close to having an orgasm in the last few months. The main problem is that visiting Blockbuster is the closest I'm likely to get to Samuel L. Jackson.

I've been getting what I think may be hot flushes. You might laugh, but it must be early menopause or watching *formula 51* too often on video, or else I've been getting myself into really embarrassing situations. You know me so you can guess what the diagnosis is.

If it's the menopause, then I ain't going for any of that HRT shit. I hear that it can make hair grow on your face, and that's the last thing I need if I'm going to get any action. What I need is hair on my head. Plenty of it. Long, silky, possibly blond. Just the way guys like it. How come these hormones can make hair grow on your chin and they don't do a thing for your head? If all the hair that I've plucked from my eyebrows, shaved from my bikini line, and waxed from my legs could all be joined together and stuck onto my scalp, then I'd have long, run-your-fingers-through-able locks.

Well, anyway, when I did look in the mirror, I was filled with horror. What if I'd somehow managed to get a date with Samuel L.? There it was on my chin: one thick, slightly curly, black hair. More the texture of pubic hair than head hair. I wonder why that is.

I suppose I'm relieved that it was on my chin rather

than growing out of my ear, or worse, my nose, but Samuel L. isn't likely to want to make love to me if I've got more hair on my chin than he has. You probably think I'm obsessed with my appearance (and Samuel L. Jackson), but I'm not. I'm just scared of frightening babies—and not ever having sex again!

My mother is nearly sixty and she doesn't have a single wrinkle on her face. Apart from laughter lines around her eyes, which don't count, her skin is soft and smooth and nutmeg brown and warm and freckled. I've seen photos of her in her teens, and if she'd thought of it, she could easily have been a model. Even now I can't swear that she wouldn't give Iman or Naomi a run for their money. I'd think she was stunning even if she wasn't my mother. You can see the way men still look at her, even the young guys. She has put on more than a few pounds over the years, which only makes her seem softer and, if you can say it about your own mother, more voluptuous. I'm sure Mom could get some anytime she wanted—but let's not go there!

Both Mom and her sister, my Aunt Bea, got the "good" hair in the family—long, silky, straightish. Mom wears it in a soft bun at the nape of her neck. When I was a child, it was a real treat when she let me comb it. Nicola and I used to fight over the privilege. Mom's got smooth, silky skin that you just want to touch because it looks so buttery, so warm and inviting. My earliest memory is of wanting to lick her cheeks. She always seems to smell of cinnamon, and her hazel eyes remain warm and affectionate even when she's mad as hell with you and her lips are set in that rigid, unforgiving line. In fact, Mom would be hideously perfect if it weren't for the fact that she nurses her resentment of my dad with passion and tenderness. It shows in those lips, the way she walks, the timbre of her voice. She blames Dad for so much. I only blame him for my hair. And my shape. Okay, my lack of height too.

I'll never be able to compete with Mom, so I'll grow old ungracefully. I'll be one of those ancient women who actually *plays* with her chin hair, caressing it like it's some sacred talisman while she silently mutters an evil incantation. I'm not going to wax my legs either. What's the point when I don't get a chance to wrap them around a man's waist? And as for the bikini line, well, it's a bit like sterile bandages—untouched by human hands.

I took a long bath this morning and noticed a couple of white spots on my chest, each about the size of a pinhead. I know it's vitiligo. I'm going to turn white! Still, that makes me feel a little better: What's the point of worrying about hairs on my face or wrinkles when I'm going to end up looking like Michael Jackson anyway?

My hair needs relaxing too. It's been way more than eight weeks, but I can't face four hours of torture in the hairdresser's chair. Darryl, my stylist, or "creative trichological technician" as he likes to call himself, will be disappointed. I'm a real challenge to him, but I sense that I'll always be a failure in his eyes. I don't steam my hair. I don't condition it. I don't steam condition it. I don't go for treatments. My parents didn't take out a hair-care payment plan when I was born. So when I do occasionally turn up at the salon, Darryl shows his pain by getting one of his assistants to hold up strands from my head as if he's afraid of catching something. He makes a point of doing this while he's treating some fair-skinned, model-type with eighteen-inch tresses that he'll be twisting around those giant pink prickly rollers. I can't help comparing the size of rollers. Like the way men compare dicks. I've never yet got past those small green ones—the rollers, not the dicks! It's as if Darryl takes my negligence as a personal affront. He's not subtle. He's not diplomatic. He knows that he doesn't need to be. We black women are masochists when it comes to hairdressers. We'll always go back, begging for more pain—and paying for it too.

"Carol, what you been doing to your head. Girl, you expect me to do something with that? Franiq'ua, show me the back." Then he'll do his sad, head-shaking, teeth-kissing, hand-on-hip act as if I've committed some major crime.

Your hairdresser, inevitably male, always seems to possess an endless, obedient supply of hair that grows on command. Whatever the latest style, he'll have it: cropped one week, ponytailed the next. Shaved, braided, twisted, locked, permed, gelled, pressed, relaxed, corn-rowed—you name it—he's got the hair to do it.

I've always yearned for long hair like Mom's, and I'm always disappointed that mine doesn't grow. Whenever Darryl wants to even trim half an inch from my head, it takes at least three of them to hold me down. I've been growing this little bit of hair for two years now, so whatever he says next time I go, he'll have to find some way to rescue what's clinging to my head for dear life. That's what I pay him for. If God had wanted me to pamper my hair, why would he have invented Darryl?

Anyway, having looked at my face, I've thoroughly depressed myself and I might as well go to bed.

It's my birthday and nobody cares. Well, Mom and Dad called. And Gabby. And Eddy. And they all sent presents and flowers. But my life is still irretrievably tragic: I'm going to bed alone.

Nicola would say that it's my own fault, but then I'm one of those women who seem to find men that my family love more than they love me. It's been nearly three years since I split with Max, and Mom, Dad, and Nicola still miss him; to them, he was the best thing since Grandma's homemade hot pepper sauce. There's very little that Mom and Dad agree on, but if there was any way they could have kept us together, be it begging, coercion, kidnapping, bribery, corruption, or blackmail, then they'd even have joined forces to achieve that end. Max Gardiner isn't in my life anymore, though I still get little pangs when I occasionally see his name in magazines; the one consolation is that it happens more and more infrequently these days. It's easiest to let everyone think that he walked out on me. It would be too hard to explain what really happened. All right, I admit that it wouldn't be difficult, but I don't think my family would forgive me for not sticking it out to the bitter end. After all, Max could do no wrong, could he?

Chapter Two

I made an appointment to see Darryl. Needless to say, he's fully booked for weeks, but as a special favor I'm being squeezed in late Friday evening. I know what that means: No woman with anything resembling a social life would accept a five-thirty appointment on a Friday since you know you won't be out before nine at the earliest, so I'll be there with all the retirees who have nothing better to do than eavesdrop on the insults that will be heading in my direction, or losers who need to get a life. I'm not a valued customer anymore. Darryl even had the nerve to pass on a message via the receptionist: *Don't expect miracles, Carol.*

I had lunch with Gabby today. She's my best female friend, but that doesn't stop me being more than slightly jealous of her. You'll understand why; if you're a true friend, that is. Gabby was dressed entirely in white. Now, how can you wear white in London? White is not a color for gray, grimy, polluted cities. White is a color for hot countries, more precisely, countries where washerwomen scrub clothes in the river and leave them to bleach on rocks in the sunlight. You can only wear white if you're rich enough to have someone else do the washing for you, or collect your clothes from the dry cleaners. Which Gabby is. Rich enough, I mean.

Her head was wrapped. Gabby is one of those women who wasn't even born in Africa or the Caribbean, and yet they always say, with a sneer in they voice, "How you mean you can't tie a wrap? Is easy!" You ever notice how they never offer to show you? Every time I try to tie a wrap, it either falls off or looks like a crumpled paper bag that got wet in a storm and the wind blew it on top of my head. So I was wearing a hat. And I sure as hell didn't look as good as Gabby in her wrap. She even wears it in that head-high, confident, elegant way that African women do. You beginning to see why I'm jealous?

Yesterday, as I said, I'd been thinking about going to Darryl. Before you go to the hairdresser, though, you have to do something to hide whatever you haven't but should have been doing with your hair. It's like scrubbing your house from top to bottom before a cleaner comes so they don't find out what a slob you are. I also wanted to displace thoughts of Max—I've heard that song about washing men out of your hair—so I got out some of those half-empty bottles of conditioner that have been languishing in the bathroom cupboard for years. When I mixed them together, there was enough for one good session. The instructions said to leave it on for fifteen to twenty minutes, so I thought an hour would be about right. I didn't have a heated cap, so I managed to find a big enough freezer bag once I'd emptied out the curried chicken that Mom had given to me. I did, at least, wash it. Once the bag was safely tied on my head, I microwaved the chicken and ate it with some hard-dough bread. I'd run out of rice. I could have had some salad, but the cucumber had turned to jelly and the lettuce was swimming in a slimy green pool. So before I could eat, I had to clean out the fridge too. You see why I don't bother to take care of my hair too often.

Anyway, by the time I'd eaten about an hour and twenty minutes had passed. I rinsed out the conditioner very thoroughly, since I know that bit's important. I sprayed it with leave-in conditioner, wondering why I'd bothered to rinse out the other conditioner, and searched in my bedroom drawers for the rollers I know I'd bought when my hair was going through another incarnation. I eventually found them, spiky blue ones. I've never understood that thing that hairdressers do where they use the roller to tug the hair from the roots up, over and over before rolling it up with a neat spin. I tried, honestly, and gave up, just doing the logical thing and twisting from the top, then sticking in a few million hairpins to keep the rollers in place. I wrapped a few yards of tape around the whole lot for luck.

I slept pretty fitfully with a rolled-up towel under my neck. I'd started out with a pillow, but it was like sleeping on a live porcupine. At about, oh, four-eighteen and thirty-nine seconds in the morning I took out the rollers at the very back and managed to close my eyes for an hour or so. I woke before the alarm since a couple of the spiky rollers had slipped down the bed and I dreamed I was being attacked by supersonic, mutant hedgehogs.

I had a couple of cups of coffee and a cigarette with my multivitamin and mineral tablets and a coenzyme Q10 for good measure before I was ready to tackle my hair. Difficult as it had been to get the rollers in, it was even harder to get them out, and most came away with a good chunk of hair still attached. Gabby's hair always looks so . . . well-*groomed* that I knew I couldn't let her see me like this. The only solution was to get the hot tongs out. I'd learned, over the years, to use them like an expert, twisting dextrously, knowing how long I dared leave them before they fried my hair. It's been a long time since I used them, though, and I managed to burn the tip of one ear, but I could cover the developing black scar with the remaining hair. I found my dryer and tried to blow-dry my hair into something resembling a style, but I had to give up the fight when the smell of burning hair induced a coughing fit. There was no way I could rescue what I'd done. I'd have to leave it to Darryl, who was, after all, the expert.

So there I was with Gabby in one of those restaurants that have stiff, pink, damask tablecloths and napkins folded to look like origami peacocks. The place smelled of camellias and the waiters seemed to be on rollerblades as they sped across the cavernous room. And I'm wearing a hat. Gabby in a wrap and me in an old hat, feeling inferior, and her with her lying self saying, "Girl, you looking good. For someone who just have she birthday. You lost weight? Your skin looking so clear. Must be inner peace. You been meditating?"

Now Gabby knows full well that I'm not the type to meditate. I've spent good money on all the books, the tapes, the CDs, and every time they tell me to lie down and relax and imagine myself walking along a beach with palm trees swaying in the cool breeze, I just start thinking back to the time I was in Trinidad with Max, or Jamaica with Max, or even Minorca with Max, or Max in Guadeloupe, Max in Bermuda,

Max in London, Max anywhere at all. And you know where that kind of thinking leads. It just leads to trouble. Nowhere else. So these days I don't even try any of that meditation shit.

"What happen to your ear, girl?"

"You looking fine yourself, Gabby. You been shopping? I haven't seen that white outfit before."

"Peter's been feeling guilty. I don't know why yet, but it must be something big. He treated me to a weekend shopping in Paris."

"You and Pete had a weekend in Paris?"

Gabby kissed her teeth. "Don't be silly. Where would Peter find the time to go shopping? No, I had a whole heap of fun. Them shops on the Champs Elysées didn't know what hit them."

I could believe it. I've been shopping with Gabby before. Now, I love spending money as much as the next one, but till you've been flashing the credit cards with Gabby, you don't know what the meaning of indulgence is. It helps when it's not her own money, but the girl don't know when to stop. She isn't just buying for herself either. If she runs out of things she wants for herself, then she moves on to buying for you. I'm not the kind to turn her down, either. If she gets pleasure from spending Pete's money, then who am I to deny her? It would be like taking away an addict's methadone. So I've got a few decent items in my wardrobe, courtesy of an ignorant Pete, one of which I was wearing today: a blue Azagury pantsuit that I trot out for important occasions and meeting Gabby in whatever fancy restaurant she chooses. I don't feel guilty because Pete is one of those guys who deserves to have his money spent.

I suppose you can guess that Pete's white. His

name is actually Peter, but I call him Pete out of spite. My revenge for the way he treats my friend. Actually, Gabby doesn't do too badly. She lives in Bayswater, in an apartment that's palatial by my standards—you couldn't actually call it a "flat" since you could fit the whole of mine in her marble-floored hallway. I usually head for the kitchen since it's the place where I can do the least damage. I don't think I'd have enough apologies to make up for a smashed antique or red wine spilled on the knee-deep, cream carpets. Gabby actually trusted me enough to let me stay one night after we'd been clubbing. Of course, Pete was away. The next morning, as I was leaving, Gabby's neighbor stopped me and asked, ever so politely, if I thought I could spare her a few hours a week. And I was standing there figuring out how much a cleaner can earn in that part of town!

Anyway, I digress. I've seen photos of Gabby and Pete together in the apartment and I don't think I've ever seen anyone who looks less like a "Pete." He's got thick chestnut hair that, I hope, might be receding under a boyish fringe, a Grecian nose, tanned skin, and the only redeeming feature, full lips that suggest a hint of miscegenation somewhere in his family history. In one photograph, I'm not joking, he's actually wearing green boots, a waxed jacket, and is carrying a shotgun. A black guy with a shotgun in south London would be surrounded by a tactical support unit in a flash.

Gabby and I both suspect that Pete has at least one mistress. There's not a lot of evidence, but he's always away (on business), gets home late (from the office), and has his credit card bills sent to work. Besides, it's what rich guys like him do. Why else would he want to spend more time than necessary away from Gabby? And that's why I loathe him.

Gabby's one of those tall, willowy, incredibly beautiful, sexy, model-types. Reminds me a bit of my mother, actually. She's over six feet tall. Statuesque. Guys are always stopping her, saying that they've seen her in some film or in a magazine, and I guess if I didn't know her, I'd think she must be an actress or model too. That's what having wealth does for you. You walk as if you don't give a toss what anyone else might think of you. If you've got lots and lots of money, I guess you don't.

You can see why Pete would want Gabby around. She'd impress anyone and certainly liven up those endless business affairs that they're always going to. She's funny, smart, and confident, and there's a hint of aloofness about her that makes people want to dig deeper. I don't think Gabby even realizes, because under the surface, she's not standoffish at all. In fact, she's warm, interesting, and *interested,* but she gives the impression of being untouchable, as if she's surrounded by an invisible force field. I've seen the field become tougher, more impenetrable the longer I've known her.

"So what's Pete been up to now?"

"He had to 'go away unexpectedly' a few weekends ago. On business. Didn't particularly bother me. I wouldn't even have thought about it twice until he suggested the weekend in Paris. Made me realize he was feeling more than usually guilty about something. Obviously, he's been putting it somewhere he shouldn't. Again. Anyway, I ended up having one hell of a good time—"

The waiter interrupted to take our order and by the

time he brought her vodka and tonic and my white wine, Gabby was ready to confess all.

"Okay, tell me everything. I can see by the look in you eye what you been up to."

She laughed. "It's not what you think. I just took a friend with me to Paris."

"You sure didn't have that good a time with no girlfriend. What friend you talking 'bout?"

"You remember the artist I was telling you about? The one I met at that exhibition in Shoreditch? From Guadeloupe?"

"Yeah, I remember. Beard, locks, eyes, accent, drop-your-panties gorgeous. But I thought you only talked to him for a few minutes. How you end up taking him to Paris?"

"He gave me his card. He's a struggling artist. I was helping with his education; taking him to the Louvre was the least I could do for the cause."

"And how much time you spend in the Louvre? About five minutes? You end up modeling for him?"

"Carol, what you take me for? The boy young enough to be my son. You think I'm a cradle snatcher?"

"I wouldn't put anything past you, Gabby. So, spill. What happened?"

That's the trouble with skinny, beautiful women. They almost have to fight the men off. It's like guys can smell when you're getting some and then they come running. I even noticed how the waiter looked at her in that appreciative way, his tongue almost hanging down to his knees while he barely noticed me. It's been so long since I got any that I ain't smelling of anything more than Chanel. If those men had any intelligence they would find it easier to go after the ones who will be begging for it. Like me. But life's like that. Don't make no sense.

"They say you can't teach an old dog any new tricks," Gabby said, trying to be enigmatic.

"What you been teaching that young boy, then? You been corrupting his morals?"

"As much as I could. And I haven't lost my touch." She made a gesture of blowing on her nails and polishing them on her jacket.

I must have groaned aloud as I rolled my eyes up to the ceiling because Gabby laughed. "When *was* the last time, Carol? You need to take care of business, girl. And here's a little something to help. Your birthday present."

Gabby handed over a small, flat, pink box tied with loads of ribbons and a French name engraved in gold on it. When I opened it, I had to close it again damned quick as I felt a hot flush coming over me. When she'd said "little," she really wasn't exaggerating. She'd got me the teeniest, tiniest, weeniest G-string I ever did see. It was exquisite. A work of art: delicate brown lace with a circle of tiny pearls in the top corners of the V. Gabby took one look at my reddened face and burst into peals of laughter, shattering the hushed sounds of the restaurant. I looked around guiltily to make sure nobody had seen my present.

"Girl, you look like one scared rabbit. You need a real birthday treat!"

Fat chance when just the sight of some skimpy underwear could bring a hot flush to my cheeks. Time was I'd be the one in Ann Summers buying sexy lingerie—for Max's benefit. It really has been too long!

When I got home, I took a serious look at myself. I

need to find me a man. Nothing too serious. Not *lurve*.
Just some good, old-fashioned, down-home sexual healing. I need a plan. First, I'll lose some weight. I only just
managed to squeeze into the Azagury this morning.
And now Gabby is expecting me to fit my ass into that
minute G-string. This is what happens when you're not
getting enough of the right kind of exercise; you put on
a little bit of weight. It wouldn't take much to shift the
few extra pounds around my waist—my doctor might
even prescribe a few hot, steamy sessions with Samuel L.

I inspected the fridge and threw out the pies, bread,
and cakes. I'm going to buy some salady stuff tomorrow. I left the chocolate because, at my age, you don't
want to lose *too* much weight. After waiting so long to
develop the curves I have, I don't intend to get rid of
them too soon. Guys like to have a little something to
hold on to; they ain't going to be staying around a stick
insect they can barely catch hold of. Or that's how I
comfort myself—when I've run out of chocolate.
Maybe I'll join a gym for a couple of months. Or else,
I need a more interesting form of exercise. Thinking
about it, I didn't put on any weight when I was with
Max. . . .

So if I'm going to find a substitute, I might have to
let Darryl have his way with my hair. I can't see myself inviting anyone back to my apartment if I have to
reveal what's under the hat. I'm going to pluck that hair
on my chin too. I examined Gabby over lunch when
she wasn't looking, and she doesn't have a single hair
on her face and look where that's got her. She doesn't
have any lines either, or the tiniest hint of a pimple.
She had a Caesar salad for lunch while I dug into pep-

pered steak with French fries and caramelized carrots and I only had a dessert because Pete's credit card was paying and I don't often get to eat in those kinds of fancy places, and what's the sense in denying yourself unnecessarily when there's rich chocolate mousse with double cream? I firmly believe that it's your duty to enjoy all the benefits that God puts on your table. Okay, so I'm in denial. I guess I'll throw out the chocolate too. Tomorrow.

Chapter Three

I had a pounding headache all day. Got to get this wrap-tying business sorted. It looked not quite right, but passable, when I left for work, but I must have tied it too tight, and since it had taken more than half an hour, I wasn't going to risk untying it in the office and starting again. So I just had to put up with the throbbing pain. And with all the comments about "going ethnic," I was damned if I was going to take it off altogether.

I work with a weird bunch of people in a small company that produces a weekly music magazine. I'm the Art Director (designer, copy editor, researcher, typist, and office cleaner rolled into one) and, even after all these years, I'm constantly amazed at the crazy variety of people you get around the music business. My boss, Oliver (Publisher and Editor), can't be more than twenty-six or -seven (sore point) and is so wired you'd think he was on something, or several somethings. I don't think he *is* since I've never caught him doing any stuff, but he just gives that impression. Might be his way of blending in with the rest of the industry. I doubt that Oliver has ever looked directly at me since each eye seems to point in a different direction and he never stands in one place long enough for either of them to catch mine. Oliver is excessively tall and gangly with a dark red Mohican and one earring that looks like a bull's eye— and that one does, occasionally, fix me with a penetrating stare. He's got his own idiosyncratic style because all this is set off by a long ginger beard that he's twisted, trained, and waxed into a Chinese Fu Manchu style. I've never seen him in anything but a variety of velour tracksuits, even before and after J-Lo made them briefly fashionable, and, my personal hate, sandals throughout the year.

I guess the reason he's the boss is that he's got an amazing, seemingly endless supply of energy—artificially induced or not. That's how he raised the money to set up *The Cream* and how he persuades investors to continue backing it. I'd have an awful lot of respect for him if it wasn't for the fact that he knows fuck all about music and cares even less. To him, this is a business, pure and simple. Plus he enjoys the perks. He gets to go to all the awards ceremonies at home and abroad, and his secretary of the moment usually goes to supply the . . . *shorthand*.

We've got a couple of full-time journalists, along with freelancers, a photographer, and Georgina, the young receptionist-cum-telephonist-cum-secretary-cum-Oliver's-current-lay-cum-daddy's-spoiled-brat. I refuse to call her George. I don't need to get that familiar.

I'm not sure where Oliver found Georgina. She just turned up in the office one day, and he must be screwing her since. Apart from low-cut sweaters and tiny skirts, she's got very little going for her. Well, actually, that's a downright lie. I think in Oliver's eyes she's got an awful lot going for her. Big tits for a start, and that's probably enough qualification for him. In fact, Georgina's one of those women who has no need for a push-up bra. She'd need a haul-up-pull-up crane. I probably hold her background against her too. We overhear intentionally loud conversations about country weekends and Daddy (real, not Sugar, I assume) bought her a place in Marylebone just so that she could taxi it to the office. No public transportation for our Georgina. I'd feel guilty about my reverse snobbery if it weren't for the fact that she's also a complete airhead with a pretty, China-doll face and long, thick, blond hair. Eddy (he's one of the journalists) and I avoid her as much as we can. You'll think we're infantile since we spend much of our lunch hours bitching about Oliver and Georgina, Eddy impersonating Oliver and me mimicking Georgina—without the hair, of course. Or the tits. Or the long legs, for that matter. We get along well, Eddy and I and whatever they might think in the office, it's not just because we're both black.

Eddy knows all the gossip in the industry, so I can always rely on him for the juiciest tidbits, most of it unprintable. I really like Eddy too. Okay, I quite like him in a comfortable, homely, safe kind of way. We might even have slept together if it weren't for the fact that something has always got in the way. I suspect we're probably better as friends. It's not awkward or anything. In fact, we joke about it and we've agreed that, if there's no one else in my life, we'll definitely do it on the day before my fortieth birthday, just to make sure that my bits are still in good working order, none of them has shriveled up, and they remember what they were made for.

It was Eddy who made me decide to put myself in Darryl's hands. "Looking good, girl!" he greeted me loudly when I arrived in the morning. But he had to spoil it by whispering as he walked past my desk, "Bad hair day?"

It's about time that brothas understand that ain't nobody's business what's going on under a sista's wrap. I guess I can forgive Eddy, though, since in that office he's a lifesaver. It's not that I've got anything against the others, well, except for Georgina and her legs and breasts and hair. And it's not even her legs or breasts or hair that get me. It's what she does with them. And whom she does it with. After all, who in their right mind would look twice at Oliver? And doesn't that beard get caught up? Not that I want to even think of where it might get caught. Or what they might do together. Yuck! I couldn't stop my mind going there for a second. It's just that Georgina seems to think that going to that place where any rational female would refrain from treading puts her in some kind of privileged position. I get the feeling that she looks down her tiny, white, pert nose at the rest of us.

Eddy and I have given up worrying about what the others say when we go off together. He's not in the office every day, so when he is, we make a point of not inviting the others for lunch. We only go to the local burger bar or pizza restaurant or, if he has his way, organic juice bar. It's not that we're being unfriendly or exclusive, but when I first started working there, you could see the way everyone watched us, fascinated by how we'd react to each other, not knowing that Eddy and I had known each other for years. So we avoided being seen leaving together for a few weeks, until we thought, What the hell, we like each other, we want to spend time together, so let's not let them get in the way. They wouldn't have thought anything if one or both of us had been white, would they? Or maybe they were just curious to see if we'd perform some sort of tribal initiation ceremony.

Strangely, I was glad that Eddy was in the office today. He was right. I was having a bad hair day. Bad outfit day. Bad mood day, really. I guess it must be the birthday and the lunch with Gabby yesterday made me realize what I've been missing.

"Where have I been going wrong, Eddy?" I asked him over pizza, fries, and a cola for me and a side salad and mineral water for him.

"Well, you could do something about that hair on your head to start."

I glared at him long enough for him to hang his head in shame.

"You black women can sure give the evil eye," I heard him mutter.

"You better be careful I don't turn you into a lizard."

It was easy for him. Eddy's head is completely, gorgeously bald. I know he has to shave it every so often, or maybe even every day, but that's nothing to what I have to go through. Besides, his style looks sexy while mine just looks ragged. I forgot to say that I have a bit of a fetish about bald, brown heads. I just want to touch them. I want to rub them, and then I get to thinking about where I could rub them and with what, and then that's likely to get me quite hot and into trouble. You see how easily I can get side-tracked into thinking about sex. It really *has* been too long.

So, I was asking Eddy for his advice. He didn't seem to think that I was doing anything too wrong.

"But I've got to do something," I whined, looking for reassurance. "Gabby seems to be fighting guys off all the time, even though she's married. It's 'cause she's so thin."

"You say she's rich too. That could have something to do with it."

"To be fair"—though I'm not sure why I feel I have to—"she's gorgeous too. She's got this long hair. She's always beautifully dressed. She bothers to put on makeup, and the thin thing is just a bonus."

"Carol, there ain't a thing wrong with you—apart from the hair. And you can get that fixed. I'll prove it to you, any time you like."

He looked at me with such a caricatured, suggestive, lecherous leer that I had to laugh. I'm sure that must be how Eddy gets a woman into bed. He laughs you into surrender. It's a better technique than many I can think of. As I dipped my fries into ketchup, all kinds of lascivious thoughts came into my head, and if I could have taken the afternoon off, I might have persuaded him to come back to my place—well, if I'd bothered to pick up the dirty clothes from the floor this morning.

When we got back to the office, all hell had broken loose. *The Cream* is one of those magazines that basically publishes puff pieces along with a lot of celebrity gossip. We're not usually into anything *too* controversial, but if the journalists do their jobs, then we sometimes get real scoops. Like being the first to announce that Brodie Wilkins was going solo or that Commander had been done for possession. Eddy's very good at his job. He's been in the business for so long that his nose for stories is acutely tuned and his contacts book is worth more than The Rock's weight in gold. I guess

that's why they can't get rid of him in spite of the fact
that he works to his own rules and doesn't take any shit
from anyone, especially Oliver.

Anyway, someone had screwed up big time—I'm
not naming names, but one of the journalists was looking shamefaced but surreptitiously glaring very pointedly at Georgina. Lawyers got involved and we had to
pull an article. An emergency conference was under
way and Eddy, superhero that he is, volunteered to find
a substitute story. He made a few calls and went off
with Patrick, the photographer. Eddy and I make a
good team, so he called to tell me how much space
he'd need and I set about rejigging the front cover and
center spread.

Of course, left to our own devices, we'd have got
the job done pretty efficiently, but I had constant interruptions from Oliver panicking and Georgina asking
brainless questions, so I was pretty ragged by the time
Eddy got back to the office. He'd dictated the article
onto a cassette as they drove back and all Georgina had
to do was transcribe it into the computerized layout.
She got so much wrong that we could have ended up
getting sued anyway. According to her, she found
Eddy's accent difficult. Poor love. I suppose if you're
brought up in the Home Counties, then a London accent
is pretty unfathomable. So I ended up doing the typing
too. I should have learned years ago not to admit that I
can type!

Gradually, everyone disappeared besides me, Eddy,
and Oliver, who wasn't being much use hovering over
our shoulders. It was two-thirty in the morning—several
shots from Oliver's emergency bottle of Scotch and a
full ashtray later—before we finally got the magazine
to bed and the disks couriered to the printer. Oliver

was gracious enough to thank me and Eddy for our hard work. I noticed, though, that he was the one covered in sweat.

Eddy and I were starving, so he offered to whip up an omelet and we took a taxi back to his place. Eddy lives in Kilburn, in one of those solidly built blocks that look as if they're private nursing homes. He's turned his apartment into a pretty cool space. Eddy's incredibly organized too. No clothes thrown around the place like in my home and no dirty dishes in the sink. Vases of flowers. And a huge tortoiseshell cat that sits purring dutifully on a cushion by the fireside, considerately attempting to blend in with the decor. Now, I've learned that in this life you have to prioritize, and washing dishes, dusting, and spring cleaning are not at the top of my to-do list. Besides, Max used to have someone take care of all that and he let me slip into bad habits. That's my excuse and you can't prove any different.

The walls of Eddy's living room are covered with original photographs of most of the biggest names in black music, and if there are any missing, it's only because they've been relegated to the bathroom. I'm always surprised that he's never bothered to get them signed, but then I guess Eddy's not that type of guy. I think he's got the photographs because he sees them as works of art, not because he's starstruck. And I suppose that's why he's got so many friends in the industry: precisely because he's not impressed by their money or fame, but only their talent.

I've spent so much time in Eddy's apartment that I feel really relaxed there, except that I don't dare to be as messy as I am in my home, but you can't have everything. It would take too long to teach Eddy the benefits of sloth. I made coffee while he started on supper, or breakfast, or whatever it was at that time of the night or morning.

I'm always interested in what other people have in their fridge, and I was impressed that Eddy's was home to vegetables, salads, sprouting beans, tofu, shitake mushrooms, and live bio yogurt. I spend a lot of time reading health magazines and am always meaning to buy all that crap, but I'm never sure which you're meant to burn and which you're meant to eat, bathe with, or slap on your face. And here Eddy was, actually *cooking* with organic, free-range, GMO-free ingredients.

I was too hungry to examine what was actually in the omelet, and sometimes it's best not to know, so I just wolfed it down and, of course, left the best till last, but by then, I had lost my appetite and only played with the salad. That's the drawback with this healthy eating—you never seem to have enough room left for the really nourishing bits.

Eddy suggested that I make myself comfortable but I didn't dare have a cigarette in his apartment, so I surreptitiously undid the button on my pants and spread myself across his leather sofa with a glass of red wine. He sat opposite looking as tired as I felt, but it was a pleasant exhaustion, infused with the satisfaction of knowing that we'd done a good job and had, not for the first time, saved Oliver's ass.

"Here's to a great team!" Eddy toasted, clinking his glass against mine.

"They don't deserve us. What would they do without us?"

"We could sure as hell do without screwups like today's." Eddy sounded more frustrated than angry. "I had to call in a few favors and you know I hate to do that unless it's for a good reason."

"You'd rather have other people owing you?"

"Damned right! You never know when you gonna need all the help you can get and I hate to waste favors on bullshit like this."

"So what kind of favors you been doing, Eddy?"

"Let's just say that I know how to keep my mouth shut."

I choked at that, almost spitting out my wine. "You're always telling me all kinds of stuff. You're one of the worst gossips I know. That's what I love about you."

Eddy's warm, brown eyes narrowed fractionally. "Carol, you know as well as I do that we all play several parts. The Eddy that performs in that office is not the same Eddy that's with you right this moment. Ain't that true?"

"Of course not."

"So the kind of things I chat 'bout with you is unimportant trivia, the sort of crap you can read about in any of them magazines, the type of things I write 'bout for *The Cream*. There's a lot that I ain't going to talk about to anybody."

"Not even me?" I looked at him with wide, would-be-innocent eyes.

He laughed. "Not even you, babe."

I know from my own personal experience that Eddy can keep his mouth shut, but I was intrigued by what he was keeping from me. That's a sure way to get me interested: Just say that you're not going to tell me something and I'm like a hound set loose after a fox, and when I catch hold of it I won't let go. I pride myself on being able to extract confidential information.

It's one of my more attractive qualities and I bow to no other woman on that score.

"What kind of things?"

"That's for me to know and for you not to even bother trying to find out."

"Eddy Stanton, you know you can trust me."

Eddy laughed at that. Unnecessarily and overlong, I felt. "Carol, you got one of the biggest mouths. You couldn't keep a secret if I zipped, padlocked, and superglued your lips together. You'd still find a way to talk."

I was hurt. Deeply. "That's unfair, Eddy. Of course I can keep a secret," I protested. "There's plenty of stuff I don't tell you."

"Like what?"

To be honest, I couldn't think of one single thing that I hadn't told Eddy. In the years that we've known each other, he has become my closest male friend, and when something is troubling me and I have to talk it through, Eddy is quite often the most available person. If he isn't in the office, then I call him or, if it's really urgent, I page him. He always calls me back. I treat Eddy a bit like a girlfriend, so whenever I get hold of a spicy bit of gossip, I talk to him first. Precisely because I know I can trust him. So it hurts that he doesn't feel the same way about me—even if he is right. I don't honestly see the sense in depriving other people. It's almost an evangelical duty to spread gossip; it makes the world go 'round.

"Like plenty of things I'm not going to tell you if you don't even trust me."

Eddy laughed his infectious laugh that would normally reduce me to giggles, too, but I was aggrieved.

"Eddy, I thought we were friends," I moaned.

He smiled gently. "Carol, you're not going to get anything out of me that way."

He stood up, refilled my glass, and stretched.

"I'm shattered, Carol. You staying?"

I had to think quickly. My first instinct was that he wasn't going to get out of answering my question that easily. My second was that I was exhausted and didn't feel like moving an inch. My third was that there was the wrap on my head. If I was going to stay, then I'd have to take it off and Eddy would get a glimpse of what was underneath. I must have hesitated a moment too long.

"I'll even turn my back while you take off that wrap!"

I threw a cushion at his head but he ducked, looked smug, and headed toward the bathroom. I heard the sound of Eddy showering. I guess he took the thrown cushion for a "yes."

I followed him and sat on the toilet seat while I finished my wine and tried to figure out how to get him to open up to me. I could only see Eddy's silhouette through the steamed-up glass. He's tall and broad-shouldered with those narrow hips and firm, round buttocks that can reduce me to a pool of jelly. I know a lot of women say that they look at a man's eyes first, or his smile or even his teeth—like he's a horse or something—but I think they're lying or just want to seem "intellectual" when they're answering a survey. At least I'm honest. I like to see how a man fills out his jeans. It's a good thing that clothes were invented; otherwise, I'd be a quivering wreck most of the time; there are a lot of fine-looking brothas out there, even if they're not walking in my direction.

Through the rippled shower glass I could see Eddy's

hands lathering his chest and then smoothing over the taut muscles in his arms. I started to think about how good it felt to be held in those arms. It was a while since I'd experienced the protection of a powerful, masculine embrace. Strong though he might be, however, I figured a man as exhausted as Eddy wouldn't be able to complete the job of showering on his own and, after all, the guy had cooked me supper; he deserved some pampering in return. Nobody can say I don't do my duty by my friends.

I was out of my clothes like an Eskimo suddenly transported to the Sahara, but I left the wrap on my head, hoping that I looked sexy and that Eddy wouldn't notice—I thought I knew how to distract him. I slid open the shower door and slipped in behind him.

"Need some help?"

"If you're offering, sugar."

I took the soap and lathered my hands. I started with his shoulders, kneading, rubbing, easing away the tension. I pressed hard with my thumbs, moving in small circles, feeling the hard muscle underneath his smooth skin that looked and smelled of sandalwood.

"That feel good?"

"Mmm."

I wrapped my arms around him so that I could soap his chest. I know he'd done it already, but cleanliness is definitely next to godliness when you get this kind of opportunity. Eddy's chest isn't bare, but not too hairy either. It's dotted with those little peppercorns that are so cute and feel so good to touch. He's a pretty sensitive guy, too; I could feel his nipples harden when I got near them, contrasting with the soft velvet of his skin. I ran my hands down, around, tracing the contours of his firm muscles. I don't know about Eddy, but I was getting carried away, especially as that position gave me the opportunity to press myself against his deliciously tight butt. The warmth I felt in my groin reminded me that I was neglecting my second favorite part of his body and I reluctantly pulled away so that I could caress his buttocks, rubbing, stroking, squeezing them and slipping my soapy finger down the crack and around the full moons over and over until he moaned with pleasure. I was working pretty hard, so I had to check that all this effort wasn't in vain. I reached round again, trailed my hands along his hairy legs, up and down, over and over, teasing the soft skin of his inner thighs until he could take no more and I reached down to cup my hands around his balls. I don't need too many hints, so I rolled them around in my slick, slippery fingers until I could feel them tighten. I desperately wanted to test how hard I'd gotten him, but I was evil enough to want to make him wait.

Eddy was standing very still, almost leaning against me, his breathing loud, and I could feel my nipples get hard as his back pressed into them. I'd got into the shower thinking that I knew what I was doing, that I could stay in control. Now, as Eddy started to move his butt in small circles, pressing himself against my crotch, making my stomach flutter with anticipation, I suspected that if he turned the tables, I'd tell him any state secrets he wanted to know.

"Babe, this is so good, but I can't take much more."

"So, what you want, Eddy?"

"You know what I want. I want your fingers right here, round my prick. Come feel how hard I am."

I didn't need a printed invitation. I grasped his thick cock that was now pointing skyward. Definitely my number one favorite part of his anatomy. I ran my thumb along the length, stroking the rippling flesh, tracing the vein that stood out, moving just as far as the bulge at the head, making him hold his breath as he waited while I gently circled it. I tightened my fingers around him, feeling hotter and hotter as I imagined him inside my pussy. You think you can't get any wetter than standing in a shower? Well, you can't imagine the places where I was getting wet. I could tell that Eddy was as aroused as me 'cos he was silent and unmoving as if frightened of what I might *not* do next. I was enjoying the sense of power.

"Eddy?"

"Mmm?"

"Eddy?"

My thumb embroidered delicate lacework around the head of his dick.

"Yes, Carol?" he moaned.

"You know what I want?"

"No, tell me."

"I want you to do something for me."

My thumb had spiraled to the sensitive tip of his cock.

He groaned and turned round to face me and stared into my eyes for a moment. Then he pulled me close, clutching my buttocks. His iron erection pressed against my belly and I had second thoughts about what I was planning to do. A flame shot through me as Eddy kissed me, the tip of his tongue searching my mouth. I gave him the right directions, then pulled away. I held my breath, needing to wait until the heat subsided a little. Eddy's eyes were transfixed by my breasts. He gently lifted them, cupping the weight, caressing the underside and tracing circles around them. He kissed each in turn, sucking my nipples into his mouth, gently nibbling, and then biting. These little shivers started to run through my body. As if he sensed what I needed, Eddy wrapped his arms around me, holding me tightly, fondling, rubbing, caressing every morsel of my flesh. His hand inched its way up my thigh. I would have held my breath even more if there was any more breath to hold. My ears were pulsing with the rhythm of my rapid heartbeat. I stopped hearing the drilling sound of the water from the shower. I was wrapped in cotton wool. Safe, secure, needing Eddy to break through the forest of thorns to rescue me.

Eddy nuzzled my ear, his hands inching closer to my clitoris, and he murmured, responding to whatever I had said—I'd forgotten—"This what you want, babe? Carol, I'll do anything. All you have to do is tell me."

"Anything?" I almost screamed as his finger hit the right spot.

"Anything, babe."

"All right. Eddy . . ."

I tilted my pelvis, pushing myself closer to him.

"Yes?"

I rotated my hips, my pussy making circles against his erection.

"I want . . ."

"Uh-huh?"

I reached down, held his straining cock and guided it between my legs. I swayed back and forth.

"Eddy . . . I want to know what secrets you not telling me."

His head snapped back and he looked at me in disbelief.

"What?"

"I want to know what kind of secrets you keeping."

"I don't believe you, woman. How you could ask me at a time like this?" The shocked expression softened and he smiled a smile that reminded me of a lion licking its lips. His eyes darkened and he lifted my chin with one finger, staring into my eyes.

"You want to know what kind of secrets?"

"Yeah, you can trust me."

"You sure?"

"Yes."

"Well . . ."

"Yes, Eddy?"

"The same kind of dark, funky secrets you keeping under that wrap!"

Eddy whipped the cloth from my head and dashed out of the shower, laughing. I followed as fast as I could, but he's taller than me and he's got longer legs, so we spent some time circling the sofa and getting the rug wet. I may be smaller, but I'm more cunning, so I managed to tackle him to the ground by leaping over the sofa. We were both hysterical until Eddy suddenly looked at me, his eyes becoming dark, smoldering, deadly serious.

"That is some scary shit on top of your head, babe."

Chapter Four

I borrowed one of Eddy's shirts this morning, careful to choose one I'd never seen him wear in the office. No sense in giving ammunition to the gossips—and whatever they'd be thinking, and whatever you're thinking, you'd all be wrong.

By the time we'd cleared up the mess of water and cushions in Eddy's sitting room and then showered off the dried-up soap it was early morning and we were both so sleepy that we collapsed into Eddy's big double bed and instantly fell asleep. It's kinda nice sleeping with his arms wrapped around me so I was all warm, cozy, safe, and prepared to be kind to the world when I woke up this morning. I seriously considered waking Eddy and carrying on where we left off the night before, but he looked so sweet and innocent and peaceful . . . and I remembered the comment about my hair.

Usually I'm a nasty bitch to be around first thing in the morning, especially before the coffee. This morning I even hummed as I showered and got ready for work. That's even though I couldn't light a cigarette in the health zone that is his apartment. Eddy was bleary eyed when he finally woke, but he got up to make me toast and not even the white fluffy stuff that I'm used to, but the healthy whole wheat slices with the crunchy bits left in. Still, a girl can't have everything. Eddy looked at me through semiclosed eyes, and though he was half asleep, he sat me down in front of the mirror, took hold of my piece of cloth, did a few fiddly things with his fingers, and the next thing, abracadabra, there was a perfectly tied wrap around my hair. I looked kind of elegant.

"How do you do that?"

"You mean you can't tie a wrap? Is easy."

It had all been going so well.

Quiet in the office today. Editorial meeting in the morning, mainly a postmortem on last night's screwup with Oliver screaming like a banshee. Dire warnings that heads would roll. Problem is that they never do. Apart from his loud voice, Oliver's kind of weak in the dictatorial area.

Eddy was out today, which was just as well since he and I might have got ourselves arrested if he'd been at the meeting. Apparently, although we weren't told, Georgina's been on trial all this time and now Oliver's decided to confirm her appointment and promote her to "Executive Secretary." Wouldn't have happened if the jury had been able to vote. Oliver did blush the color of his beard, but Georgina didn't have the sensitivity. Today her neckline seemed to have made a rendezvous with her hemline and they were obviously due to meet in the not too distant future. Give it a week or so and she'll be Chairman or Chief Executive or some other shit like that. I guess I shouldn't object to a woman using her every asset, but if I'm honest, I resent them abusing assets that I couldn't get in a million years. Particularly big, baby-blue eyes, long blond hair, endless skinny legs, and untanned skin. Where's the level playing field?

Executive Secretary my ass. I gave Georgina my most evil look as I watched her wrapping her long blond hair around her fingers, but it was a waste of time since she wasn't looking at me, but staring into space with a vacuous look on her face, and so she didn't immediately turn into a cockroach as I'd planned. I wondered which part of Oliver's anatomy she wrapped that blond hair around to get him this much under her thumb—probably a very apt turn of phrase.

I got some petty revenge when I left the office. My sleeve "accidentally" caught a folder on Georgina's desk and as I had an urgent appointment I couldn't stay to pick up the debris scattered on the floor. I smiled to myself as I watched her on her knees scrabbling to retrieve slides, photographs, cuttings, and cassettes. Oliver was just coming in to the office, so I figured that he'd be able to help her straighten things out. At least they'd probably have fun trying. I felt a subtle glow as I contemplated how considerate and helpful to others I can be when I try.

I went home and changed before going over to Mom's—the urgent appointment. I wasn't about to invite an interrogation by turning up wearing Eddy's shirt, even though I felt so comfortable in it. It still had that clean, masculine, sandalwood scent of Eddy. If I closed my eyes, I could make believe that Eddy's arms were still embracing me. I sort of liked the way Eddy had tied the wrap so I left it on.

Mom lives in Balham, south London, which is where I grew up. We've all kind of stayed in the area, apart from my one sojourn in Notting Hill, 'cos it's where we know. I feel less at ease the farther north I go: The bricks get lighter and so do the complexions. I'm okay in Soho, where our office is, but definitely not myself in places like Cockfosters, and I wouldn't even know how to get to High Barnet if it wasn't at the end of the Northern line. I don't even know if it's still London. Funnily enough, it's fine once I get out of London itself; I've even ventured as far north as Manchester without too many side effects. So we've all stayed south of the river. Mom, Dad, Aunt Bea, and my sister, Nicola. It's sort of nice that we're so close and can pop over to each other's homes whenever we want. It's good because I couldn't stand to actually *live* with any of them. Now, don't get me wrong, I love my family, but sharing a house with them would be like voluntarily walking into the lion's den, lying prostrate on the dining table, and smothering yourself in antelope gravy.

Anyway, the reason I had to go over to Mom's is that Nicola is getting married in a few months and Aunt Bea is making the dresses. Tonight was the second fitting for the bridesmaids.

It took thirty-five minutes to get to Mom's house even though she only lives about five miles away. The jams and roadworks were horrendous, but I love driving in London, and the more traffic, the better. Once you learn the unofficial rules, it's almost relaxing, even though you have to be alert all the time. You go into automatic pilot, vying for road space with taxis, vans, trucks, and cyclists. You stare grimly ahead to avoid letting anyone move into the six inches of space in front of you. Even the abuse that you swap with other drivers is only halfhearted and routine. It's all part of a game that only London drivers play. Or maybe I'm addicted to exhaust fumes.

I took the time to psyche myself up. Things have got a little bit uncomfortable between me and Nicola recently because I guess I haven't been able to hide my feelings about her fiancé too well. When I told her that he was a rat-faced, low-life, devious, untrustworthy, two-timing, slimy piece of shit who should never have been kidnapped from the rest of his family in the primordial swamps, I'd had a drink or two. Somehow Nicola got the idea that I don't care for him too much.

I'm in a difficult position and it's a bit complicated, so bear with me. An old schoolfriend's aunt's cousin's daughter used to be married to Vince (the fiancé) and so I've heard thirdhand or fourthhand all kinds of stories that I can't repeat to Nicola since I've got no real evidence. I've dropped enough subtle hints, though.

Nicola tells me that Vince left his wife because she was too demanding. Yeah right! She demanded that he should stop screwing around. Nicola trusts Vince because he hasn't pressured her for sex and she's determined to save herself for marriage. (I don't know where she got her genes. When she was five I persuaded her that the stories about the stork were true and that she'd just been delivered to our doorstep one day. Now, I'm not too certain myself.) I'm sure the reason Vince hasn't been pressuring her is 'cos he's getting it somewhere else. I've heard the rumors. Apparently he's got a thing about leggy blondes. He couldn't even be original! Come to think of it, he does remind me of a black Rod Stewart.

I'm not helped by the fact that Mom likes him. Usually her instincts are sharp. But when she first met Vince, the lizard had dressed up in a smart suit and turned up carrying red roses for her. I thought he was a greasy sleazeball, but he must have pressed all the right buttons because Mom looks on him like the son she never had crossed with Saint Valentine himself. She won't hear a word against him.

I guess it's what he does for a living: He creeps. I describe Vince as a used-car salesman because that's what he looks like. He's usually dressed in gray trousers, white shirt, navy blazer, and striped tie, which doesn't really go with the black complexion. It wouldn't surprise me if the tie was from an old school that he never actually attended. That would be just like Vince. It's hard to describe his personality because there's not a lot of it. He's all about illusion. He doesn't seem to have a family, a history, any beliefs, or even an opinion, except what he thinks you want to hear. It's even hard to remember what he looks like when he's not standing right in front of you, but I guess he must be good-looking since, like me, my sister has inherited the matrilineal trait of impeccable taste in men—physically at least. I think Vince has a beard and moustache, but I know that in the past he's shaved one or the other or both off without anyone noticing. I suspect that, at some time, his ancestors must have come from Trinidad or Guyana or some place like that because he's got curly, almost Indian hair that he wears a little too long. I know he's got sharp, white, shiny teeth because they're always on display when he's around our family. I keep trying to count those teeth since I'm convinced there are far too many for his mouth. He's a couple of inches taller than me, so you wouldn't exactly call him tall, and he's neither fat nor thin, just average. What *is* striking, though, is that he has huge, downward-slanting eyes fringed with thick, dark lashes. I remember the eyes because Vince seems to think they're his ace in the hole and that he can use them to seduce anyone. They don't do shit for me. To be fair, Vince is not a salesman at all; he runs a car showroom, but I prefer to think of him as a used-car salesman.

Well, I think I managed to smooth things over with Nicola without having to say anything nice about Vince, but I've got to learn to keep my damned mouth zipped. I told Eddy that I could keep a secret so maybe it's time I start practicing. And it's not really any of my business. It's not as if Vince has murdered anyone or anything like that. At least, not that I know of. Most guys try to spread their seed around as if it has an imminent sell-by date. So, as long as he treats my sister right, I'm best staying out of it.

"Carol, you're late. What happen? Bea's here waiting on you. You all right?" Mom hugged me and pushed me into the living room before I could even attempt a response. The room was chaotic with bronze silk, floral carpet, pins, plastic-covered leather sofa, scissors, beads, antimacassars, babies, doilies, children, glass baubles, and frantic adults. Aunt Bea was presiding over all of this and she bustled over to me, not even taking the time to greet me before starting to strip my clothes off. If she wasn't my aunt, and female, I might have enjoyed the experience.

I make huge allowances for Aunt Bea. She looks so

much like Mom that she benefits from the leftover love. They're both tall and willowy with long legs, and Bea has a perfect, sylph-like figure. Nicola and I must have got our shape from our father. The few differences between Mom and Aunt Bea have become more pronounced as they've got older. As Mom's outline has filled out and softened, Aunt Bea's has become more angular, the sharpness of her silhouette in stark contrast with the warmth that exudes from her. It's as if Mom has been feeding off Aunt Bea, and maybe in the last decade or so that's been true, emotionally at least.

Nicola gave me a restrained hug. I can see I've still got a bit of crawling to do. She's looking good these days and I told her so. There must be no end to what the love of an honest man can do since the love of Vince has transformed my little sister. She's been pretty determined with this dieting and she's lost about thirty pounds and is getting sickeningly shapely. We made a pact at New Year's to lose the extra weight, but I've had little success. There have been other things on my mind, like chocolate, cakes, cream, and chips. So that's my diet in a nutshell: I need to cut out any food that begins with C.

Being fitted for a dress is almost as bad as going to the hairdresser. There can hardly be any greater shame than standing half naked in the middle of a crowded room and having Aunt Bea grab hold of an inch or two of extra padding to show that you've put on weight and there ain't no way you goin' to be squeezed into this dress come the wedding day. I felt so ashamed that I was even more determined to stick to whatever diet Nicola had been using. I can't let down our side of the family, and bronze silk isn't the most flattering fabric if you've got the odd ripple or two to hide. The under-nines in the room began to giggle behind fingers spread too wide, the way that children do.

"Sis, I like your African wrap," Nicola rescued me before everyone else could join in. You only have to mention the word "weight" and every woman, young or old, suddenly becomes an expert and is ready to offer a variety of prescriptions: high-fiber, bananas, protein, baked beans, kiwi fruit, acupuncture, jogging, cross-training, aerobics—all words that I understand in theory, but have had little experience with. It's like sitting in church on Sunday listening to a sermon about forgiving your enemy: you know the theory makes sense, but it's damned hard to put into practice.

"Aunt Bea, you think the bridesmaids could wear something like that? I been wondering what they should do with their hair. Carol, you can show us how to do it?"

I gave Nicola the evil eye. If I'd ever had the temerity to believe that I'd been forgiven for my comments about Vince, I was disabused. Nicola knows full well that anything that has to do with manipulating hair or decorating it with fabric does not run in our family. My mother can't even canerow.

"Listen, girl, I'm going to the hairdresser tomorrow, and I promise I'll look after my hair. I'll steam it. I'll condition it. I'll get it trimmed. Treated every week. I'll wash it in asses' milk, coat each strand in eighteen-carat gold, and wrap it in the finest silk. By the time we get to your wedding, you goin' be so proud of my hair that you won't want me to hide it."

Nicola raised a skeptical eyebrow, but I think I just about got away with it. Besides, I'm damned sure that Nicola wasn't intending to wear any wrap on her own head. She happily trots off to the hairdresser every week even though she doesn't need it. She calls it pampering. I call it mental and physical torture that should be outlawed under the Geneva Convention.

It seemed like hours before Aunt Bea and all the others had gone, leaving me, Mom, and Nicola alone at the kitchen table. Mom had cooked saltfish and callaloo with fried dumplings so the diet I'd started thirty minutes earlier went straight out the window, but it was a cold evening so I needed some carbohydrate fuel to keep me from freezing to death on the way home. Naturally, Nicola only picked at the callaloo.

"How you getting on with the preparations, Nicola?"

"Well, I'm not panicking anymore, Mom. The church is arranged, the hotel's booked, I've chosen flowers, Vince is organizing the cars, you're dealing with the catering, and we've finally sorted out the guest list. We'll send out invitations this weekend." There came the pause that I'd been expecting. Nicola and I had agreed that there was only one way of broaching the subject—come right out with it. "Of course, I've invited Dad."

Mom was quiet for a heartbeat or two and both Nicola and I avoided looking at her, concentrating instead on our plates.

"You have to do what you think is right, child." She couldn't seriously have expected Nicola to do anything else.

"I'm not going to ask Dad to give me away, Mom, since you brought us up, really. I'd love it if you would."

"Me? How can I give you away? That's a man's job." You could tell, though, that Mom was touched. Under her dark complexion there was a delighted flush and she became coy and girlish in her happiness. Her generation just couldn't accept gifts outright without making some protest.

"Mom, this is the twenty-first century. I wouldn't want anyone else to do it."

"Did you ask Pastor Michaels?"

"Yes, he's got no problem with it. Will you think about it?"

"Of course, I'll think about it, darling."

Nicola turned her attention to me, changing the subject too abruptly for my liking. "So who you bringing with you?"

A trick question as well as a way of leaving Mom to her own thoughts. Nicola knew full well that I didn't have anyone I wanted to bring with me. But a wedding is the kind of occasion where you just can't turn up on your own. The main reason all the distant relatives come is to find enough gossip to sustain them until the next christening, birthday, wedding, or funeral. I made the mistake of turning up to the last two family events without a partner and now all the great-aunts and cousins three times removed *know* that I'm a lesbian. Not that they would ever mention that word or even really knew what a lesbian does, but they've started to take me to one side, pat my hand kindly, and inquire after my health, both physical and mental. After a few minutes' intense interrogation, they move away to commiserate with "poor Josie" (Mom) who is "so worried that she might not live to see she grandchildren dem."

It didn't help that they all knew about Max. There was no way that I could have kept our relationship secret, even if I'd wanted to, since his name was in the papers nearly every week. So knowing who Max was, and frankly, how *hot* he was, they all figure that there must be some dark reason why he left me, i.e. my lesbianism. In a million years they'd never consider that I might have been the one to do the leaving.

I could always ask Eddy to come with me to the wedding as a big, huge, fat favor, and he'd do it, but I'm not sure what he'd want in return and he wouldn't know what he'd be subjecting himself to. After such a long drought, the prospect of a new man to interrogate would only bring out the worst in my relatives. It would be like throwing a newborn lamb to the vultures.

"Don't think you goin' come to my wedding alone, Sis. After Barbara's christening party my phone didn't stop ringing for days. Everyone wanting to know when was the last time you had a man in your life. You know they all had someone they were longing to fix you up with, so you owe me one for protecting you." I heard that word *protecting* and began to seriously wonder where this idea of me being a lesbian had really originated. Had that been Nicola's way of fending off the relatives? "I lied for you and I'm willing to go on lying, but you couldn't just do me this one tiny favor of bringing someone? Someone presentable. Is my special day, Sis. I'll give you the money to go to one of those escort agencies."

"Nicola, behave yourself. Don't be so rude to your sister."

"I'm not being rude, Mom. I'm just trying to help."

"I don't need your help. I've got plenty of men I could bring."

"Name one."

I'm *so* bad at lying. All the deception genes must have passed to Nicola because she does it so well. I racked my brains and came up with very little. Eddy was beginning to look more woolly and frisky every minute.

"And don't even think of suggesting Eddy. I know the guy's your friend, but this would be asking too much of him. If you two aren't going to get it together, then it would be too cruel to inflict all of the aunts on him." It's eerie the way my sister can read my mind. It frightens me sometimes. I worry most when I'm thinking vile thoughts about her or Vince. "Anyway, I'm inviting Eddy and he'll probably want to bring someone else, so there!"

Eddy? Bring someone else? "I wasn't even going to mention Eddy. Nicola, you don't know everything."

"Oh no?"

"There happens to be someone new in my life at the moment. Why you think I'm going to the hairdresser tomorrow?"

I thought that would convince her. Nicola knows that I won't willingly go to Darryl unless there's some very good reason. And in Nicola's mind that reason would have to be a man. Of course, Darryl does Nicola's hair and that's one of the reasons he's so mean to me: he doesn't believe that my unruly hair is genetic but rather a result of neglect.

"Well, who is he? Tell me all."

"You'll just have to wait. You're a jinx, so I'm not saying anything to you."

"He doesn't exist, does he?"

"He does too."

"Doesn't."

"Does."

Please! The depths to which I sink when I'm back home with Nicola! Anyone would think that we were children again. Mom obviously does.

"Stop fighting you two or you won't get any pudding."

"I don't want any, anyway."

That was Nicola, not me. She's such a goody-two-shoes these days and she's so selfish. When Mom had gone to the trouble of making bread pudding, with custard, too, it was damned rude to refuse. So I had to eat Nicola's helping, too, just so as not to upset Mom.

"So you hear from him, then, Nicola? Him let you know, say him coming?"

That came from left field and rescued me. We all knew who she was talking about. Mom never mentioned Dad's name; but we could always tell by the tone of her voice and the way she said "him," sort of weary and resigned, sharp and caressing all at the same time.

"I spoke to Dad a couple of days ago. Of course he's coming. And Pauline and the kids. I couldn't not invite them, Mom. Jason refused to be seen dead in a pageboy's outfit, so Rosa followed suit, but of course, they'll come."

"Of course, child. I don't have no problem with that." She said it in the same way you'd say to the hangman, "Oh no, go ahead. I had a bit of a sore throat anyway."

Mom prides herself on being a true Christian and I wouldn't expect her to say anything else. But I know that underneath it she detests the woman she always calls Pauline Brickell even though Pauline's been married to Dad for ten years now and they've been together for who knows how much longer. Anyway, she's Pauline *Shaw,* but Mom won't acknowledge that. I can't really blame her since Pauline did sort of steal Dad away, but I can't help liking Pauline either. She

has a wicked sense of humor and drinks like a fish. A
bit like me really. Of course I don't say that to Mom.
I'm not one for rubbing salt into the wounds and I
firmly believe in allowing people to wallow in their
own self-pity as long as they're enjoying themselves.

Mom's a bit of a drama queen, so this was her cue to
start clearing the dishes, as loudly and wearily as possible. I was generous and allowed her to wallow some
more. Besides, while she was elbow deep in washing-up
liquid and slamming the plates onto the rack, she
hummed some old-time spiritual to herself that was
bound to soothe her soul. Mom isn't a regular church-
goer, so I don't know where she gets these tunes from.
Must be passed on through the genes. The day I start
humming "That Old Rugged Cross" is the day I know
I'm turning into my mother for real. Anyway, the
mood Mom was in she didn't need to be bothered with
me and Nicola hovering around her with tea towels.

"You know she doesn't like the idea, don't you," I
whispered to Nicola, making sure that Mom was out of
earshot.

"Of course, I know. Washing up has never been so
loud, but what can I do? I love Pauline and the kids.
They're our family too."

"Sis, it's your wedding day. It's only going to happen once. . . ." I surreptitiously crossed my fingers behind my back. "So you have to do what's going to
make you happy."

"You calling me selfish?"

"You know I'm not. Nicola, there's nothing else
you can do. Mom's just going to have to get through
the day the best she can. It's only one day, after all."

"Well, you know what would make me *really* happy
on my big day?"

"What?"

"To see you fixed up with someone. Carol, there's this guy . . . I've talked to him about you—"

"No."

"Just hear me out—"

"Nicola—"

"Sis, I'm not asking you to marry the guy, just to meet him."

"No way in a million years."

"He's a really great guy."

"Not if you tied my body to a rack and tortured me with a red-hot poker."

"Trust me, Carol. He's just your type."

"Not if you pulled my eyelashes out one by one with rusty tweezers."

"Sis, just for me?"

"Not even if you tickled the bottom of my feet with a feather duster."

"Please, Carol. It would make me so happy."

"Even if you confiscated every bar of chocolate in my apartment and forced me to eat boiled okra."

"All right. Fair enough. If that's the way you want it, I'll just tell Mom about that night you snuck out with Rob Elliott."

"Okay, I'll do it."

Chapter Five

Why did I let my sister sweet-talk me like that? It's not even as if anything happened with Rob Elliott. And I'm thirty years old, so I shouldn't be scared of my mother finding out. We were both thirteen at the time and didn't know much about anything at all. It's just that we were the studious nerds in our year and everyone else seemed to be getting up to mysterious things in the bathrooms, under tables, in fields, on the backseats of buses, and sometimes in locked bedrooms. It was all very vague, but whatever they were doing, they made me want to be doing it too.

Rob was sweet really, if a bit of a dork, with huge eyes that always looked as if they were about to fill with tears. I kinda liked that, but you can see why he got picked on. That and the fact that he always did his homework on time and got the best marks in the class. Actually, even I could see why the others were out to get him. Mom really liked Rob because, as luck would have it, his mother was one of her friends from work so they pushed us together since we were both from "good" families and could be trusted together. We could be trusted because we didn't know any better. We used to get teased by the adults about what a lovely couple we made and at church we'd usually be paired off as ushers. If you want kids to just say no to sex, then push them together at Sunday school. I was *playing* at being "good," but I suspect Rob was the real deal. Because there was no way of escaping him, I decided the only thing to do was corrupt him.

It took a lot of guile and persuasion to get Rob to do anything the least bit underhanded, so sneaking out to a late-night movie must have seemed like one step on the road to damnation. I had to get Nicola to cover for me and make sure that the front door wasn't bolted when I got back, so that's why she's got a hold on me now. In the end, neither Rob nor I knew what we were supposed to be doing, so we just held hands for a long while until they got sweaty. When we attempted to kiss in the back row it was unbelievably awkward since Rob was six inches shorter than me and I got a crick in my neck. Besides, gluing my lips to someone else's for five minutes didn't do much for me and I ended up having nightmares about the film. We didn't know that you weren't actually supposed to *watch* the movie and choosing a horror movie was not the smartest idea Rob ever had.

Then to add to the misery, I couldn't actually admit to my ten-year-old sister that we hadn't done anything. It would have got around like wildfire, so to satisfy her curiosity, I made up all kinds of physically impossible feats, the sorts of things that only the fertile mind of an inexperienced thirteen-year-old could come up with. That's why I can't log on to Friends Reunited now. Not because of anything that we did, but because of what everyone *thinks* we did. In fact, Rob should be grateful to me since the whole saga did wonders for his reputation, as well as perpetuating all the stereotypes about black men. How was I to know?

In a way, though, it's Rob's fault that I'm now forced to go on this blind date with Nicola's chosen victim. You're probably thinking that I should be grateful for small mercies given the dearth of eligible men on the scene. Well, you don't know Nicola as well as I do. Think of Vince and you'll understand why I'm not looking forward to meeting this guy. Ironically, Nicola occasionally reminds me that it was through her that I met Max. That's supposed to be some kind of recommendation. Well, I know Max a lot better than she does.

Not to say that Max wasn't physically acceptable. In all honesty, he was probably the most devastatingly sexy man I'd ever met. I wondered why Nicola was leaving him for me. This was long before she met Vince and she insisted that she just thought he was more my type.

I haven't mentioned that Nicola runs a secondhand bookshop in Streatham specializing in black history and culture. Well, it's really half a bookshop since she shares the space with a brotha who sells African artifacts. Max came in a couple of times in search of books on music, so that was introduction enough for Nicola to invite him to her apartment-warming party. There's sisterly love for you; he could have just been released from a mental hospital, but the fact that he was interested in music and could read meant that we must have a whole heap in common. Mind you, Nicola must have been the only woman in the country not to have recognized Max on sight.

So when Max walked into her apartment, he made me go quite literally weak at the knees in the same way that Samuel L. Jackson obviously does, but Michael Jackson couldn't. More Quincy Jones than James Earl Jones. More Lenny Kravitz than Will Smith. MC Romeo rather than Ja Rule. I think you get the general idea. So my palms began to sweat, my knees gave way, my nipples got hard, and my panties were wet. Not the most attractive combination, I admit. Anyway, Nicola eagerly introduced us and I was supposed to attempt a rational conversation with him. The only thing I could think of saying was, "Oh Lord, what's a world-famous, rich, talented, sex god like you doing in a house party like this?"

I guess Max must have been used to that kind of reaction since he didn't treat me like the bumbling, slobbering idiot I actually was. You see, not only was Max a walking, bottled aphrodisiac, but he was also lead singer in one of those up-and-arrived R&B bands that would have been considered to be manufactured if the term had existed then. So, inevitably, he had women throwing their underwear, their phone numbers, as well as their bodies at his feet. But I didn't find that out until later, and by that time Max and I were an item. And we were tight. None of them girls could have come between us. When I think back, sometimes I could scream aloud at what a waste it all was. It's best not to. Think back, I mean.

Going to the hairdresser today at least took my mind off my worries about finding a date for the wedding. I'm almost beginning to believe that men are the more intelligent sex—and it would take a whole heap of evidence to convince me of that. Plus, it would have to be evidence compiled by a woman. But when was the last time you saw a brotha in one of these fancy hair-dressing salons? That might be proof enough! Time was, they used to sit with us getting their hair relaxed or permed. Nowadays, it's only a few guys having their hair cornrowed—the rest get a quick trim at the barber, or else they have those patterns shaved into their hair, and even that can't take more than half an hour or so. You see, they *have* evolved.

Well, there was a guy there today. It's funny how, once someone raises the subject of A Man In Your Life, your senses become heightened and you start looking, checking out possibilities. I don't mean just a passing glance; you really begin to scrutinize them from top to bottom, weighing them up. When this guy came in, Darryl was examining the remainder of curls at the back of my neck, so I could only see the trainers and the bottoms of the brotha's jeans. Darryl greeted him with a "Hey, man!" and I could hear one of those hand slaps that guys do. You can't tell a lot from trainers because everyone wears them these days, even my sixty-year-old dad. You really need to see what *shoes* a man wears to work or when he's in a suit. I steer clear of gray leather myself, or anything with a gold chain. Untrustworthy. Like thin upper lips. Or eyebrows that meet in the middle. Anyway, I could tell the brotha was going to be tall, because there was a long, almost endless expanse of black denim, and I skipped past the crotch area, just noticing along the way that he had slim, but definite, hips. Lots of men these days grow so long and lean that they seem to miss out on hips altogether. I like hips myself. They suggest that there might be a manly butt to go with them.

As Darryl tilted my head back a little, I managed to get as far as a chest wearing soft black cotton and, thank God, no hint of jewelry around his neck. That's another of my no-nos. I'm a bit put off by a man who wears more jewelry than me. I was enjoying what I was seeing, though, and fantasizing all sorts of possibilities. I was definitely hoping to check out more of him, though if you twisted my arm, I could have been persuaded to take what I'd already seen of the package, but I was still intrigued. When you think about it, a hairdresser's is as good a place as any to meet your life partner; if he's seen you with your hair all messy anyhow and he's still interested, then that's a reasonably solid foundation to build on.

So, I was just about to glimpse this intriguing face when Darryl jerked my head back. If he'd asked, I would have risked further humiliation just to get a glimpse of the face. I didn't have the choice, though, so I gritted my teeth while Franiq'ua washed and conditioned under Darryl's watchful eye. You can't expect someone who charges $165 for a relaxer to actually *wash* the hair as well. Still, even though my neck was bent into an unnatural position, Franiq'ua's massaging fingers felt good as she shampooed my hair. The firm, rhythmic pressure eased the tension from my shoulders and I almost moaned aloud. I could have turned into a liquid puddle on the floor as I drifted into a warm languor. The sharp needles of cool water brought me to my senses quickly enough, and as Franiq'ua wrapped a warm towel around my head I remembered about the stranger. I looked up only to find that he'd gone. I was strangely disappointed. I'd begun to feel a bit of stirring in my loins, wherever, precisely, they might be.

I'm ashamed to tell you about the next half hour,

but I did warn you what I'm like about having my hair cut. As I expected, Darryl got Franiq'ua to expose my shame to the audience of women in the salon.

"Let me see. Lift a strand up. And one from the back. Now the side. Hmm."

I could tell that "hmm" wasn't an approving "hmm" or an appreciative "hmm." I hadn't really been expecting a gold star from Darryl, but the state of my hair must have been even worse than I could have imagined, because Darryl actually left the (long-haired) client he was working on to come and stand behind me. He lifted a single tendril with the end of his comb and then even touched it with his own hands, holding it as if it were about to communicate some incurable disease. My heart started to beat faster when he called Gregory down. Gregory is the rarely-seen owner of the salon, and if Darryl is asking for his advice, then things must be deadly serious. Gregory touched my hair too. I should have felt honored. They didn't actually say anything to each other, just shook their heads sadly. The next thing I knew, a circle of women had formed around my chair and they all suddenly become haircare experts.

"Oh my God!"

"Girl, you ain't been taking care of your hair."

"I thought mine was bad when it started to break, but thank God it wasn't as bad as that."

"Yes, but you caught yours in time and you did something about it."

"She could have saved that with Elasta."

"No, I prefer Hair Rescue Serum. That's what I does always use."

"What she goin' do now? Too late for all that."

"I would just start all over if I was she."

"Wear a wig." One of them laughed, but the rest

looked at me with deep sympathy and in deadly earnest as if they were viewing a newly deceased corpse. I began to understand that that was exactly what they were doing; the hair on my head was truly dead and we were now only discussing the cremation arrangements.

Darryl looked at me in the mirror and shook his head. "Carol," was all he could manage.

He was like a hospital consultant. I fully expected him to take my hand, but he didn't. "There's nothing more I can do. I'm sorry." A hairdresser saying he was sorry! I wanted to plead for a donor to come forward. "It will have to go."

That's when I disgraced myself. It might have been the stark way he told me or the looks of sympathy from the other women as they turned away, not wanting to share in my bereavement, but I felt my eyes well up. My bottom lip began to tremble, my nose began to tingle, and a single tear made its way down my cheek. It was like the women were performing in a well-rehearsed ballet. They each rushed to their abandoned handbags to return with a tissue. I took them all 'cos I knew I was going to need them. I wasn't discreet. I sobbed uncontrollably as someone put her arms around me. I wailed. I admit it, I bawled. Loud and long.

"Don't cry, darling."

"But, but, but . . ." I stammered. "It took years to grow it this long."

"I know, sweetheart, but when was the last time you looked at the back of your head. Is not a lot of hair left there."

I wept. I sniffled. I howled until there was not a drop more liquid to be wrung from my body. Gregory turned the sign on the door to "closed." I don't suppose he wanted any potential clients to think that he'd done this to me. Franiq'ua brought me coffee. Darryl went to the pub next door and got a medicinal triple brandy.

"Come now, sweetheart, you've had a bit of a shock, but is no need to be going on like this." The woman could have been my mother.

I sniffed in reply and swallowed the brandy. I took a deep breath.

"All right, Darryl. Let's get it over with."

Everyone returned to her rightful place, but I could see that over the tops of their magazines, the women were keeping an eye on me. I don't know whether they were fascinated by what Darryl might create or whether they were just terrified that I might succumb to another bout of high-energy mourning.

Darryl didn't snip with the scissors. He hacked. I made sure that I produced the occasional sniffle just to remind him that this was serious shit and he wasn't to take any liberties. To distract myself, I flicked nervously through the pile of hair magazines that Franiq'ua brought. She could at least have censored them and torn out or defaced all the models with long hair, but I endured that reminder with only the odd, deep, heartfelt sigh. I brightened a bit when I thought I might end up looking like Beverley Knight. Darryl snipped again and it was more likely to be Halle Berry, but, hey, that's nothing to complain about. You can tell that whenever I look at those pictures in hair magazines, I always think that I'm going to end up looking *exactly* like whoever the celebrity might be. I don't mean that my *hair* will look like theirs. No, I mean that I will suddenly be transformed into Halle Berry. Hair, face, body, money, Oscar, husband (no, on second thought, scratch the husband), talent, the lot. That's why I'm always disappointed. It's not totally Darryl's fault.

When I looked in the mirror again, I finally understood that I wasn't going to look like Halle Berry. More like Errol Brown from Hot Chocolate. Still, we have to be grateful for small mercies, and when more hairs appear on my chin, then I can form a tribute band.

I couldn't really look when Darryl had finished. Hairdressers like you to spend hours admiring their handiwork, but I didn't have the heart for it. I'd been there for four hours, my emotions had been wracked and I needed to escape from everyone who'd witnessed my humiliation as well as my sex change. I left a huge tip to make up for any loss of business that I'd caused, put my hood up, and skulked out as fast as I could. My head was bowed to avoid looking anyone in the eye, so it was inevitable that I was going to bump straight into a pair of trainers, denim jeans, and black cotton shirt.

"Hey, sexy lady, where you going in such a hurry? I been waiting for you."

I looked up into a face that reminded me of Craig David, maybe because of the elaborate goatee. I've always been a bit suspicious of Craig David's beard. Like it was there to cover up something a bit dodgy going on with his chin. And then he shaved it off. And grew it again almost immediately. Point taken? This guy's hair was braided. I don't normally go for that on a man—too vain somehow—but it suited him. My stomach did one of those little somersaults. Definite orgasm potential.

"I wanted to see what you'd look like when they finished with you."

I was more than a little surprised. He couldn't have been more than about twenty-four. Beautifully smooth bronze skin, full lips, chiseled features with high cheek-bones that suggested he should be one of those "heroin-chic" models, long dark eyelashes, and big eyes that brought to mind Rob Elliott. That was the problem re-ally: I knew I'd do anything he asked.

He put an arm around my waist and led me to a spot under a streetlamp. He pushed back my hood.

"Wow! You look incredible. Short hair on a woman is *so* hot." He ran his fingers over my scalp, tracing the contour of my head. Why was I letting a complete stranger do this? "You've got a beautifully shaped head. Just right for that style. You are one gorgeous babe." That's why!

Tears prickled my eyes again and my throat was too choked for speech. That's what I hate about really short hair; it makes you feel so vulnerable, so exposed, so weepy. I decided he'd taken pity on me.

He reached for my hand. "Come and eat. You must be hungry. I bet you've been in that place all day."

"I don't go out with men who have longer hair than me." I sniffed.

"Well, that rules out most of us," he teased, smiling at me. And it was that smile that warned me that he might not be as young mentally as he looked physi-cally. "Come on. You need to chill."

What did I have to lose? I'd just allowed another man to cut off the hair that I'd labored over lovingly for years—well, all right, I hadn't exactly lavished care on it, but I still expected it to do the decent thing and stay in its rightful place—on my head. I certainly deserved a little ego boosting. He had said all the right things so far, so I was looking to forgive his youth. Be-sides, his eyes did remind me of Rob Elliott and I didn't want to make him cry.

As I mentioned before, no self-respecting woman under the age of sixty or so has an empty schedule on a Friday evening, so the Caribbean restaurant he led me to was packed with crowds of young people gearing up for a night's clubbing. The place, not much bigger than my own living room, was hot, smoky, and noisy, and we had to squeeze past some seriously revealing party outfits to get to a table in the corner.

Now, I'm not a mother, so I don't have to worry about embarrassing my kids with the clothes I wear. Nicola thinks my dress sense is outrageous and she has been known to send me home to change when we've been out together. Today I had on a very short micro leather skirt with fishnet tights and a figure-hugging sweater cut low to make the most of my ample cleavage. Looking around me, though, I was well overdressed compared with the young girls wearing very chic, expensive, wispy bits of nothing. I was beginning to feel frumpy and middle-aged.

"Hell!" he said as I took off my coat, staring with a deliberately suggestive look in his eye. "Well worth waiting for!"

I blushed again. I wasn't used to such open appreciation, so I studied the menu chalked on the blackboard. I could feel his leg move between mine, pressing against my knee. I didn't know whether it was deliberate or just that there wasn't anywhere else for his long legs to go since the place was so packed. I couldn't decide between the curried goat and the ackee and saltfish. I had to concentrate on that to avoid looking at him or registering the fact that I could feel the heat of his skin through his jeans.

My hand was resting on the table and he reached over to gently stroke it with one finger. It was an idle gesture, but it surprised me and made me all the more aware of his nearness. He was tall, spare, rangy, but confident within his skin. I think that's why I could forget his youth, because he acted with the self-assurance of a man twice his age. For a moment I wondered where his confidence with women came from, but I didn't really want to know. I'm not naïve enough to think that his every action was anything but practiced. I was enjoying him, though, and wasn't intending to examine the molars of any gift horse. It helped his cause too, that I could see several of the girls in the restaurant eyeing him up appreciatively, the same way I had done earlier in the salon. He was polite enough to ignore them all, though I knew he was aware of them. Instead, he gave me his full attention.

I think you'll understand how insecure I was feeling when I left the salon. I know you've probably been there too. It's like you hand over your most precious treasures and they come back shattered. I was practically bald-headed. One consolation, I guess: at least it took my mind off getting older, even though it's a bit like amputating your leg to take away the pain of a bunion.

So there I was, lucky enough to be rescued from imminent despair by a handsome young man who seemed hell-bent on showering me with compliments and making me feel hot and horny. Well, what would you do? If you say you'd walk away, may you rot in hell 'cos I ain't goin' believe you in a million years.

The chance of our being served within the next hour or so seemed slim. This had been a day for waiting around. Hairdressers, restaurants, take-aways—even in a country as cold as England the Caribbean pace of life doesn't change one bit so it's best not to fight it. Those of us who are born here just have to learn to feel the flow, to chill. Is a part of we heritage we ain't goin' give up without a fight. My companion went to the bar and snagged a couple of bottles of beer, which we drank straight from the bottle. I was getting into the role. Now that I looked like a man, I might as well behave like one.

He leaned across the table and whispered in my ear, "You're all woman, you know. I love to watch your lips around the neck of that bottle." I could feel the warmth of his breath against my cheek and, as he moved, the pressure of his knee against my thigh. This was no accident. The heat started to percolate throughout my body, right up through my stomach, my breasts, my neck, flooding my face until I knew I must be shining like a beacon. I almost choked on the beer.

"Why you embarrassed? You know how sexy you look. What you expect a guy to do? You getting me horny as hell. Don't worry. Look around. No one paying us no mind."

He was right. The restaurant was too busy. Anyway, I wasn't really able to take in what was going on around us. I couldn't look into his eyes because the lust in them was too blatant. Instead, I concentrated on his lips. That was best since I couldn't be sure that I heard him properly amidst the din. I lip-read to reassure myself that what I thought he was saying wasn't just wishful thinking. It wasn't. His lyrics should have come with a Parental Advisory sticker.

"I'm so glad I waited for you. When I walked into the salon I couldn't see your face, just those shapely, sexy legs and that very short skirt. Can you imagine what that did to me? You know what effect you're having, don't you? That's why you women dress like

that. You want us guys to get so stiff that we'll beg for
it. I know you were looking at me. You couldn't take
your eyes off my hard-on. It's all for you. I could see
you staring. Were you getting hot? Was your pussy
getting wet? Knowing you were watching only made
my cock harder. Did you see that?"

I didn't like to tell him that I'd only been staring
because I couldn't move my head. I didn't remember
any erection, but the thought of it was certainly affecting
me now. I felt a pit-a-pat in my stomach, if not butterflies, then at least caterpillars. I guess it was the thought
of having such power over him.

"Yes," I lied, beginning to enjoy the fantasy. If
that's all it took to keep him saying these good things
to me, then so be it.

"You knew I'd be waiting, didn't you?"

"Yeah, that's why I was running out the door."

"I knew your face would be like the rest of your
body. Beautiful and sexy as hell." He slowly licked his
finger and reached over to caress the contours of my
mouth. "Sexy, warm lips. I know just where I'd like to
feel them."

He took my hand in his and licked the palm, circling it with his tongue. Instantly, a jolt of fire shot
through me. It woke the butterflies and sent them skit-
tering in every direction. I caught my breath. I felt a
fluttering in my groin, surging upward to my breasts.
He certainly knew what he was doing since his eyes
stared into mine as he kissed each finger in turn. There
was no mistaking what those eyes were asking and I
couldn't stop mine replying, even if I'd wanted to.

"Tek you order?"

A rather sullen waitress chose this most inconve-
nient moment to approach our table. Casting a malevo-

lent glance in our direction, she held a pencil poised impatiently over a pad. I didn't hear or care what he ordered. I just wanted the waitress to go. Right now. If necessary, I would have wrestled her out the door, but she didn't show much more interest in us and progressed to the next customer.

"I think I know what you want," he said. I pretended that he was talking about the food.

He took my hand again, thumb hypnotically circling my palm. "We have to wait till you're ready, though." I watched as his eyes slowly traveled to my breasts. I was acutely aware that my nipples were like bullets. He watched with a hint of amusement on his lips. I couldn't stop what was happening and could only attempt to cover myself with my free hand.

"Don't do that," he ordered abruptly. "Let me see." I slowly took my hand away, but as I did that, I became more aware of the other people in the room. He'd said that no one was paying attention, but either it was my imagination, or a whole heap of men were mesmerized by my protruding nipples. I could have died with shame but I was strangely excited too. He turned to follow my gaze and smiled as his eyes returned to meet mine.

"You should be proud. It makes me feel good that all them other guys are getting hot, but none of them can have you."

So I wasn't imagining it! They *were* all watching me. Half of me wanted to get up and run out of the place in shame. What if any of these people knew my nosey aunts, or, heaven forbid, my parents? The other half of me, though, stayed rooted to the spot, curious about where all this would lead, confident that nothing much could happen in the middle of a crowded restaurant. Could it?

The waitress brought our food, slamming it down on the table. I don't even know if we got what he ordered, but the food was delicious; tender pieces of jerk pork, spicy with pimento, allspice, and hot scotch bonnet pepper. I could sense that he was watching every movement I made. Sweat began to bead my forehead. The heat wasn't all coming from the food.

"You eat the way I imagine you make love. Like you want to savor every single moment. I bet you like to take it nice and slow."

This guy was completely outrageous. I couldn't even eat my food without him making something suggestive of it. I couldn't let him get away with it.

I put down my fork. "I like my meat hot. I ain't never found anyone who makes it hot enough for me."

I'd done it now. I could see his eyes spark with the challenge. He wiped his lips with a napkin, folded it, and rested it on the tablecloth, slowly smoothing out the creases. When he looked up, he smiled at me and I felt his knees part to separate my legs. My heart leaped to my throat with sudden trepidation. What the hell did I think I was playing at?

He spread my legs wide and then was still. He looked at me with a determined set to his mouth. He raised one eyebrow slightly in question. As if responding to some invisible signal that I'd unwittingly given, his hand disappeared under the table. He ripped at my tights. I gasped. I felt the almost imperceptible touch of a finger against the silk of my panties. I was suddenly breathless. Literally. I couldn't make a sound.

"You see why I like short skirts."

He waited for a moment and then stroked me softly. "Well, well, I knew you'd be wet." I couldn't deny that I was enjoying what was happening; there was no way of hiding the fact. His finger continued to caress, to fondle, to tease, and I found myself shifting against the leather seat, tilting my hips toward him, lifting my butt so that he could pull down my tights. He knew what he was doing, and as he hooked his finger under my knickers and moved the fabric to one side, I bit my lip to stop myself from moaning aloud. He grinned as he lightly touched my clitoris, making me want to scream. He'd found the right spot but now that he had, and knew it, he wanted to torture me. He just let his finger hover there. I was determined not to move either. I was desperate to feel his touch, I wanted to thrust against him, but this was a battle that I wouldn't let him win. I didn't stir a millimeter. I simply stared into his deep brown eyes for a moment.

"So," I said, as calmly as I could. "What do you do for a living?" That surprised him. He wasn't expecting me to have such self-control.

"I'm a masseur."

He was lying and we both knew it. But he'd thrown down the gauntlet. The gloves were off. I considered slipping my feet out of my shoes, but decided against it. I shifted to cross my legs and I know he thought I was giving in. The momentary sensation of his touch almost made me surrender, and he grinned in triumph; but I'm made of strong stuff. As I crossed my legs, I made sure that my stilettoed foot grazed his crotch. I heard his sharp intake of breath and he pulled away. Two can play this game. I ran the pointed toe of my shoe along the seam in his jeans, following the contour of his balls and his much-appreciated erection. His eyes widened in shock. *That wiped the smile off your face*, I thought. Except that a blissful smile did suddenly colonize his features. I continued to play with him until he leaned back in his chair. I missed the feel of his touch on my skin, but I knew I'd won. I reached forward until my fingers found the hard-on that he'd promised me and I trailed one finger along the length, taking the measure of him, not unimpressed by what I found.

"All for you, baby, all for you," he muttered, almost delirious. I pressed harder against him, searching until I found his zipper. I reached inside the thick material of his jeans until I could feel the heat of his flesh, the hardness of him in my hand, the throbbing of the vein as the blood rose to his face.

"So . . . tell me what massage can do for me," I teased as I wrapped my fingers around his straining erection. I knew he couldn't speak. I freed his cock from its confines and could only imagine what it looked like as, blindly, I traced the shape of it, impressed by the length and the thickness. I reached deep into his jeans and cupped his testicles, weighing them in my hand, rubbing my thumb around them like they were juggling balls. I'd been neglecting his cock and it was bouncing against my hand, demanding attention, so I took care of it, stroking, squeezing, making tiny circles around the tip with my thumb until he moaned aloud and gripped my wrist, pushing me away from him.

It had only been a temporary truce. His hand was back on my flesh, rubbing gently with the heel, round and round until I thought I couldn't take any more. Then his finger was inside me and my mouth opened in a silent "oh" of surprise. He laughed aloud, but I didn't care. I just wanted to feel more of him, so I rocked my hips. And then there were two fingers inside me, then three, moving in and out, stopping only to feather against my clitoris, then in and out again, repeating the rhythm, over and over, harder and harder, faster and faster until I closed my eyes, wanting to raise the white flag, to shut out everything around me, to shut him out, to concentrate on just the longed-for sensation, the delicious tingling that flooded my breasts, my vagina, my womb, the heat that swirled through me, the pleasure that made me want to scream. I bit my lip, hard.

"That hot enough for you?" I heard him murmur.

When I finally opened my eyes and looked up, he was gone. No one was looking in my direction. In fact, all the men seemed to be averting their eyes.

I quickly rearranged my clothing and put my coat on. I stood on shaky legs and tried to pay the waitress. She told me that it had all been *taken care of.* I swear to God she had a smile on her face. I prayed fervently that it would crack and shatter into a thousand pieces. I got out of there as fast as I could.

Chapter Six

When I woke this morning, I wondered whether I'd imagined last night. I tend to daydream a bit, but I don't think even my imagination is that fertile. And I still had a warm, fuzzy feeling in the groin area. It really *has* been a while! I'm a bit surprised that I allowed things to go that far. But I don't feel bad about it. In fact, I'm amazed that I still have it in me. I feel quite proud of myself. I used to be the kind of person who never takes chances. That was before I met Max.

I surprised myself by waiting for months before I ended up in bed with Max. Not because I really wanted to wait, but because I suspected a certain smugness about him. And I didn't want to become another groupie on the bedpost. And then he was away a lot. I ignored the flowers, didn't return his calls, was usually busy, and generally refused to respond when all my senses were screaming at me to ravish him. I wanted to make him beg. What stunned me was that, in the end, that's exactly what he did.

"Girl, please tell me what's wrong with me. My mother loves me. My sister loves me. My dog loves me. Even my goldfish love me. What I done to you to make you treat me like this? Carol, I don't know what else I can do. Tell me, I'm begging you." He was down on one knee in front of my office desk. He'd somehow managed to charm his way past reception and now all my colleagues were staring in my direction, the women with baleful, accusing looks in their eyes. "Go on, Carol," one of them shouted. A whole chorus followed, "Give the guy a break."

All this was before *The Cream*. In those days I worked in a huge, open office in a rather conservative insurance company. Believe me, Max was doing me no favors. My heart sank when I heard a discreet cough behind me. I turned to see my straightlaced boss, all pink and flushed and smiling benevolently. "Carol, I think you could have an extended lunch hour, don't you?"

Lunch was more of the same pleading over pasta served with envious looks from the waitress. Then a walk in Green Park with his constant litany interrupted only by requests for autographs. All of which only made me more wary. What kind of intimacy could there be with someone whose life was lived in the public eye? That and my belief that his ego didn't need feeding any further. I still hadn't agreed to go out with him by the time we got back to the office and, for a moment, I caught a glimpse of that Rob Elliott–type look in his eye. Something began to melt.

"I won't give up you know, Carol," he shouted as I walked through the revolving doors into the elevator and back to my desk. Every single woman in the place looked as if she wanted to string me up.

I could have strangled Max that afternoon. He didn't know how long it had taken me to blend into the background, to get to the point where I could just get on with my job without being singled out and then leave at the end of the day without anyone paying any special attention to me. That afternoon the office was abuzz. It was only then that I understood quite how famous Max was. I thought those guys in their gray suits, men and women, must lead a wild secret life outside the office. It turned out to be simpler than that; most of them had younger siblings or children who had posters featuring Max on their bedroom walls. So I was the talk of the whole building and everyone suddenly wanted to be my new best friend.

I was still seething when I finished work. I refused the many offers of drinks and just wanted to escape to the sanctuary of my home. I walked out of the elevator accompanied by the most persistent of my colleagues. And there he was, sitting forlornly in reception, surrounded by what seemed like every bouquet of white roses that London had to offer. The receptionist came over to whisper that he'd been waiting all afternoon. I took one look at his puppy-dog face and sighed. Then I felt a grin tug at the corner of my lips and soon I was laughing. Whichever way you looked at it, the whole situation was comical. Max looked confused at first, then he laughed, too, walked over, and kissed me full on the lips, to the accompaniment of enthusiastic applause.

I took just one rose and Max distributed the rest to my colleagues and anyone he encountered on our path to the car that was waiting outside. Turned out that he had a gig that night. He'd missed rehearsals to camp out in my office building all afternoon, but he assured me that he had all the inspiration he needed. Max made me feel special. I could almost smell the hormones rising from the thousands of women in the audience who desired him, and as he gyrated on stage, raising the temperature higher and higher, I wasn't immune to his spell. And then he did something that guaranteed that I'd end up in his bed. He dedicated the last song of the evening to "the only woman I want in my life: Carol." He sang, kneeling by the side of the stage, gazing into my eyes. I challenge any woman to resist.

I guess last night's encounter took me back to those days with Max. My instincts had told me that I wasn't in any danger and the thrill of public sex was a powerful aphrodisiac. I suppose it was always like that with Max, as if we were constantly being watched.

When I got back home, I spent a long time looking at myself in the mirror and decided that I could go some way toward forgiving Darryl. I was getting to quite like my new half-a-centimeter-long hair. I could even see what my anonymous sexual partner had meant. There's something intriguing about the severe masculine cut when matched with soft, feminine contours. And if that's the effect it has on men, then I definitely won't complain. Safe sex doesn't get a lot better. We didn't even exchange names.

There was a message on my machine from Gabby. "Tried to call you last night. Guess your cell was switched off. How did it go at the hairdresser's? Anyway, pick you up at seven."

Shit! I'd forgotten that I'd agreed to go to a fancy

gallery opening with Gabby tonight. She gets invited to loads of those events that you see written up in *Hello!* or *OK!* magazine. You know how you always see one black person in those photos? Well, it's likely to be Gabby, so you already have an idea of what she looks like. When she invites me, the organizers probably worry that we're going to riot! I've been with her to a couple of these occasions now and they're good for those fancy canapés that always have smoked salmon and olives in there somewhere—and it means that I don't have to cook.

Gabby said a cocktail outfit would do fine, so I squeezed myself into a dark green raw silk, V-necked dress with onyx beads scattered randomly here and there. I wanted to put on some makeup but had to make do with a few drops of water on a dried-up mascara wand and the same old red lipstick that I've worn for about fifteen years now. I even got out the rollers, brushes, and hot comb until I remembered that I no longer need all that stuff. I smoothed my hand over my unfamiliar head and the feel of my new style brought back memories of the young stranger that I don't need to dwell on here.

Gabby picked me up in a taxi at seven forty-five and she looked as stunning as ever. Try as hard as I might, there's always something that lets me down. While I wore my practical, old, black coat, Gabby had on a beige leather shawl-type thing that was soft enough to be silk. Underneath I could see a few wisps of material draped strategically to cover all the naughty bits. My mother would never have let me out of the house dressed like that. Gabby had on the highest, spikiest stilettos that it's possible to wear without the help of a pair of crutches. She could get away with it, though, since she's the kind of woman who can get in and out of cars without revealing the color of her knickers.

The new gallery was in Old Bond Street and our taxi had to wait in line until each celebrity stepped onto the metaphorical red carpet. I was quite excited at the sight of the waiting photographers and managed to slip out of my old coat before we got out of the cab. I was still caught out by the flash of lights and I cussed myself knowing that I'd end up in the background of some photograph looking like a giant panda with Gabby tall and elegant in the foreground. You know the type of thing: . . . *the exquisite Gabriela Chapel accompanied by one of China's last surviving Giant Pandas arriving at the opening of the new Ponti Gallery* . . .

I was determined not to be fazed, though, so I dumped my coat as quickly as I could and hovered for a while at Gabby's shoulder while a whole group of admirers flocked around her like Trafalgar Square pigeons to breadcrumbs. I felt a little surplus to requirements and decided to leave them to it. I'm not brilliant at these kinds of events, so I headed straight for a waiter carrying a tray of champagne and found a secluded corner from which to survey the room.

I told myself to make the most of the evening. It's not often that I get to meet so many famous and influential people, so I watched the way Gabby operated, planning to do whatever she did. But Gabby didn't have to do much at all; she just stood there looking gorgeous and enigmatic and men swooped on her. Well, that wasn't going to work for me, so I had to find my own way. I reminded myself that I had a new hairstyle, makeup of a kind, business cards in my bag, and a glass of alcohol in my hand. I looked right and left and my spirits lifted when I recognized a friendly face in the center of a small group. I couldn't quite remember where we'd met before, but he had a sympathetic air so I made a beeline for him with an unthreatening smile plastered on my face. I held out my hand with a confident "Nice to see you again. How are you?" He took my hand, holding it with both of his own.

"Good to see you too. You know Alison . . . Bill . . . and Clive?" They all looked at me expectantly, so I introduced myself. "Carol Shaw." This circulating business was easier than I thought. We chatted easily about this and that, mostly soaps that we watched on television. I soon worked out that the guy I'd recognized was called Stephen Saunders and the name rang definite bells but I still couldn't place him. Gradually, the others drifted away and I was left alone with Stephen. It was so weird: I felt as if I knew him so well but *how* was a mystery. He was so charming too. You know the type: distinguished-looking with hair graying at the temples and genial crinkles around his eyes, the sort of white guy that grows up to be Santa. He seemed fascinated by my conversation, intense blue eyes glued to mine, and I had just launched into a critique of the latest medical drama I'd become addicted to when someone bumped into me and sent me flying into his arms. It was the concern in his eyes that tipped me off. Dr. Coram Staines, Medical Director of *St. Stephens*. No wonder he had such a sympathetic look in his eyes. He was quite practiced at it. That's exactly how he always looks when he has to tell someone they only have days to live, a frequent occurrence on that particular soap opera. I surreptitiously felt my pulse and then my forehead as my cheeks burned. I'd never met him before! There I was treating him like some long-lost buddy when I'd only ever seen him on television. I could only stutter "I'm so sorry" and rush to the bathroom to splash cold water on my face. I calmed down and decided that I was going to stay there for the rest of the evening. The rest of my life. I'm not really safe left on my own.

Gabby came looking for me and she only laughed when I told her the story. "Come on, Carol. I'm sure he didn't mind at all and you can't stay here all night. They don't serve drinks in the bathrooms and, anyway, there are some people I want you to meet."

"As long as you warn them first. Tell them that I've only just been released and I still need care in the community."

Gabby took my hand and practically dragged me out. She led me around the room as she sought out her particular targets, a couple of youngish guys talking animatedly over by a huge fireplace.

"Carol, meet Adrian and Julian. I've told them all about you." I prayed that she hadn't. "They work in the music business too." And with that, she was gone and I stood there feeling as if I'd been thrown in the deep end of the pool. That was Gabby's technique. Sink or swim.

The guy she'd introduced as Julian threw me a lifeline, "We were just discussing all these *Pop Idol*–type programs. Adrian's convinced that they're reviving the industry, but he would say that since he's one of those corporate sharks who only look for the dollar signs, whereas I'm an independent talent scout and I can see the harm these manufactured bands are doing. Nobody's interested in real ability anymore. Gabriela said you work for a music mag. What do you think?"

"I'm not really into teeny-pop, so I don't bother

with all that stuff. Of course, we cover all the angles
the record companies come up with to get publicity for
those acts. It sells. All we have to do is put one of the
winners on the cover and we're guaranteed sales. But
we try to cover some real music inside the magazine
too."

"So what do you call 'real' music?" the one called
Adrian asked with a definite sneer in his voice. I couldn't
really understand the hostility.

"Well, I've always been into black music—"

"You mean *urban* music," he interrupted in that
patronizing kind of way that white guys have when
they've spent five minutes learning a little itsy bitsy
nothing about black culture.

I took a deep breath. "Urban, garage, soul, retro-
soul, funk, house, deephouse, disco, hip-hop, trip-hop,
rap, swingbeat, R&B, bluebeat, reggae, ragga, lovers',
dub, Brit funk, jazz, jazz funk, blues, Motown, Philly,
rhythm 'n' soul, drum & bass, techno, rare groove,
afrobeat, calypso, soca, world, call it what you will."
I pulled myself up to my full height and tried to look
down my nose at him, even though he was at least six
inches taller than me. I could see Julian smiling in appreciation and I continued, "I also enjoy folk music or
country music or any music that has a heritage and
something to communicate. I can even find myself tapping my feet to some manufactured bubblegum music.
Those kind of *Pop Idol* programs only promote the
bubblegum, though, and the problem is that eventually
the bubblegum loses its taste and you spit it out." *When
did I get to be so pompous?*

"So, you're an expert?"

"No, just someone who really appreciates music."

Julian laughed out loud. "Good on you!" Adrian walked away, muttering something under his breath.

"I'm so sorry," I apologized, to completely the wrong person. "I don't know what got into me. That was so rude."

"Don't worry. I was trying to make the same point before you came along. Just not quite so eloquently. Adrian's company has just signed a deal to make one of those talent search programs so he's probably feeling sensitive. It was all his own idea and, can you believe it, they're going to do a kind of *Soul Idol*. He was so enthusiastic about it that he was making me feel quite nauseous. I think you just popped his bubble."

"Oh God, then I was even ruder than I thought."

"Well, I really enjoyed it. Let me get you another drink."

I needed more alcohol. In only an hour or so I had already managed to offend two people. If Gabby was hoping to influence people or make any friends, then she'd invited the wrong companion and she should get me out of there as soon as possible. I looked around for help, but Gabby wasn't anywhere to be seen and Julian was heading toward me with glass in hand. At least there was one person who wasn't taking the first opportunity to get away from me.

I took the time to study Julian as his route was interrupted by several people who stopped him to chat. He looked early thirties, tall with hair so blond that you wondered if it came out of a bottle and blue eyes that fixed on anyone he talked to so that you felt you were the only person in the room. I noticed that most of those who greeted him were women, invariably equally blond, wearing diaphanous slivers of material that revealed surgically enhanced bosoms that they pressed against his arm. I don't know whether it was because of the kind of admiring attention he was getting, but I suddenly found myself looking at Julian in a new light. The kind of light that makes your nipples tingle. I was surprised since he's not my type, but I was quite enjoying the feeling. I wondered whether this was something to do with the previous evening. Was I going to be thinking about sex every time I was in an open space with a vaguely eligible man?

I was standing there gazing at Julian when a hand sneaked around my waist. I looked round and there was Adrian, slightly the worse for wear, leering at my cleavage.

"I think we should look at the art. That's what we're here for, after all." He took my arm and led me into a large room crowded with people ignoring the huge paintings decorating the walls. I was mesmerized by the swirls of gold and purple, the tiny black figures overshadowed by the tumultuous shards of sparkling light. The swaths of color were strangely arousing and for no apparent reason I thought of last night's encounter. I could feel the heat rising from my crotch up through my breasts and flooding into my face. I could vaguely make out Adrian's voice.

"Let's talk more about your theories about music. I'm interested in what you were saying." I'm not really sure that's what he was interested in at all, since he couldn't take his eyes from my breasts. But talking to him was safer than thinking the thoughts that were entering my head. God help me!

I dragged myself back from the paintings and was just about to launch into a speech worthy of a PhD dissertation when a figure straight out of a Noel Coward play, complete with smoking jacket, rushed toward me and grasped my hand, "I saw you looking at my work."

I was quick enough to realize that this must be the artist. "I love your paintings—"

"You are the only one who has taken the time to look, mademoiselle." Even without the "mademoiselle" his precise speech and accent plus the fact that he would not let go of my hand had told me that he wasn't English.

"I looked earlier," Adrian protested. Then the next thing I knew Stephen Saunders walked into my eye-line.

"Adrian, Marcel, I see you've met my friend Carol," and he stroked my arm in a most suggestive way. I felt kind of flattered that he wanted them to think there was something between us, but before I could get my head around that, Julian finally arrived with the glass of champagne that was now more than welcome. Before I could take it all in, there was another man approaching our group, then another and another until I was queen bee at the center of a swarm. What the fuck was going on? A whole heap of men all around me. Yes, and true to form, not one single one paying any real attention to *me*; no, more interested in comparing their dicks. There I am drowning, needing air, and all of them showing off their breaststroke. I stood on tiptoe and searched frantically until I caught Gabby's eye. She winked at me and I mouthed "help!" She walked over and took my hand, hauling me out of the scrum.

"What is this shit?" I asked when we reached the safety of the bathroom.

"What do you mean?"

"Where did all those guys come from? One minute

I'm standing there like a vicar in a lap-dancing club, the next minute I'm drowning in a sea of testosterone!"

"You been getting some lately?"

I blushed, thinking of the stranger last night.

"You see," Gabby said, not waiting for a verbal reply. "They can always tell. Is like honey to the bee. Just enjoy it."

I wondered if that's why Gabby was always surrounded by men, but it seemed rude to ask.

"So who is he?" Gabby wasn't going to let go.

"Nobody. I mean, nothing. I haven't been doing anything."

"No?" That raised eyebrow was so eloquent.

"Could I lie to you, Gab?" She didn't answer.

You know, guys always wonder why we girls go off to the bathroom together. Most times, it's to get away from men and have a chance to breathe. When I checked my lipstick and mascara and opened the door, there they all were, standing outside, waiting. This was a really new experience for me and I felt like I was being stalked. I wondered if Gabby was right, or whether this was all to do with my new hair. My life had started to change as soon as Darryl had cut the straggly mess from my head. That must have been an omen.

I decided not to analyze, to just enjoy the moment in case it never happened again. I would follow Gabby's lead. Before I could think about it, I found myself in a taxi with Gabby, Julian, Adrian, Marcel, and Stephen heading toward the bright, but slightly seedy, lights of the West End.

Another new experience. I'd never been to one of those "businessmen's" clubs and had never really wanted to, but I was seduced by the twinkling lights at the entrance that reminded me of Christmas and tinsel and presents under the tree. It pays to hang out with well-connected folks since we were immediately ushered past the queue to a seating area that commanded a perfect view of the dance floor. Bottles of Cristal soon appeared. What was I to do? It would have been rude to turn teetotal.

You've been to the red-light district in Amsterdam, so you know what I mean when I say that, in spite of the alcohol, I felt more than a little awkward sitting there while the scantily-clad lap dancers gyrated in front of the men. Without exception, they were gorgeous—the dancers, not the men—with the kind of bodies that you'd sell your soul for, the type of bodies that were designed to arouse. Even me. I've never felt the urge to indulge in any kind of sexual activity with another woman, but, objectively speaking, a woman's body is infinitely more attractive than a man's. What these girls were simulating was definitely erotic. But I guess the reason I felt ill at ease was that their eyes were glazed and they seemed so detached and I knew what that felt like. I'm sure you know what I mean too. Don't pretend you've never had the experience where you just have to let him get on with it and imagine yourself somewhere else. Anyway, the guys I was with didn't seem to recognize that look. They were well into the whole atmosphere of the place and didn't even notice the photographer hovering nearby. I did. And he recognized me too. It was Patrick from *The Cream* and it felt good to see a familiar face in this alien environment.

"Carol! I didn't know this was the kind of place you come to."

I didn't know whether I should take that as a compliment or not. Did he mean that he thought the place was beneath me or above me?

"I didn't expect to see you either, Patrick."

"Oh, I'm a regular here. Don't you recognize the place from the photos we've used? This is where I get some of my best scoops. A few glasses of champagne and they don't even notice me."

"I hope you don't include me in that."

"You'll have to wait until Monday to find out, Carol."

"Would you like a drink, Patrick?" I poured a glass from one of the several bottles nestling in ice buckets.

"Carol, some of the best in the business have tried to bribe me and I can tell you a glass of champagne is not enough. You'll have to try harder." He moved closer. I wondered if Patrick had been drinking already, because suddenly his presence didn't seem so reassuring. He leaned toward me, leering at my cleavage. I couldn't stand the lack of subtlety so I happened to trip and spill his drink down his front.

"Patrick, I'm so sorry," I said in a flat monotone.

He smiled, but we both knew that it wasn't an accident. I looked at Patrick again—the first time I'd really looked at him in ages. Overlong graying hair, slightly seedy army surplus jacket designed to hold all the paraphernalia he carried with him, jeans, slip-on shoes—precisely the kind of disguise every sensible paparazzo adopts these days. The difference was that his was soaking wet.

For a moment, I felt guilty, but only for a moment. I smiled, knowing that the smile didn't reach my eyes. Patrick scuttled off to the bathroom to get cleaned up, reminding me of a hermit crab.

By the time I turned back to my table, the dancers

had moved on and Adrian's attention had returned to me. I noticed that looseness around his eyes and lips that suggested he'd had a bit too much to drink, and not for the first time, but he managed to speak reasonably coherently.

"So, Carol, you know everything there is to know about urban music?"

I sighed. "I didn't quite say that. I know quite a bit about different types of music. That's part of my job. It just happens that my personal taste leans toward black music."

"Don't be so sensitive," he remarked. Moving to put an arm around me but put off by the look in my eyes, he rested it along the back of the seat.

"I'd still like to pick your brain. You know we're starting a new talent show, *Soul Sensation*? I'd like to talk to you more and see what you think. Kind of like my own personal focus group."

Adrian said this while looking me straight in the eye, so I had to take him at face value. You can't really complain when you've been moaning about something and then someone who could make a difference actually wants to listen to your opinions. I took the card that he handed me and gave him mine. I had another sip of champagne and decided I'd had enough of polite conversation. I took Adrian by the hand and led him to the dance floor.

Looking round, you could see that the club was aimed at the over-twenties, well, over-thirties. So they were playing the kind of stuff that's good to move to: Mary J. Blige, Incognito, Funka-delic, and even a smattering of Nas, P. Diddy, or Busta Rhymes when the DJ thought no one was really listening.

You know what I'm like when I get started. At first

Adrian was looking at me as if I'd started breakdancing in the middle of the Royal Opera House and he wanted to pretend that he wasn't with this lunatic. I wasn't letting him go, though, and he'd swallowed enough alcohol to soon get into the spirit himself. I could always rely on Gabby who joined us, dragging Marcel along with her. (What is it about Gabby and artists?) Soon the dance floor was full with everyone getting hot and sweaty and down.

I'm not in the same physical shape that I used to be and it wasn't too long before I needed to take a breather. I stumbled back toward our table and on the way bumped straight into Eddy. I didn't know this was the kind of place he went to either, but I should have guessed that where Patrick was, Eddy was sure to follow.

He handed me a cool drink. Then, with one finger, lifted my chin, turning my face from side to side. "Glad you took my advice, babe. You look sensational. Couldn't believe it was you out there on the floor. Girl, you sure were getting down," Eddy teased. "I ain't seen that kind of movement since . . . well, since my last woman passed out from ecstasy."

"You should sue your dealer! Don't flatter yourself, Eddy. You ain't ever seen that kind of movement around you," I teased, batting my eyelashes at him in a vampy kind of way.

"You know, sugar," Eddy leered, "maybe you need some more practice." He dragged me back to the dance floor and we put on a show of some outrageous bump and grind till we both collapsed laughing and retreated to our seats.

Gabby followed soon after and I introduced her to Eddy. They'd each heard me talk about the other so it was like they knew each other anyway. I began to feel like a fifth wheel and I was suddenly hit by a wave of exhaustion. I looked at my watch and it was four-thirty. I was dead on my feet and needed some beauty sleep. Gabby, Eddy, and I shared a cab. I debated going home with Eddy but I was sort of solitary tired and they dropped me off first. I crashed into bed, dog-tired, surprised that I'd had such a good time and knowing that I'd wake up with one hell of a hangover.

Chapter Seven

It bugs the hell out of me that guys can look so fresh when you know they've been overdoing it over the weekend. They don't even have the advantage of makeup, and yet their eyes are still bright and their skin so bloody healthy. I hated Eddy today. I don't know how much he drank on Saturday, but he sure didn't deserve to look as good as he did this morning. Must be all those beansprouts and tofu and soya milk, the kind of stuff that you normally feed to cows. Still, when was the last time you saw a cow with a hangover? Today I'm definitely heading for the health food shop on the way home. Well, on second thought, not if it makes me look as smug as Eddy did. He made me so mad that as I walked past his desk on the way to the morning meeting I deliberately ignored him, although he wasn't even looking in my direction.

I was only half awake so it took me a few seconds to realize that the dozen or so 6"x 9" photos of the brazen, scantily-clad celebrity shot in a variety of compromising poses were, in fact, pictures of me taken the night before. Me with Adrian. Me entwined with Julian. Me grinding with Eddy. All tossed casually on the table laid out for our meeting. I got my brain into gear fast and just managed to snatch the last of them up before the rest of the team came into the room. I guessed this was Patrick and Eddy's idea of a joke.

It was more than a little difficult to concentrate on the rest of the meeting since I was congratulating myself on my dexterity and thinking the most evil thoughts about my colleagues. I came to when Patrick was handing round the photos he'd taken that were candidates for our "celebrity outings" section. While everyone else was swapping tidbits of gossip, I tried to focus on the visuals, on choosing pictures that would look good in the spread. Everyone agreed that we'd have to use the one of a married boy-band member getting up close and personal with a lap dancer. I just had to choose the best shot. It was while I was scrutinizing the half a dozen pictures spread out before me that I noticed the figure in the background. I held my breath for a moment as I stared hard, wanting to be mistaken. These were shots that Patrick had taken before I arrived at the club and there, sitting at the bar, gazing deeply into the eyes of a blond girl (she couldn't be more than nineteen or so) while he rested a finger on her bare arm, was Vince. You remember Vince? Nicola's soon-to-be-husband. I felt the heat rising to my face with righteous anger. I'd been justified in disliking him all along. The old goat couldn't be trusted. But how was I going to let Nicola know when she was so protective of Vince and wouldn't listen to anything I had to say about him?

I got through the rest of the meeting in a blur. I

walked out with the pile of photos and took them to my desk. I glanced through them again, looking at my notes to work out where they'd fit in the various spreads. We didn't yet have all the copy, but I could do a rough layout and I had an idea of what images I'd need from our library. A job for Georgina if I could trust her to follow my simplest instructions. I jotted down on a notepad exactly what I needed in words of one syllable and handed it to her, pointedly ignoring Eddy as he smiled smugly at me. Patrick was sitting on Eddy's desk, and I just knew by the way he kept glancing in my direction that they'd been plotting together. I guess Patrick was getting his own back for the spilled champagne. Pathetic, really.

I spent the next few hours at my computer, managing to forget my worries about Nicola and my annoyance with Eddy as I manipulated the images. I kind of get wrapped up in what I'm doing when I'm working on a layout. It's a bit like putting together a jigsaw puzzle. I make sure there's a perfect fit. I wasn't too absorbed, though, to miss my opportunity when I saw it. As soon as Patrick left and Georgina went down the corridor to the library, I stormed over to Eddy's desk with the photos of me that I'd concealed in a folder. He didn't hear me coming until I slammed the folder down on his desk. He jumped backward and looked up at me in shock. I've been told that I'm a scary sight when I'm angry. I swell up and descend on my prey like a menacing Gorgon. I really wished I could turn Eddy to stone.

"What the hell—"

"I guess you and Patrick thought it would be funny to embarrass me in front of everyone!" I hissed at him, not wanting to attract any unnecessary attention.

Eddy looked innocent, but that didn't fool me. I've seen that expression on his face a million times before.

"I don't know what you talking 'bout, girl."

"Don't add insult to injury by lying to me, Eddy Stanton."

He opened the folder, continuing the pretense of innocence. He took the prints out, examined each one carefully, one by one. When I saw the growing look of amusement and appreciation on his face, I realized what I'd done. Eddy really hadn't seen the photographs before. Now, I'd set a trap for myself and supplied the bait.

Eddy looked from the photos to me. "I ain't never seen such a sexy woman before, honey," he drawled. His eyes met mine; then he looked back at the pictures and shook his head slowly, examining each one with intense interest. I tried to grab them from him, but he saw the move coming and managed to keep hold of one. "For my collection, babe."

"Eddy, give that back to me. You goin' make me so mad."

"Why? Because I appreciate a beautiful woman when I see one?" He looked up at me, an oddly serious expression in his eyes.

"Why did I let you see them?" I wailed as I walked back to my desk. I sat and held my head in my hands. Apart from the remaining effects of sleep deprivation and alcohol abuse, shame made me want to run away and hide.

Georgina came back into the room and sat looking at me curiously. Eddy was muttering behind his partition, in a way that was meant to be heard by me, "Sure is hot . . . fine brown sister . . . wouldn't throw this one out of bed . . ."

Suddenly, he shouted across the partition, "Carol?"

"What?"

"Who *is* the woman in this picture?"

From: <adrian_carlisle@09tv.co.uk>
To: <carolshaw@thecream.co.uk>
Subject: Soul Sensation
Carol,
Remember our conversation? Can you make
a meeting this evening? Around eight? Give me
a call.
Adrian

A little presumptuous to assume that I didn't have a busy social life, but it was a Monday evening and only the television beckoned. There would be no harm in just talking to him. I sent off a quick reply. I got my coat and left the office, this time *really* ignoring Eddy.

When I got back from a dull and solitary lunch, there was a straggly daisy, complete with dirt-caked roots on top of a note on my desk.

> *Don't know what I done wrong, but*
> *since we black men have to pay for the sins*
> *of the world, let me take you for a drink*
> *tonight. E.*

I agreed to go out with Eddy so that he could make up for his rotten behavior. I made him sweat for it, though, ignoring him throughout most of the afternoon. I've made pointedly ignoring men a fine art, but I needed to talk to someone about Vince. Eddy was still laughing at me when we got to the bar round the corner. It doesn't take much to make Eddy laugh at me and I could kick myself for giving him more ammuni-

94 *Jade Williams*

tion. We found seats in the crowded, smoke-filled room and I made no move to buy drinks. He was going to have to pay big time. I was only ordering double brandies too. That's my hangover cure. Eddy was still amused and thought he was *so* funny, striking poses while he waited to be served that I knew were meant to remind me of how Patrick's lens had caught me. I lit a much-needed cigarette and inhaled deeply. Eddy didn't like cigarette smoke, but I was in no mood to accommodate him.

"Just you wait, Eddy 'Cleverdick' Stanton. One day, I'll get my own back on you. Even if I have to pay a hit-man," I muttered beneath my breath.

"That's all the thanks I get for treating your hangover with this fine cognac. What have I done anyway? Apart from telling you what a hot, luscious babe you are?"

"I'm not in the mood for sarcasm, Eddy. Besides, I need to talk to you about something serious."

"Who said I wasn't being serious?"

"Eddy!" I stopped him with a look.

"Okay, babe, this must really be serious shit," Eddy said, taking my hand in his. "What is it, sugar?" My irritation melted away at the concerned look on his face.

I showed Eddy the photo of Vince.

"What makes you think this is anything important, Carol? She could be someone he just got talking to. Or an old friend."

"Eddy, you're a guy. Just look at the way he's looking at her, the way he's touching her arm. What do you think?"

"I think he's been caught with his pants down. What can I do to help?"

I knew that I could always rely on Eddy when I

needed him most. I went over all the stories I'd heard about Vince. The evidence sure did look incriminating. Eddy, though, was the sensible one in this conspiracy.

"I don't think you should say anything to Nicola." Eddy had met my family on a few occasions now and Mom treated him like an honorary son. He treated Nicola like a younger sister and I could see the worry in his eyes. "You know I got my invitation this morning."

"Who you going to bring?" I asked. As if that was the most pressing question at a time like this, a time when I was hoping there wouldn't be a wedding at all. I suppose I'd been comforting myself with the thought that, if I didn't find anyone else, I could always take Eddy.

"Haven't had time to think yet," he brushed my question aside. "I tell you what I think we should do. Let me talk to Patrick, see if he knows anything about this guy. I'll ask around—don't worry, I can be discreet. Let's make sure of our facts before we do anything else."

I sighed and took a huge gulp of brandy. I felt a little better knowing that Eddy was helping. It didn't solve the problem, but it did take a bit of the weight off my shoulders. If Eddy could dig up enough dirt, like if Vince is a closet transsexual, or likes to wear a nappy, or even that he sleeps with his teddy bear, then I'm sure I can get the wedding postponed, if not called off altogether.

"So, Carol," Eddy continued, "what the hell were you doing with the guys in those photographs?"

"Adrian and Julian? Absolutely nothing." I pleaded innocence, until I realized that I was being teased. All the same, I'll never look at tabloid photographs in the same way again. I insisted that it was just the angle at which Patrick had caught me.

"That's what they all say," Eddy responded, smiling at me as if I were some naughty child caught stealing from the candy jar.

We got into a bit of a row about tabloid journalism. Eddy maintained that he only writes salacious stories about guys who deserve it, and he reminded me about all the secrets he was keeping and those he'd kept in the past. That made me pause for a moment, but I'm still not totally convinced. I asked who appointed him judge and jury. Who is he to decide who deserves to be protected and who doesn't? I believe that I don't have the right to judge anyone else (except Vince), but I was on shaky ground since I'd always trusted Eddy to do the right thing. He's got his own, idiosyncratic sense of morality. In fact, that's why I enlisted his help with my current dilemma.

Anyway, we got to talking about Adrian and the new *Soul Sensation* program and I saw the light go on in Eddy's eyes that says "Radar Alert: Potential Story." I kind of wished I hadn't said anything because Eddy started to ask all those Who, What, When, Where, Why questions. I didn't have a lot of answers but mentioned that I'd be meeting Adrian later. I started to wonder how ruthless Eddy could be. Would he use me, his friend, to get a story? I was in a serious place in my head, kicking myself for not thinking before I opened my big mouth, once again, when I dimly realized that Eddy was talking about Gabby. I wasn't sure how she'd got into the conversation, but he'd obviously asked a question that demanded a response. I played for time.

"Why you interested in Gabby anyway?" As if I didn't already have the answer. Gabby is a stunningly beautiful woman. A man would have to be dead from the waist down not to fall under her spell.

"She seems like one helluva smart lady."

So what about me? Doesn't Eddy think I'm smart? Why was I even asking myself that question? Was I feeling the slightest hint of jealousy? That's ridiculous since Eddy and I don't have that kind of relationship. I really do care about him, as a friend. Sure, we lust after each other from time to time, but there's nothing serious in that. We've never really been desperate enough about sex to go through with it, right? I mean, if we had been, then we'd have found the time and the space and not let any interruptions get in the way. Wouldn't we? And I've always known that there would, one day, be a special woman in his life. I just haven't let myself think about it much. When I'm at his place I don't go 'round listening to his answering machine messages or seeing who his letters are from. So I can't be jealous, right? It just isn't like that with us. When it's your best friend he's interested in though . . .

"Yeah, she's smart. And beautiful. Sophisticated. Kinda sexy. Long hair . . ." I stumbled to a halt, not really wanting to talk about Gabby anymore.

Eddy ran his hand over my head, trailed a finger along my jawline, and lifted my chin. All kinds of feelings surged through me at his touch. I wanted to cry. It was the alcohol. Empty stomach. Short hair. A sense of losing Eddy and a hint of desire. I've got to watch myself in these open spaces.

"What is this thing you have about long hair, babe?"

"Is not just me. Is all you men. You all want women with long hair. That's why so many of the brothas go with white women. I don't think is anything besides the long hair."

"You underestimating we. Maybe they don't give us as much grief as you sistas."

"Only because we know we deserve nothing but the best."

"Girl, your problem is that you don't recognize the best when it in front of you."

I didn't know whether he was talking about women in general or me in particular, but he said it with a slow smile on his face.

"You want to come back to my place?"

"You changing the subject?" I asked.

"Yes, but you want to come back to my place?"

I was tempted. I looked at Eddy. I wanted to feel my naked skin against his. Right there and then if necessary, but I'd arranged to meet Adrian in his office and I don't like to go back on my promises. I swallowed the rest of my drink and left Eddy to his own devices. He was looking very thoughtful.

In the end, I *think* I'm glad I agreed to talk to Adrian. I'm not sure. He wasn't anything like as arrogant as he was before. What a difference being away from the safety of the masculine herd makes! I got the sense that he was feeling overwhelmed by the commitments his company had taken on and was looking for a lifeline wherever he could find one. I suspect I'm one of a host of people he's been talking to.

His office gave off an air of controlled panic, a sense of the strain that he was under: sticky notes covering every spare centimeter of wall, his desk straining under piles of papers, video cassettes, tapes, photographs, cold coffee cups, full ashtrays, a slight hint of stale sweat underlying the heavy, smoke-laden air. I felt at home.

Adrian poured me a glass of wine. We both lit cigarettes and he refilled his half-empty glass of Scotch. I wasn't really expecting it, but he immediately launched into a justification of *Soul Sensation*, the program he was making for one of the major network channels. After the success of other talent-search–type programs like *Pop Idol* and *Fame Academy* it was only a matter of time before *Soul Idol, Rap Idol, Blues Idol,* or less likely, *Jazz Idol*. We'd joked in the office about *Grunge Idol*, *Karaoke Idol,* or even *Busker Idol*. Adrian seemed to be trying to convince me, or himself, of his company's commitment to the series. I don't understand why he felt the need.

"There really is so much talent out there that doesn't get recognized. We came up with the idea because we believe that to be true. We all know there are unfairnesses in this business, and this is our small way of trying to address that." He looked at me with an expectant smile on his face. What exactly did he hope for? A gold star? Who was he telling about "unfairnesses"? I guessed that was his euphemism for "racism".

"And how much will you make out of it?"

He had the grace to look a little shamefaced, but not very. "You have to believe that's not why I'm doing it, Carol. How can I prove that to you? Look, let me show you what I mean."

Adrian took my hand and led me to a darkened room set up with a huge television screen, a video, a very expensive stereo system, plus a couple of comfortable-looking armchairs.

"Carol, just take a moment to listen to some of the

tapes we've been sent by the kids out there. They're so excited. So hopeful. Maybe this will convince you of what I'm saying."

Before I had a chance to respond, he'd started a tape. For the next half hour as the enormous speakers boomed, I was subjected to a huge variety of vocal talent, from the downright painful to the tear-jerkingly beautiful. I was holding my breath listening to a young sista with a voice suggesting centuries of pain and suffering when Adrian stopped the tape.

"You see what I'm saying?"

"Adrian, you don't have to convince me that there's a lot of unappreciated talent around. That's not the point I'm making. It's just that I don't see what good programs like this do. So you crown someone the king or queen of soul. What difference does that make in the end? All the others still go back to the obscurity they came from."

"So what do you suggest we do? Nothing? If you think you've got all the answers, if you really want to do something to make a difference, why don't you join the show? I'd love you to be one of the judges."

My mouth fell open. (I really must do something about this infirmity!) I was so shocked that I didn't know what to say.

"If you really do care about music like you say, and you really want to make sure the series achieves something, then here's your chance. You can say all the things you want on the program. To a huge audience. No censorship, I promise. People in the industry might even sit up and listen. Isn't it worth a try?"

"But I don't know anything about television," I managed to squeak.

"You don't have to. All you need to do is be your-

self. We'll take care of the rest. You're bright, beautiful, and opinionated. You seem to know your subject. I
suspect people will want to hear what you have to say."
Where did he get the idea that I was "opinionated"? I
like to think of myself as shy and retiring.

I was still wary. His initial arrogance had done little to make me warm to him. And it's all too easy to be
set up in the media. Maybe he just wanted to get his
own back and see me fall flat on my face.

"One problem I have is that these kinds of programs can turn into freak shows. You set people up to
be laughed at." I'd have to think about his offer.

"That's not what we're about. Trust me."

"Adrian, will you give me a bit of time?" I needed
to talk to Eddy.

"Of course. I'm serious about this, Carol. I think
you could make a real difference to the show." I
needed to talk to Eddy real bad.

I got out of there as fast as I could and called Eddy
on my cell.

In the cab on the way to his flat, I tried to work out
how I was feeling. I was smiling a lot. To be honest, I
was really flattered. I hadn't gone to Adrian's office
expecting anything like this. I had intended to pour
scorn on the whole project, to convince him that he was
being patronizing and ineffective, a corporate drone interested only in the profit margin. Now, I'd been seduced; not by Adrian, but by the talent and the hope I
heard on those tapes. And here was someone promising me that I could make a difference! All right, I was
seduced by the idea of my fifteen minutes, or in this
case, five hours of fame too.

I expected Eddy to laugh, to be dismissive. I thought
he wouldn't understand how tempting an offer like that

could be. Once he'd heard me out, though, he went into the kitchen, then returned with a bottle of chilled champagne, which he proceeded to open. He poured two glasses, clinked his against mine, and we both took a sip before Eddy stared into my eyes and kissed me warmly on the lips.

"I'm really proud of you, girl."

"I haven't said I'll do it yet." He wrapped his arms around me, his body pressed dangerously close to mine. "Doesn't matter whether you do it or not. At least someone else recognized your ability. You know you can do anything you put your mind to."

"Eddy, you sound like my mother!"

He kissed me again. "Does this feel like your mother?"

It was safer to ignore him. "But seriously, Eddy, you know I've never done anything like this before. How do I know I'd be any good at it? And who am I to be making decisions about another person's future? I could say the wrong thing and ruin lives. And I'm not a singer or anyone important in the music business. What the hell do I know to think I can judge people?"

Eddy took my hand and pulled me down to the sofa. "Just the fact that you're worried about all this means you're the right person in my mind. You think all them others worry about ruining people's lives? And who say them know anything more about black music than you? You work in the industry and you know what you like. You have the guts to say what you think is right. I'm serious, Carol. I know the best when I see it."

He was teasing me now, but so gently that I couldn't hold it against him. "You're a good friend, Eddy." I found myself wanting to stay with him, but I suddenly remembered about the conversation we hadn't been having about Gabby, so I reluctantly called a cab, finished my drink, and left.

I called Gabby as soon as I got home. I was still so excited that I had to tell everyone. I guess I wanted them all to convince me that I really could do it.

"Carol!" she shrieked so loud that I had to hold the phone away from my ear. "Girl, go for it. You've got to do this. I don't know Adrian well, but I know he's so serious about his business that he wouldn't have suggested it if he didn't know you could do it. You'll be brilliant. Promise me you'll let me be your personal stylist. I can see it now . . ."

I had to laugh to myself as I let her daydream. I suppose I was coming down on the side of giving the program a try. I was reassured by Gabby's excitement. She kept on talking, making me smile with her generous enthusiasm. I wanted to bring the conversation 'round to Eddy. I wasn't exactly sure why.

"I've been talking to Eddy and he says the same as you, except for wanting to be my personal stylist, that is. He's a good friend."

I suppose I wanted to subtly let Gabby know that I didn't have any claim on Eddy. We were the best of friends and had occasionally shared a bed, but I didn't have any exclusive rights to him. Gabby and Eddy were both my friends and I had to clear the path.

"He seemed like a really genuine guy. We talked a lot in the cab back home. I really liked him, Carol." That's all I needed to know. I'd suspected that Eddy liked Gabby too. For some obscure reason, I felt a real pang of disappointment, but I was just being stupid and tired. The day had been filled with too much emotion and I was coming down from a high. I needed a good night's sleep and maybe a few teetotal days.

Chapter Eight

As it was, I didn't sleep at all well. I dreamed about appearing in front of millions of people with my skirt tucked into my knickers or stumbling down a sweep of stairs and landing flat on my arse. You might call them anxiety dreams. I knew that I'd have to just make a decision, call Adrian and present myself with a *fait accompli*.

Of course, without really wanting to, I thought about how Max had dealt with his fears. You've probably seen his performances, either live or reruns on those *I Love the Nineties* programs. He's rarely seen in public these days. Max is now a cult figure, an icon who is used to sum up an era. When we first got together, though, his career was still on that rising curve. I look at photos of those times with wonder and regret. He looked so fresh-faced, although, with hindsight, I can see a shadowy wariness in his eyes even then. I guess it was all part of the vulnerability that made me want to do anything to make him happy.

* * *

That night, I was the one with the smug look on my face as I watched the waiting groupies skulk off. Max held my hand tightly as if he was scared that I'd run away. And I might have. I'd been whisked straight from the office, still in the gray business suit, without a scrap of makeup and with hair that was showing unhappy tendencies even then. And there was Max, stud, love-god, rejecting all these glamorous babes. For me. He didn't do it as if he was making a gesture, either. It just felt natural. Most people have forgotten about it now, but I've kept the press clippings from that night. I was a "mystery woman" at the time, though it didn't take long for the press to track me down. We used to be photographed together wherever we went. Many times I had to use subterfuges like wigs, hooded jackets, and ridiculous aliases in order to spend some quiet time with Max. I guess the press lost interest when I stuck around and became a fixture.

We went back to Max's hotel that night. We were both nervous. I hadn't intended this; hadn't thought about what I'd do at this moment; hadn't invested in pills, potions, or condoms in any shape, form, or flavor. Max told me later that he was petrified because this was *exactly* what he'd planned, but he was terrified in case he disappointed me. I suppose when you're as famous as he was, you think you have an image to live up to. If I'd known, I would have reassured him that he didn't have to prove anything.

We listened to a recording of that night's concert. At first, I thought it was really tacky—wanting to listen to yourself sing, I mean. Showed a lack of humility, somehow. Then I realized that he did it precisely because he felt anxious about his performance. He was listening for the errors, for how to get it right the next time. Max poured me a drink and lay back on the bed, concentrating hard. I sat in an armchair at first watching him and then closing my eyes, overcome again by the power of his voice, the seductive depths that moved me each time. I visualized him up on stage and I opened my eyes to look at the real presence, wondering again at how I came to be there. The tape got to the point where Max was making his dedication again. He turned off the machine and, suddenly, he was serenading me. The kind of thing you see in those old-fashioned movies. I had to shake my head. Here was the famous Max Gardiner, gazing into my eyes, singing just for me. Shivers went down my spine. And then I listened more closely. The words were of the "Roses are red, springtime is breezy, your nose is big and your socks smell cheesy" variety. He could see the shock in my eyes and started to laugh hysterically. "Got you, didn't I?" he gasped. I stood up and began to punch him gently, joining in the laughter. As tears coursed down his cheeks, he suddenly pulled me onto the bed and wrapped me in his arms until the laughter subsided.

Then he was kissing my neck, my ears, my eyes, my lips, and I was straining to press my body against him. I guess I'd waited too long for this moment, because I was tearing frantically at his shirt, desperate to get as close to him as I possibly could. He was biting my lips, pulling my skirt down over my hips with one hand, unbuttoning his trousers with the other. I was on top of him, under him, straddling him, clasping his hips with my thighs. Then frustration got the better of me and I was rising above him, undoing my bra, taking his hands and pressing them to my breasts while I fumbled to release his straining penis, not wanting to wait to feel the hardness, the strength. I leaned down to kiss him furiously, needing his closeness, wanting his desire to overpower all my senses. I was uncontrollable. Rubbing my body against his, raking his skin with my nails until he cried out in pain, clutching his buttocks, drawing him nearer. I knew that if I didn't feel him inside me, I'd soon lose all control. I writhed against him, wanting him to be as enflamed as I was. "I want you, now," I pleaded.

"Take it easy, honey. We've got all the time in the world."

"No, we haven't. Max. Please. Now."

I took hold of his cock, guiding it to the entrance to my pussy. Rubbing myself against him. Thrusting. Taking control. "Honey, what you doing to me? I'm so horny, I can't wait."

"I don't want you to wait," I whispered.

"You sure?"

"Sure."

He thrust into me hard. The whole length of him giving such pain and pleasure that I couldn't tell one from the other. Wanted more of both. Then he was on top of me, pulling out, right to the edge of ecstasy. "No," I begged him. "Don't stop." He held me there, enjoying his power, resisting me. "Max," I screamed.

"Mmm?"

I opened my eyes. What I saw in his eyes puzzled me a little. His look was intense, but there was no triumph. There was powerful desire and something deeper, something a little scary.

"Carol, I want you. More than I've ever wanted anybody."

"Well, take me then," I teased.

"I'm serious. I really want you."

There was something in him that moved me powerfully. "I'm serious, too, Max. You can have me."

He moved again, hard, grasping me to him, his hold tightening as his strong rhythm grew and the blood was pounding in my head as he moved inside me and I caught his rhythm and we surged together until I felt as if my body was about to shatter into a million tiny pieces of pure, unadulterated pleasure and he was moaning gently, whispering my name. We were struggling, not for dominance, but to overcome the demons of fear—fear of inadequacy, fear of rejection, fear of not loving enough. Then he was screaming my name in one long crescendo and my body was squeezing his, tighter and tighter until the sweetness overtook us in a surge of ecstasy and we melted together, wringing the last drops of joy from each other, and I subsided into the warm safety of his arms.

We held each other gently, Max nuzzling my ear until sleep overtook him. I lay awake looking at him, knowing that, much as I wanted to feel his body next to mine, to keep the insecurities at bay, I'd never sleep while his nearness distracted me. I eased out of the single bed and tiptoed to the other one, covering myself in the blanket, no substitute for his arms. I soon drifted into a relaxed sleep, only to be woken by Max crawling into my bed. "I missed you, honey," he muttered entwining his body with mine. I resigned myself to wakefulness.

I'm never likely to achieve the kind of fame that Max had to endure, but the memories still make me wary. All the same, it's going to be hard to turn down Adrian's offer. My family would never forgive me.

Before I could call her, Nicola rang, wanting to *talk*. She didn't want to speak on the phone so, since she was going to see Dad after work, she wanted me to come too. We arranged to meet at her apartment. I wondered whether she'd found out something about Vince, but I put the thought to the back of my mind since it made me feel ridiculously happy and I didn't want to jinx the possibility.

I had a chat with Oliver. Being a judge on *Soul Sensation* would mean time off work—a lot of time—so I needed his agreement. I hesitated to ask just in case he laughed. That's all it would take for me to lose the fragile confidence I'd built up overnight. Oliver did laugh, but with pure delight. He made a move toward me as if he was going to hug me, but the disgust on my face must have deterred him. He coughed to hide his embarrassment.

"Carol, that's fantastic! This will be great for business. There's just one condition: *Soul Sensation* will have to guarantee us exclusive access to all the backstage happenings. And tickets to the final show, of course." I was touched by his concern for me. That was so typical of Oliver, grabbing any opportunity to get his face on television. I couldn't see Adrian refusing Oliver's conditions; he'd want as much publicity for the show as he could get.

I took a deep breath, picked up the phone, and called Adrian. He sounded relieved, and that made me feel good. It was a boost to know that he wanted me in the show that much. There would be much to finalize in the next couple of weeks, he said, but in principle, we had a deal. I did a little dance around my office cubicle and then sat, staring into space, my heart pounding. What the fuck had I just done?

I don't know how I got through the rest of the day at work. Only half my brain concentrated on what I was supposed to be doing. The rest just kept repeating, over and over, "I'm going to be on television!" I was glad that I'd arranged to meet Nicola. I had to tell someone else.

"Sis, what happen? You looking so excited."

I wanted to appear calm and grown up in front of my little sister, but the silly grin that kept appearing on my face must have given me away.

"Come on, Carol, tell me. You met a new man?"

"Why does everything have to be about a man?"

"Because you know that's what you want."

"Isn't."

"Is."

"Isn't."

Can you believe this is the woman who sees herself as a serious judge on a program watched by the whole nation?

"So what is it, then?"

"I'm going to be on television."

Nicola's mouth dropped. (Must be something genetic.) And then she grabbed hold of me, her screams getting louder and louder with excitement.

"What you going to be doing?"

"You have to keep it secret 'cos it's not absolutely finalized yet."

"Promise."

"Cross your heart?"

"Cross my heart."

"I'm going to be a judge on *Soul Sensation*."

Nicola grabbed me and screamed again. We twirled

around the room together like we used to do when I was about six until we collapsed, out of breath, lying flat on the floor.

When we could speak again, Nicola looked at me. "What's *Soul Sensation*?"

I explained.

"I can't believe it. My sister going to be a star."

We stared at each other for a second and laughed some more. I looked at my watch. "Nicola, we better hurry up if we're going to Dad's. Remember, not a word to anyone."

I drove to Dad's house in Streatham. We were quiet until we came to a standstill trailing a long queue of traffic on Trinity Road. I suddenly remembered that Nicola had said she wanted to talk. I braced myself.

"So what you wanted to talk to me about, Sis?"

"God, Carol. I was so excited that I nearly forgot. I just wanted to tell you that I've arranged it."

"Arranged what?"

"The date."

I'd completely forgotten about the blind date. I wasn't in any mood to even think about a date, but I'd agreed to it, even if it was under duress. Nicola continued, a sly look on her face, "This Saturday evening."

"Nicola, what make you think I'm not busy."

"You know with your sad-assed love life you're never busy on a Saturday evening."

I hated her for being right. How pathetic my social life is. But all that's going to change when I'm a TV star!

"So who is this guy?"

"Not telling you."

"So how am I going to meet up with him if I don't know who he is?"

"Don't worry. Just be in Bougainvillea at eight on Saturday. There's a table booked. He'll find you."

I sighed with a certain amount of irritation. By the time the traffic started to move, my mood was much more sober than it had been. I slammed the car into gear and roared off, determined to get through the lights before they turned back to red. I drove with a controlled recklessness, just so that Nicola wouldn't get too comfortable. I needed to wipe the complacent smirk from her face.

Dad's house is always full of noise and activity. Pauline's incredibly lively, always on the move, and the children are at the age when they have to listen to music at full volume and in separate rooms. Dad opened the door and gave us both a big hug.

"Dad, guess what? Carol's going to be a judge on *Soul Sensation*!"

I dug Nicola in the ribs. Hard. So much for her promise of secrecy! Dad started to shout until Pauline came running.

"Pauline, guess what? Carol's going to be a judge on *Soul Sensation*!"

"Rosa, Jason, come down here right now. Guess what? Your sister Carol going to be a judge on *Soul Sensation*!"

Suddenly I'm standing in the middle of a madhouse with everyone running 'round and 'round the sitting room screaming, stopping only to jump up and down on the sofa, until they all ran out of steam.

"Listen, folks. This is meant to be a secret. Nothing's signed or sealed yet."

"We won't tell anyone. Promise." And leading the chorus was Nicola!

"By the way," asked Dad, "what is *Soul Sensation*?"

Over supper Pauline, Nicola, and the kids planned every detail of my television appearances from makeup and clothes to what opinions I should hold and who should win—even though they didn't yet know who the contestants were. According to them, they'd seen enough of these programs to know the winning type. Everyone had their own view. While they continued arguing over the washing up, Dad and I went out into the garden to have a quick cigarette. Pauline doesn't let him smoke in the house, so the garden is his retreat. Dad put his arm around me as we walked down the overgrown path. Looking at the colorful weeds that threatened to swamp the flower beds, I wondered if Dad's sole interest in the garden was as a nicotine sanctuary.

"You know I'm really proud of you, girl."

"I'm really nervous," I confessed. "I'm not sure I can do it."

"You can do it, Carol. All you have to do is be yourself. None of them others you see on the TV any better than you. I'm sure you'll make a good job of it."

I hugged him. "That makes me feel better, Dad. Thanks."

"Soon I can stop worrying about my big girls. You'll be making your fortune in television and Nicola getting married and her husband can take over worrying about she."

"Humph!"

Dad knew how I felt about Vince. Although he'd never come out and said anything, I knew he had his doubts too.

"Don't be like that with your sister, Carol. She

grown and she make her own choice. We have to trust that she know what she doing. Is she life, Carol. You can't live it for her."

"I know, Dad, but—"

"No 'but.' I know you want to look after your sister, but you not her mother, you know. You and she did always fight, but I know you love her—"

"That's why I don't want her to be with *him*." I couldn't tell Dad about the photos. He's one of the most peaceable people I know, but he can be roused when he sees a threat to any of us. I've only seen his temper once or twice in my whole life, but Dad can be like a tornado, destroying everything in his path. I'll only tell him if he really needs to know and I hope Eddy and I can avoid that.

"If you love Nicola, then you have to support her choice. None of us is perfect, girl. We all make mistakes." He looked at me. Did I see guilt in his face? Or reproach? "All you can do is to be there for she if she need you. Promise me that, Carol."

"You don't have to make me promise, Dad. You know I'll always be there for Nicola. I'm doing everything I can for my sister."

Dad looked at me with a question in his eye. It's strange how the mention of Vince can spread gloom over the happiest of occasions. I just hope it won't be like that on the day of the wedding—if we ever get that far.

We simultaneously stubbed out our cigarettes and Dad took my hand as we walked back to the house. "How's your mother?"

"She's fine, Dad. Just the same as ever."

"How she feel about me and Pauline coming to the wedding?"

"You know Mom. She's upset, but she's enjoying every moment of it." Dad laughed. I wasn't being disloyal to Mom. I knew that Dad still had a great deal of affection for her. So he wasn't in love with her, but that didn't mean he could just cast aside everything they'd shared for so many years. Dad was hopeless at trying to hide his feelings; you could read on his face exactly what he was thinking, and I could tell that he was genuinely concerned about whether his presence at the wedding would distress his ex-wife. He once admitted to me that he never stopped caring about Mom and that Pauline had proved herself to be the woman for him when she made it clear that she understood and wouldn't expect anything else of him. One of the reasons that I was so fond of Pauline was that she accepted the feelings he still had for Mom. She'd said that she wouldn't have loved him so much if he'd been able to just throw Mom aside like a used rag. On the surface they were so different, Pauline and my father, but a few hours in their company and you knew that they were meant to be together. I don't try to justify his behavior, though, since we've all had to live with the consequences, but I've made my peace with him in my own way.

"So, Carol, Nicola tell me you have a special date on Saturday." Pauline winked at me as we walked into the kitchen. "What you goin' wear?" She laughed. I guessed that Nicola had let her in on the secret of whom I'd be meeting. "Girl, you need something really special for this one." Her peal of knowing laughter filled me with dread.

I left Nicola discussing wedding arrangements and spent the rest of the evening with the kids in Jason's bedroom listening to Cam'ron, Big Brovaz, and 50

Cent, the latest CDs they'd bought. I wondered whether
Dad and Pauline had ever listened to the lyrics of this
stuff, but the music was too loud for me to inflict my
views on misogyny on my young siblings. Besides, if
I'm going to be a judge, I'll have to stay up to date
with what young people are into and keep an open
mind. And anyway, that shit's really addictive, so we
were soon all dancing crazily around the room.

I was determined not to make too much effort for
the date, just to spite Nicola. The last few days at work
have been hectic with more than the usual screwups
and complications before we could put the magazine to
bed. I was really in no mood for a date, but hell, I had
to eat, and I'd promised. Actually, much as I'd like to
be thought of as a tough cookie, I wouldn't have been
able to stand my date up anyway. I'd always imagine
how I'd feel, sitting forlorn in a crowded restaurant—
without my anonymous friend. Besides, I'd have to
emigrate if Nicola spilled the beans to Mom.

I took a long, leisurely bath, scented with patchouli
oil. I could have stayed there, fallen asleep, and drowned.
But at least my corpse would smell nice. Well, you can
see how much I was looking forward to meeting this
stranger. At just the thought of the word *stranger* I felt
the heat rising to my face at the recollection of the
Caribbean restaurant. I don't think I'll be able to look a
plantain in the face again. I smiled to myself, though.
A secret part of me was luxuriating in the brazenness,
the flirting with exposure, the hint of danger. Then
Max's image floated in front of my eyes, so it was time
to get out of the bath, pull myself together, and get on
with the evening. I hadn't even heard my cell ring, but

there was the inevitable text message from Nicola: *For God's sake, make an effort. I know you! You'll regret it if you don't. Trust me.* As if!

I dressed entirely in black to suit my mood, debated whether to risk my luck by wearing the birthday G-string, decided against it, slapped on some lipstick and mascara, and took a taxi to Bougainvillea since I planned to drink as much alcohol as the restaurant stocked. That would be the only way to get through the evening. It's not that I don't trust Nicola . . . Well, actually, I *don't* trust her. We have completely different tastes in most things, especially men. All you need to do is look at who she's marrying!

Bougainvillea is a newish French Caribbean restaurant that's opened on Northcote Road. At least Nicola hadn't forced me out of my natural south London environment. I've never been there before, but the reviews have been superlative, which means that it probably won't last long. Luckily, it's not one of those pompous, chichi restaurants, and the waitress who greeted me had obviously been warned to expect a lost-looking black woman who might be about to bolt. She was friendly and welcoming as she led me to the reserved table. The place was luxurious but relatively small and intimate, shades of coral and pale yellow dominating with orchids on each table. I was feeling remarkably at ease after a few hasty sips of a rum cocktail. There were four or five couples and a raucous party of about twelve at a huge table in the center. They must have been celebrating a birthday or an engagement or something since they seemed in the mood for fun—unlike me. The lighting was at a lowish level, but not so dark that you'd have difficulty identifying what you were eating. I began to think that I wouldn't mind if my date didn't turn up at all. I was quite enjoying the atmosphere on my own and particularly the alcohol. I told myself that I needed to keep a clear head, so I delved into the depths of my glass to retrieve the copious chunks of fruit. They would help to stave off the pangs of hunger and provide the "healthy" part of my meal.

"I love to see a woman enjoying her food! Hi, Carol."

I looked up into the biggest, deepest, brownest, most soulful eyes you could imagine. I knew what people meant when they described eyes as "twinkling." Apart from that, his face was one of the most delicious I'd seen in quite some time. He literally took my breath away and I couldn't respond for a few moments. He laughed. "You don't recognize me, do you?"

I reddened with embarrassment. "Am I meant to?" He nodded. "Um, could you give me a clue?" I played for time.

He didn't reply, but sat opposite, that maddening grin on his quite gorgeous full lips. I wasn't used to being at such a disadvantage. I looked away, racking my brains. There was definitely something familiar about him and something at the back of my mind told me that if I gazed into those eyes long enough, I'd be able to place him. I didn't dare, though, since those same eyes were sending a warm, delectable flutter bubbling around my stomach.

"This is really embarrassing . . ." I said.

"Think scary movies."

Don't tell me this was going to be another of those actors. I really didn't want to make a total idiot of myself like I had at the gallery opening. He could easily be a film star, but surely I'd remember one as scrumptious as this. He must have seen the blank look on my face.

"It was a long, long, time ago, Carol."

Something began to prickle in the depths of my consciousness. "How long?"

"Think homework. Think Sunday school."

"Oh my god! You can't be. Not—"

"Rob."

"Not Rob Elliott? I don't believe it!"

This time I made sure that my mouth didn't fall open, but I still must have seemed completely dumb. Looking at him, I really started to wish that I'd made an effort for this date. I was wondering if I could sneak off to the bathroom and take off my bra or do my face properly, but I hadn't even bothered to bring any makeup with me. The only thing I could do was gulp more alcohol. Rob was laughing out loud now.

"I'm so sorry. You've changed so much. You're . . . you're . . . absolutely gorgeous."

Shit. Did I really say that out loud?

"Why, thank you, Carol."

"Oh, I didn't mean to say that. It sounds so rude. Like you weren't gorgeous before. But then you weren't. Not that you were ugly or anything like that, but—"

"Honestly, Carol, I won't take offense."

"Nicola didn't tell me."

"I asked her not to. I didn't think you'd come if you knew it was me."

"Why on earth not?"

"You think I don't remember what a jerk I was at school? Hell, *I* wouldn't want to meet up with me."

"You weren't that bad."

He looked me in the eye and smiled wickedly. "A

young girl sneaks out of her home to be with you and what do you do? Nothing! That's how much of a dickhead I was!"

We both laughed and that kind of broke the ice. I decided that I might quite enjoy the evening, after all.

We had lots to talk about, finding out what we'd both been up to since we'd lost touch. In fact, we have quite a lot in common. Rob's a lawyer now and he specializes in media and intellectual property. He represents a load of writers and musicians so there weren't any awkward gaps in the conversation.

It was hard to concentrate on what Rob was saying, though, because I kept trying to convince myself that this was really the same boy who'd been such a nerd at school. I could make out fleeting glimpses of the old Rob Elliott, but he'd certainly filled out well. He must have had a growth spurt since he was much taller and much broader and much hotter than I remembered. When he took off his jacket, he looked like someone who worked out regularly. I was impressed. His chin was covered by a neatly trimmed beard, but it didn't look as if there was anything weak underneath. My eyes kept going back to those sexy lips as he spoke and he still had long, long eyelashes. Curiously, he no longer looked as if he was about to burst into tears. Instead, I could imagine Rob making a lot of women cry.

All too soon, I heard Rob saying "I'm really glad that Nicola arranged this, Carol. It's been good to see you again." I looked around the restaurant. It was virtually empty. I hadn't even noticed when the party of twelve had left and I didn't remember eating any food, though I suppose I must have. And I certainly didn't remember drinking as much as my sense of balance implied.

"It's been good to see you too, Rob." I really meant it. For once, Nicola had come up trumps, though I don't think I'll admit that to her. I *so* hate it when she's right.

Rob paid the bill and took my arm as we left the restaurant. He led me to a minivan. It was smart. A Mercedes, but still a minivan. I realized with a sense of disappointment that we hadn't talked about his love life. I didn't know if he was three-times-married with seven kids. The minivan suggested just that.

I got in and gave Rob directions to my apartment. He drove well and confidently, keeping his eye on the road and only glancing at me now and again. Shit. If I'd had my wits about me, I would have pried a bit more. What had happened to my famed interrogation skills? Now, part of me was wondering how much of a mess I'd left in my apartment and the other half didn't know whether to invite him in at all. I'd be mortified if I asked and he thought I was some kind of slut. Actually, the way I was feeling *I'd* think I was a slut. Keep thinking wife and kids, wife and kids, I told myself. Perhaps he'd only wanted to meet me out of curiosity. Maybe he'd discussed it with his wife and kids. *I can't wait to see her. The girl who tried to seduce Daddy when we were only thirteen. Flat as a pancake. Looked like the back of a bus. Just think: I might never have met Mommy. It'll be a bit of a laugh. I'll tell you all about it when I get back. Ha-ha!*

Rob pushed a few buttons and the cool, sensual tones of Maxwell soared into the air. I wondered if this was some kind of not-so-subtle coded message. To me, listening to Maxwell's *Embrya* album *is* foreplay.

When he finally stopped outside my flat and we'd waited for those few awkward seconds, I plucked up courage and asked if he'd like to come up for a drink. There was a heartbeat's silence, during which I had time to regret the impulse, and then Rob said, "You understand that if a girl sneaked out to meet me now, I wouldn't waste the opportunity . . ." I think I understood where he was leading and my stomach gave a little flip. I got out of the car and he took my hand as we walked to my door.

I didn't turn on too many lights in the living room. I couldn't remember whether I'd be revealing anything embarrassing, so it was best to err on the side of caution. I poured us both drinks and sat next to him on the sofa, surreptitiously checking to make sure there weren't any stray items of clothing tucked behind the cushions.

"It's *really* good to see you again, Carol."

"You too."

Rob put his arm around me and did what I'd been hoping he'd do all evening. He leaned forward and brushed his lips against mine. I instantly felt a shock of pleasure, unexpected in its intensity, sear through my body. Damn! Either Rob Elliott had turned into one very sexy hunk or my hormones were going haywire. Anyway, it frightened me and I found myself retreating a little as his tongue flickered against mine. He must have sensed my hesitation and he pulled away, leaning back on the sofa, one hand gently caressing the back of my neck.

"So how comes you not married, Carol? Whenever I thought about you, I always imagined you with a husband and a whole heap o' pickney."

I laughed. "How you know I'm not married? Maybe I locked my husband in the cupboard for the evening. No, seriously, I think I've been enjoying my life too much to get 'round to it." That was only half a lie. I didn't add that no one had ever proposed. "How about you?"

"Oh, been there, done that."

"Divorced?"

"Not yet. But officially separated."

I looked up at his face, but it was hard to see in the dim light whether there was any pain, guilt, or regret there. I was strangely glad that he admitted to at least one marriage. When guys get to our age and they're not married or haven't had at least one serious relationship, you start wondering what's wrong with them. Whether they're lying. Or worse, lying to themselves.

"Any children?" I asked, wondering about the minivan.

"No, thank God. We kind of never got around to it."

I was curious about the reason for the breakup, but the moment didn't seem right to ask. I burrowed farther into his chest, relaxing against him while feeling the pounding of my heart as the warmth he generated sent a shiver of excitement through me.

"Cold?" Rob asked, holding me tighter and maneuvering our bodies until we were lying stretched out on the sofa.

I shook my head and he kissed me again. This time I was prepared for the sensations and I responded eagerly, wrapping my arms around him and pulling him even closer, inhaling the intoxicating scent of alcohol with an undertone of nicotine. I could feel the throb of the pulse in his neck and sensed his growing excitement as he pressed his body against mine. Rob's tongue was exploring my mouth, his hand tracing the line of my collarbone, making its way down to the buttons on my dress. He lifted himself on one elbow, pulling away to

watch what his fingers were doing. As his eyes moved
to the swell of my full breasts, I felt my nipples contract. Rob breathed deeply. "You sure have grown up,
Carol Shaw," he smiled, pushing the straps of my bra
down so that he could lift one breast out of the cup. He
was all seriousness and deliberation as he caressed my
skin, then gently feathered my nipple, circling with
one finger. He bent down to kiss me again as he rolled
my nipple between finger and thumb and I felt it hard-
ening, responding immediately to his practiced touch. I
heard a momentary *What the hell you think you doing,
Carol Shaw? A good meal and a whole heap o' rum
cocktail and you throw youself 'pon him like some low-
down dirty whore* at the back of my mind, but what the
fuck? It had been so long and we'd established that we
were both free and single. I couldn't help myself. I
arched my back, pressing my breasts ever closer to him.
He bent down and, so gently I could almost believe I
imagined it, his tongue whispered across my nipple.
Then, just as suddenly, he stopped, just sat there looking at me. I moaned out loud.

    Rob laughed. "What's the matter, babe?"

    "How could you do that?"

    "What?"

    "Just stop like that."

    "What do you want me to do, Carol?"

    So that's how he was going to play it. Was he
going to be one of those guys who want you to beg?

    "Nothing," I said, smiling to myself as I saw the
surprise in his eyes. I righted my clothing and sat up.
Rob sat upright too, looking puzzled and perhaps a little hurt. I took a long sip of cognac and stood up. I
walked in front of him, swaying my hips mock-siren
style, then circled behind him, reached over, and loos-

ened his tie. I began to massage his shoulders while leaning over to kiss him gently. I could feel the knot of tension in his muscles, and now it was his turn to moan as I probed harder.

"Mmm. Feels good." He closed his eyes, almost delirious with pleasure as he relaxed beneath my touch. I removed his tie and unbuttoned his shirt so that the warmth of my palms could ease away any lingering tightness. He was melting, like honey in my hands. I stopped for a moment and moved so that I could sit behind him, my thighs straddling his hips as I continued to massage. I waited for the instant when his eyes started to close in contentment and I reached round to gently caress his nipples. I could see his eyes fly open and I moved myself around so that I was across his lap, my crotch resting against his. I continued rolling his nipple in one hand while I gently blew on the other. I heard his sharp intake of breath as both nipples hardened. I barely touched him with my tongue and his hands instantly moved to my shoulders, nails digging into my skin. I continued, first licking one nipple, then biting and sucking until I could feel his erection getting stronger. I pulled away from him.

"What you doing, Carol?"

"Nothing."

"Why did you stop?"

"What you want me to do, Rob?"

It took a moment for him to understand; then he laughed, grabbed me, and started tickling me until we rolled off the sofa onto the carpet, giggling like little children.

Rob was suddenly serious. "I'll tell you what I want, Carol. I want to see your naked body, those gorgeous tits, I want to touch every part of you, taste each little bit of your body. I'll make you moan. Scream. I want to make you so hot and wet that you'll beg me to take you."

"I don't beg no man for nothing," I protested; but, oh God, my mind was getting the begging bowl ready. He rolled on top of me, pinning my body to the floor. Then he was feathering my face and neck with butterfly kisses. And then . . .

And then, damn it, the doorbell rang. We were both silent and still, hoping we'd imagined it. Then it rang again. And again.

I scrambled up, trying to make myself look as decent as possible. I snatched at the intercom.

"Yes?" I barked.

"Carol, it's Eddy, I need to talk to you."

I buzzed him up, glancing in the hallway mirror and wiping off smeared lipstick with the back of my hand. Damn Eddy Stanton! Just because I wasn't getting any with him was no reason to stop me getting it with someone else! I could hear his feet pounding up the stairs as Rob buttoned his shirt and stuffed it back inside his trousers.

"Work colleague," I mumbled.

As I opened the door Rob stood and I was just about to make the introductions when Eddy reached out a hand to him.

"Rob, man, long time."

"Whassup, Eddy?"

I should have guessed they'd know each other. I poured Eddy a brandy, my resentment at his sudden appearance fading gradually. I had to remind myself that I frequently called Eddy at any time of the day or night and had been known to turn up unexpected on his doorstep just because I needed a shoulder to cry on. I could almost laugh at the whole situation.

Anyway, it was obvious that the moment (you know, *the* moment) had come and gone and after a few minutes of polite chitchat, Rob got up to leave. At the doorway, he kissed me briefly on the cheek and said he'd call. I felt a little disappointed, but I turned my attention to Eddy.

"Did I interrupt something, babe?" There was a wicked smile on his lips, but his eyes were serious.

"Nothing important," I lied.

Eddy lifted one skeptical eyebrow so I threw a cushion at his head. "So, what's so urgent?"

"It's not *that* urgent. How was I to know you'd have company? When was the last time? Prehistoric days?"

I raised the appropriate finger.

"I thought you'd want to know what I found out."

I sobered up immediately.

"I talked to Patrick first. Don't worry, he doesn't know who Vince is, but he says he's seen him with the blonde before. I went to other clubs. Same story. Blondes. Seems like that's his thing. Doesn't arrive with them, but sometimes leaves with them. We don't have anything concrete, but Patrick will keep an eye on him."

"You didn't tell him why?"

"No, he just thinks it's a story I'm working on. Patrick can be discreet." I found that difficult to believe.

"What am I going to do about it, Eddy? Nicola will be devastated. I think she really loves him, even though he's such a fucking loser."

"Carol, calm down. I know what you're like. This

time, I don't think you should rush into anything. We don't really know what's going on."

"Don't we?"

"We can't be sure. There just might be an innocent explanation. Let me do a bit more digging. It does look like Nicola's going to get hurt, but we have to be sure of the facts."

"There's only a couple of months to the wedding."

"Don't do anything hasty, Carol. Let me deal with it. Trust me."

The thing is that I do. Trust him, I mean. I didn't feel exactly ecstatic about the situation, but I'd sleep a little easier knowing that Eddy was on the case. I hate being the little woman relying on a man, but just occasionally it feels good to have broad shoulders to lean on.

"Thanks, Eddy," I said. "Part of me hopes Vince isn't doing the dirty on my sister because if he is . . . I'll personally nail the bastard's balls to the nearest bedpost."

Eddy winced. "You might have to get in the queue. Anyway, babe, let me get out of here fast. I can see that scary look in your eye."

I laughed at the mock expression of fear on Eddy's face. He gave me a quick hug. "Don't worry, sugar. I'll take care of it."

I went to bed seething. As well as everything else, I could blame Vince for the fact that I was spending the night alone. I'm only now beginning to see how *satisfaction interruptus* can be a really effective form of birth control.

Chapter Nine

Nicola deserves Vince. She called me at seven-thirty this morning to find out how the date went. Seven-thirty on a Sunday morning! According to her, she was so excited for me that she couldn't sleep. Just to teach her a lesson I played it totally cool.

"Oh, Rob? Yeah, it was nice to see him again."

"Nice?"

Women hate that word *nice* when you're talking about what's supposed to be a hot prospect. What exactly does it mean? Did he have bad breath? B.O.? Gray leather shoes with a gold chain? I knew it would annoy Nicola.

"Yes, he was nice."

"Nice? Girl, you blind? What you talking 'bout 'nice'?" Nicola kissed her teeth in disgust. "The man is sex on legs. If I wasn't already taken, I would go after him myself. Every woman I know lusts after Rob, and all you can say is him 'nice'? What wrong with you, Carol? You had a libido bypass?"

"If so many women after him, then how you manage to pry him away from them to set up a date with me?"

"I had to get down on my knees and beg him. I told him how desperate my older sister was. I promised if he did this one tiny favor for me, then I'd introduce him to my best friend."

"Ha, bloody ha!"

"So tell me the truth, then. What happened?"

"We had a very pleasant evening. Good food. Enough wine."

"And then what?"

"Then nothing. He went home. I went home. It was . . . nice."

"Is that all?"

Nicola sounded so disappointed, but I couldn't resist punishing her further. "What else you expect? Nicola, what kind of a girl you think I am?"

"Sis, I already know what kind of girl you are. That's why I was so hopeful that Rob might still be there."

"Sorry to disappoint you."

"Oh well, it seems as if I must have got the wrong impression, then." I could hear the note of triumph in her voice. What on earth could she know that I didn't?

"What you talking 'bout?"

"I'm just wondering why Rob bothered to call so early this morning to get your e-mail address."

She put the phone down. I just don't know where the girl got that devilish streak. Obviously it bypassed me.

The butterflies had turned into pigeons stomping in the pit of my stomach and I was immediately and completely awake. I leaped out of bed and rushed into the living room to turn on the computer. While it booted, I made a coffee and lit a cigarette to steady my nerves. It was a long time since I'd felt this way about any guy. It was important to my newly found self-esteem that Rob should want to see me again. I know he'd said he would call, but I'd had my doubts, especially since I'd forgotten to give him my number. How dumb can I get? I wonder how many times that's happened before. Actually, that might explain all the lowlifes who didn't call. Suddenly that made me feel a whole lot better. Anyway, thank God we'd been fixed up by Nicola; otherwise, he might never have been able to get hold of me without facing the possible humiliation of just turning up on my doorstep.

"Last night took me back to old times. Older woman trying to corrupt my morals again. You must try harder. Tuesday evening? Rob."

Older woman? I'd forgotten that Rob's a few months younger than me. Smiling, I went back to bed. Keen enough to e-mail me so early on a Sunday morning! I hugged the knowledge to myself and drifted back to sleep.

Max had been equally keen, even after we first slept together. Part of me had worried that he was only attracted to me because of my seeming lack of enthusiasm and that, paradoxically, once I began to fall for him, he'd lose interest. But it wasn't that way. If anything, his need for me only deepened, and it wasn't too long before I'd moved in with him and left work at the deadbeat insurance company. Rob had bought a house in Notting Hill, well, Ladbroke Grove, really. Painted white, with a shiny black front door that you could see your reflection in and floor-to-ceiling, first-story windows with balconies that overlooked a leafy square. Max said he'd bought it to make a statement. He'd grown up in a similar house, not that far away in Shepherd's Bush, but that building had been divided into studio apartments. He and his mother and brother had been crammed into a room smaller than the bathroom in his new house. And his grandfather had talked about coming to England and trudging through these same streets day after day looking for accommodation and having those shiny black doors slammed in his face.

Now this had become one of the trendiest and most expensive parts of London. It was hundreds of mental miles away from my beloved south London, but the need to be with Max was like a physical illness, and although Nicola teased me about "withdrawal symptoms," the pain of too-frequent separation was unbearable. Besides, he turned the attic into a darkroom where I could concentrate on turning my hobby of photography into a career. Max promised that he'd do anything so that I could be with him and he was as good as his word. We were like upended bookends, Max ensconced in the basement recording studio, me in the attic. I rarely ventured into his territory, not because he made me feel unwelcome, but whenever the guys from the band were together down there, the smell of testosterone mixed with sinsimilla was overpowering and they all looked at me with polite curiosity as if I were E.T. It didn't seem worth the effort of negotiating the videophone and security locks. It wasn't till later that I'd understand the importance of those locks.

I traveled with him. Took hundreds of photographs of Max and the guys in seedy dressing rooms and at lavish awards ceremonies. I still have them, locked away in a trunk. I don't go there at all these days.

It was through the photographs that I met Eddy. The first time I saw him at one of Max's gigs, he was like an oasis of calm in the backstage insanity. I was drawn to the solid, rocklike figure who seemed to be encased in a bubble of tranquillity. I snatched a photo and he turned, smiling at me as he heard the whir of the shutter.

"You must be good," he remarked. "Is not often anyone gets to take my picture."

"I'm sorry. That was rude of me. I should have asked, but I couldn't resist it. You look so out of place in all this madness."

"You don't look as if the men in white coats are after you either."

He was waiting for an interview with Max. He gave me his card and I tucked it into the back pocket of my jeans. Over the next few months, we saw each other at one venue or another. I got the feeling that Eddy had more than a casual interest in Max but put it down to a journalist at last recognizing the true extent of my lover's talent. A talent that Max himself never truly believed he possessed.

It was when I moved in with Max that I started smoking. I'd hardly noticed before that offstage he was rarely without a cigarette between his slender fingers. I slipped into the habit. It didn't take me long to understand that the diffident little boy who had first seduced me was closer to the real Max than I could possibly have imagined. I guess I was taken in by the posters, the videos, the articles in music magazines. There were hordes of adoring individuals surrounding Max: managers, PR, lawyers, musicians, security, women and still more women, all wanting a little piece of him, all willing to shower him with love, and still it was all ephemeral, so intangible to him. Funnily enough, living with Max made me more confident; even though he was cocooned in all this adoration, he chose to come back to me, like a homing pigeon, unflattering though the comparison might seem. Of course, if you've ever seen him perform live, you'll find it hard to believe that underneath the showmanship, the extrovert posturing, the exhibitionism, Max was painfully insecure. I tell myself that's what led to our problem.

There was a message to call Adrian when I got to the office this morning. I caught him just as he was rushing out.

"Carol, thanks for calling. Sorry it's such short notice, but can you make a meeting tomorrow evening, around seven? You'll get to meet the team and the other judges. Bit of brainstorming."

What, a choice? A dull meeting at a TV production company or the chance to finally get some action. I quickly dismissed the lascivious vision that popped into my head and agreed to the meeting before I could change my mind. I knew that Adrian's question, though phrased like a polite request, was, in fact, a subtle command. I hung up and e-mailed Rob to turn down his very tempting invitation. Still, it won't do any harm to make him wait. Keep him on his toes, wondering if maybe I'm not as eager as he is.

I was actually quite glad of an evening alone in my apartment tonight. I've been so busy recently that I haven't had time to think. Doesn't seem like only a couple of weeks ago I was fretting about how uneventful my life was and envying Gabby. Now look at me: new haircut, new job, potential new man. Mercury must have moved out of my house of spartanism and celibacy. I had a long, hot bath, washed my hair, moisturized my skin, and wrapped myself in a terrycloth robe. I poured a glass of merlot and lit a cigarette. I was enjoying being alone. I luxuriated in the quiet, the opportunity to sort out my emotions, the peace. I picked up the phone and called Gabby. I needed to tell her everything that had happened.

I'm still in a state of shock. I should have listened to my instincts when they were telling me to steer clear of *Soul Sensation*. But where were the omens, the writing on the wall, the portents? The spirits that guide me should know me well enough to have taken out a billboard advertisement or screeched sinister words in my ear. They should know that I don't respond to subtlety.

I arrived at Adrian's office only a few minutes late and was the first "civilian" to arrive, so over warm white wine and drying, curled sandwiches, I got to know the team. There seemed to be scores of them: runners, researchers, producers, directors, production manager, editors, cameramen, designers, and dressers, and it took me quite a while to work out who was who, let alone what exactly they did. My fellow judges arrived one by one at fairly lengthy intervals. There are four of us altogether and the next to join us was Quentin Royle. I think he must have been chosen as the "good guy." He's an agent, fiftyish, overlong silvering hair, attempting the casual youth look—six-pack, unlaced trainers, and low-slung jogging pants. Totally unobjectionable (apart from the jogging pants) and eager to please.

More intriguing was Gary Sargeant, the DJ from Phat FM. Gary's the flavor of the month at the moment and impossible to avoid. You'll have seen him on television, read him in the papers, and of course, heard him on the radio. His face is on billboards advertising anything from aftershave to jewelry. He's striking. Cheekbones that look as if they've been chiseled from granite. Narrow, sleepy, slanted eyes that make him seem catlike and mysterious. A full, generous mouth that contradicted the hint of danger in the eyes. Skin the color of butterscotch. And the cutest, Pharrell Williams–type smile. Unlike most celebrities, he's as tall as he seems in photos and on television. I could guess why Gary had been chosen. He could be relied on to be controversial, to be at times right-wing and reactionary. Many times on radio I have heard his young-fogey act and been outraged, but not quite enough to phone in to his show. I guess I've never taken him seriously enough since he's only young. He can't be more than about twenty-three.

Gary seemed pleasant enough, though, shaking my hand firmly and looking me straight in the eye as he told me how glad he was that I was on board. He seemed genuine. I wondered what Adrian had been telling the others about me.

"I know *The Cream*," Gary said. "Respect to Eddy. The best in the business." Could I not get away from Eddy's sphere of influence?

It was getting late, and even though we were still waiting for the final judge, Adrian, who must have done management training, got us all sitting round in a circle so that we could each introduce ourselves to the others. Gary winked at me. I tried to concentrate as each member of the production staff explained in words of

one syllable what exactly their role was. I nodded as
wisely as I could and soon everyone was talking as if I
understood what they were saying about recces, locations, sets, call times, single-camera shoots, and studio
dates. It all even began to sound logical. I should have
understood then that as soon as I began to relax, to feel
at ease, that's when thunderbolts roar and lightning
strikes.

I don't know whether he'd chosen his moment to
make a dramatic entrance, or whether chronic lateness
was just a symptom of his lifestyle, but it was as we
were all about to say polite farewells that the fourth
judge made his overdue appearance: Max Gardiner.
Believe it or not, my mouth didn't fall open. I think my
jaw clenched involuntarily because I could feel the
ache in the muscles around my mouth as a smile froze
into place. As Adrian led him around the room, my
heart pounded and my nerve ends tingled. I wanted to
take flight. It'd been well over three years since I'd
shared a space with Max and, as I've said, my guardian
angels had given me no inkling that I would so soon
have to deal with the emotions that he still managed to
arouse.

While they were doing the rounds, I had a bit of
time to work out what the hell I was going to say to this
man who'd once been my whole world, but all I could
do was stare at him as my brain turned to mush. Max
looked at least ten years older than the last time I'd
seen him. His hair was now dreadlocked and, surely
prematurely, gray. Once prominent cheekbones were
now razor sharp, overhanging sunken cheeks, and as
he completed his tour of the room, I could see that his
eyes were huge and haunted, his full lips now thrown
into relief by the obvious weight loss evidenced in his

narrow face. I felt a prickle of hot tears behind my eyes as I struggled to maintain some kind of composure. Max didn't look at all well. But he was still charismatic, a fine-looking man.

As it was, I needn't have worried about what to say. When Adrian mentioned my name in introduction, I looked into Max's face, only to realize in the fleeting instant that his eyes met mine that there was no hint of recognition in his glance. Nothing as he dropped his gaze. I wanted to weep.

"Max . . . It's been . . . It's been a long time," I managed and thought I saw a brief furrow of puzzlement between his brows. And then he'd moved on to the next person and all I could do was stand stock still like some brain-dead idiot.

"You look as if you're in shock. You a big fan?" I heard Gary's voice from a distance. Thank God he was too young to remember anything about my personal history. I pulled myself out of my stupor in time to respond.

"Oh, isn't everyone?"

"Yeah, the guy's a legend. Didn't know I was going to be working with the great Max Gardiner."

"No, neither did I."

"Well, I'm really looking forward to this. You ever worked in television before, Carol?"

I can't tell you how grateful I was that he'd changed the subject. "No, I didn't understand most of what they were saying in that meeting."

"Don't worry about it. Eddy called me. Made me promise to look after you. The first thing is not to let them screw you when it comes to your contract. They're bound to try."

Gary told me how much they were paying him,

which kind of shocked me. Then he itemized the other demands he'd made: dressing rooms, first-class hotels, clothing allowance, expenses, personal drivers . . . I'm sure that's fine for him, but I don't believe they'll agree to the same terms for me when I've no experience at all.

"They'll try to tell you that you're not a big name," he said, reading my mind. "Remember that they really want you. They need your skills and your knowledge. That's what they're paying for. And they need the credibility that we give to the program. That's the most important thing. Make them pay; otherwise, you'll let the side down. Don't ever question your abilities, Carol. Eddy told me what an incredible woman you are and I trust his judgment."

There's no escaping Eddy's web. Who does he think he is? The Godfather? I wondered if he was calling in a favor. I have to admit, though, I'm really grateful; I need a helping hand to navigate the media waters.

I thanked Gary for his help, said good-bye to Adrian, and slipped away. I got a cab home. If I'm going to be earning the amounts that Gary's talking about, then I can afford to spurn public transport now and then. Besides, I desperately wanted to get back to the solitude of my flat. I didn't want to think, but knew that I would. If I was going to fall apart, I wanted to do it in private.

For a while, I led the kind of dream life that most women would kill for. In fact, many of the groupies would have been happy to poison me in return for time with Max. In reality, he was away a lot, touring, but I was just as often on a train, in a car, or in a plane on my way to meet him on the last date of a tour ready to jet away to an exotic holiday somewhere. Life was almost perfect.

When I was left alone in the Notting Hill house, I worked hard on my photography, building up a freelance career, even occasionally working with Eddy, who was generous enough to use his contacts to throw work my way. I had the nights to miss Max, to build the frustration and sexual longing to a frenzied pitch, so that when we met, a ferocious mutual desire would erupt, leaving a gentle, seductive pleasure in its place, which we'd work on for the next few days.

Looking back, I can't pretend that there weren't signs that I should have noticed, but I was too busy being ecstatically, complacently, blissfully happy. Max was drinking. A lot. He took a bottle of vodka on stage with him. We'd always agreed that drinking vodka was like sucking crude oil straight out of a tanker, but the bottle would be empty when he came off stage. That alone should have been a clue.

Gradually, Max was losing his allies and closest friends. I listened, bristling with anger as he explained how band members, his agent, who also happened to be his brother, the record company, and his lawyer were ripping him off. Everyone wanted a piece of Max and he had to watch his back. I was fiercely protective of him, and at times it seemed like it was the two of us against the whole world. The two of us and my family, that is.

Of course, Mom had no idea who he was and, at first, treated Max just like any other no-good, rampant dawg in heat come sniffing around she dawta. I expected Max to quail before her Gestapo-like interrogation, but he charmed her by teasing her mercilessly.

"Mrs. Shaw, my intentions toward your daughter

are only honorable, but if I did catch sight of you first, you know I would never have even looked at she twice. You've stolen my heart." He fell to one knee, hands on heart.

Nicola and I held our collective breaths.

"Young man, you too feisty for your own good." But Mom laughed, playfully slapping his arm away as he tried to hug her. Max later told me that she reminded him so much of his own mother that he couldn't take her fierceness seriously. I think Mom fell a little in love with Max from that day. Of course Nicola was in seventh heaven. She saw herself as the fairy godmother who had brought us together, transforming me from Cinderella into Mrs. Domestic Goddess.

Dad was a little more wary, less immediately susceptible to Max's charm, but he soon fell under the spell when he saw how Pauline and the kids responded to him. I remember wandering down to the garden shed and stopping outside to eavesdrop on the two of them. Dad was listening to one of his old-time reggae tunes and they were both crooning along in companionable harmony, occasionally stopping to laugh. Hearing them together made me smile. It was all kind of chicken and egg, really. The fact that my folks ignored Max's wealth and fame meant that he relaxed with them, and the more at ease Max was, the more charming he became. With Max I learned an important lesson: If you're not sure a relationship is going to last forever, keep your man away from your family—they'll never entirely forgive you if it all falls apart.

I did start to notice how long it was taking Max to come down from the high of performing. We'd spend more than half the night awake listening to recordings of the shows, analyzing his vocals, with Max picking

away at the tiniest error, rewinding, rubbing a sore spot
until it hurt. Finally, he'd disappear for a walk on a de-
serted moonlit beach, or an eerie city street, or if we
were at home, into the gloom of the basement studio.
And it was only then that I'd sleep. I wondered when,
if ever, Max slept and, naïve idiot that I was, I continu-
ally made him herbal teas!

I guess Max, so sure that my love was uncondi-
tional, became reckless. He had to, I suppose, since I
was so completely blind.

It was a gray, cold October evening. We'd usually
escape English winters, but Max was staying put, os-
tensibly to work on a new album. Most of the time he
was alone in the studio, but I figured that since he was
writing he needed the solitude. Eddy seemed like a
fairly constant presence in our house at that time. Max
trusted him, and they were working on a project together: the definitive biography of Max Gardiner. I understood, even then, how difficult a task this was for
Eddy. Max was prickly a lot of the time, becoming ob-
sessive about his music and, more often than not, when
Eddy arrived for an agreed interview, Max would be
too busy to talk. So Eddy would hang around the kitchen,
waiting to seize his moment. That was when our friendship developed. I realized later that Eddy was also trying
to protect me, to forewarn me, to soften the blow that
would inevitably fall. He was worried for Max too. I
think he wanted to be there in case anything happened.

In the end, nothing too dramatic did happen. I woke
one morning, startled from a nightmare and cold without Max's body beside me. I looked at the luminous
figures of the digital clock. Five thirty-seven. Only
half awake, I slipped into one of Max's thick jumpers
that hung over a chair and made my way, bare-footed,

down to the basement. The fact that the door was ajar should have alerted me to something being wrong; Max never, ever, left that door open. I could hear vague muttering as I descended the carpeted stairs and wondered who was with him. It wouldn't be so unusual for one of the guys in the band to be working with Max, even at that time of the morning. As I got nearer, I could hear words, Max's voice, not making too much sense.

". . . can't get away with it. I won't let it happen. Look at this paper. He think I don't have the evidence. If it take till kingdom come, I goin' get it all back." His words slurred. "That's how much she tief from me. And my own brother with she! That, and the royalties from the first record. I got all the proof I need now. I know how I goin' deal with it. If they think I going to involve the law . . ."

As I got to the entrance, the acrid smell hit me first, sharp, stinging my eyes, making them tear. And when Max lifted his head to look at me, it was the first time that I saw that glassy, staring look of nonrecognition that terrified me on that occasion. In less than a second I took in the state of the studio: papers, videos, CDs covering every inch of the floor, Max cross-legged, the notepad by his side filled with nonsensical doodlings, the empty vodka bottles, overflowing ashtrays, the gas cylinder and the blackened crack pipe.

I got Rob's number from Nicola this morning. I hated to do it because I knew she'd be feeling smug and self-satisfied. I didn't want to send an e-mail message, so I called him. He sounded rushed, but pleased to hear from me, and there was maybe just a hint of self-satisfaction in his voice. I could forgive that, though. After all, hadn't I felt the same when I got his e-mail message? If I'm honest, too, I wanted Rob's attention. I was in danger of free-falling into the black hole I'd found myself in post-Max. I needed to grab hold of any prop to shore up my confidence.

"Rob, I just wanted to call to let you know that I'm not avoiding you, it's just that my schedule is so busy at the moment."

"Day and night?" he asked.

"I'm going to be away quite a lot. I've agreed to be a judge on *Soul Sensation* and . . ."

"Wow, Carol. I'm honored that I knew you before you were famous."

"Don't tease. I feel self-conscious about it already."

"I'm serious. You're going to be mega-famous. You need a lawyer?"

"Never mix business and pleasure."

"Seems like there's not going to be a lot of time for the pleasure part!"

"That's why I'm calling you. Do you fancy a movie or something tonight?"

"I've got meetings until late. How about tomorrow?"

"Okay, do you want to choose the film?"

"Will do."

I put the receiver down and looked up to see Eddy peering over the partition. I knew he'd heard most of the conversation.

"How long you known Rob?"

"A hundred years. Since we were kids. Why do you ask?"

"I just wondered how much you know about him. You never mentioned him before."

"No, we've only just hooked up again. How do you know him?"

"I've had dealings with some of the acts he represents. I don't know the guy well. Be careful, Carol."

"Eddy Stanton, you turning into my father or something? Or maybe you jealous," I teased, but Eddy didn't laugh. Anyway, I felt awkward discussing Rob with him. Fortunately, Eddy must have sensed that since he immediately changed the subject and asked how the meeting had gone the previous evening. I thanked him for asking Gary to look out for me. I looked around the office. I wanted to tell Eddy about Max, but knew that Georgina had one ear on our conversation.

"No worries, babe. I promised you that I'd look after you." He walked round the partition and took the seat on the other side of my desk. He lowered his voice.

"I know you're going to be busy, Carol, but I want to find a date when I can take you to a club. A Saturday night. I want you to invite your Dad too. I'm trying to arrange a kind of party."

"And you want to invite my dad?" I didn't think Eddy and my father were *that* close. Certainly not close enough to hang together.

"I think it would be good to have him there." I understood.

I fished my new schedule out of my bag and we fixed a date several weeks away. I could guess that Eddy was plotting something to do with Vince.

"What are we celebrating?"

"Oh, the future." And he was gone, out the office door.

*   *   *

Gabby called. She was still raving about my soon-to-be success, but I think the real reason behind the call was a fishing expedition. She wanted to know more about Eddy. I'd tried to push the thought of the two of them together to the back of my mind, but more often than I wanted, the image rose to the surface. Each time, I felt more uneasy. I found myself being protective of Eddy and so not very forthcoming. I sensed the irritation in Gabby's voice, but I was caught in a hard place. Why am I so reluctant to let go of Eddy? I think he and Gabby could get on really well. Okay, she's married, but Eddy knows that, so whatever he might or might not do with Gabby is his business. They're both adults, so I should really butt out.

"What about Pete?" *Call that butting out?*

"What about him? You've never worried about Peter before."

"I suppose it's Eddy I'm worried about. He's my friend. I don't want to see him get hurt."

"What makes you think I intend to hurt him?"

"People do get hurt, Gabby."

"Carol, if what you mean is that you want to keep Eddy for yourself, then all you have to do is say so."

It's just that now, more than ever, I really need Eddy. Max's reappearance in my life has brought back a thousand unwelcome memories. I owe the person I am now to Eddy. Sure, Gabby was there for me, but it was Eddy who hauled me through and then put the pieces back together. Eddy who understood what I was dealing with. I guess I should have explained that to Gabby. I don't know why I didn't, except that the conversation had taken a wrong turn.

"You know it's not like that with me and Eddy."

"So what's your problem, girl?"

My thoughts turned to Rob. I had no right to be selfish. "I don't have a problem. Honestly. Eddy's a fantastic guy, Gabby. Take care of him."

I put down the phone feeling very much alone. I needed comfort and affirmation, and whom was I going to get that from? I walked into the bathroom and looked at myself in the mirror.

"Carol Shaw, you're a big girl now! Big in more ways than one. You can do this. Max was in your past. You didn't let him ruin your life before. Now you have your lucky break. Don't let Max Gardiner spoil it. You have to do this program. You know you can do it." Of course I could. Maybe.

Rob picked me up from work, brought me flowers and chocolates—which, of course, I'll resist since I have a will of iron. He had booked a table at an intimate little bistro around the corner from the movie theater. He was solicitous, charming, attentive, and amusing company. I wondered how he'd managed to develop into every woman's dream from such inauspicious beginnings. Must be the fact that he grew up in a household full of women who would have used the subtle tactic of beating the shit out of him if he'd disrespected any of them. I remember the muscles on his older sister. I said as much to Rob and he agreed that she still terrified the life out of him, but added that his younger sister probably had more impact; he could never bear to see her cry and would have done anything to stop her tears. I let slip that it must run in the family since I'd always felt the same way about him. Rob looked shocked, but laughed, shaking his head.

"I don't believe I was such a dork."

"Do you ever look at old school photos?"

I should have known better than to leave the choice of movie to Rob. I should have remembered that men aren't genetically programmed to be able to pick a watchable film. Rob apparently expected me to be thrilled that he got tickets for the latest Die-Hard-My-Dick's-Bigger-Than-Yours epic. It was completely mindless, so it gave me a chance to watch Rob out of the corner of my eyes and to think some fairly delectable thoughts.

He was affectionate, too, a relaxed arm around my shoulder as we watched the movie, his thumb absently caressing my neck, my jawline, my earlobes. And of course, here we were together in a public space—red rag to a bull it seems where I'm concerned. I was determined to control my raging hormones, but it was difficult, especially when I wasn't in the slightest bit interested in what was happening on the screen. I looked at Rob's strong profile, that warm full mouth, and I knew that I wanted to feel the caress of his lips on my body again. Rob must have sensed my thoughts since he pulled me closer and I relaxed against him, feeling the heat rise from his skin. As a group of over-testosteroned hulks pounded each other in full Techni-color, his hand moved downward until his fingers found my breast, squeezing gently until he could sense my excitement. Now his thumb was circling my nipple with a hypnotic rhythm while his eyes remained glued to the screen, almost as if his every movement was in-voluntary. This wasn't the Rob Elliott I remembered from our last outing to the movies. I was a little shocked. What kind of woman did he think I was? Or had Nicola been talking? Then I remembered that I'd shown him exactly where I draw the line the last time we met. You can't blame me; I've been stimulated in so many ways in the last few weeks and always left frustrated. I have to take every opportunity that comes my way before I explode.

I allowed my hand to rest on the inside of his thigh, unmoving. I wasn't going to rush anything. I intended to thoroughly enjoy the sensuousness of the moment. Gentle arousal. No rush of passion, just pure, unhurried eroticism. Besides, I didn't want to do anything that might deny my pleasure later. Rob's hand covered mine, moving it slowly farther up his thigh until I could sense, without touching, his own growing excitement. He didn't ask for any more, just turned to brush a fleeting kiss against my lips. I could have stayed there forever, especially when his hand moved to my inner thigh, stroking gently, up and down, his thumb edging farther upward and me sliding farther down in my seat, praying that he'd get the message. He was proving to be as slow on the uptake as he'd been back in school. I had to grab his hand, directing it to my sensitive, desperate clitoris, closing my thighs around it. He looked at me for a moment, eyes glazed, and then turned back to the screen. I wondered if his mind was on the job in hand.

Seemed I'd chosen the wrong moment to try to get his attention. I was competing against the climax of the film with lots of shooting, blood, and gore. How could a girl win? I was tempted to do my own thing, but the lights came up. Ironically, I was disappointed that the film was over.

Rob drove me home and apologized for his disastrous choice of movie. I assured him that I'd really quite enjoyed it—up to a point. He walked me to my door and held my hand, tugging me toward him as I struggled to unlock the door. I turned to him, fully expecting him to follow me in, intending to finish what we'd started. After all, it wasn't as if we'd just met; we've known each other nearly all our lives. He kissed me, and it felt very much like a good night kiss. He pulled away.

"Carol, I've got to go. I wish I could stay, but I've got to meet up with a client. Honey, I'll call you. Soon."

I glanced surreptitiously at my watch. A client at twelve-thirty? Still, none of my business. And then again, it was probably for the best since I didn't know anything about his life since school. Or about his wife. My body was still yearning for him while all these thoughts were going through my head. But I wasn't going to beg—well, I was so horny that I might have if I thought it would do any good. But he looked determined. Besides, I had an early start ahead of me, plenty to think about and enough sensations to get me through the night. I said good night. What else could I do?

I opened the door to go in, but Rob pulled me back to him. He gazed at me with those huge, sexy, brown eyes. I could see him forcing them to well with tears.

"Carol, if you don't give me one more kiss, I might just burst into tears."

I laughed and gently closed the door.

Chapter Ten

The last few days flashed past in a blur. I know I set off for Manchester at some ungodly hour on Wednesday morning. The production company sent a car to pick me up—part of the deal I'd negotiated with Gary's advice ringing in my ears. At least I could try to read the notes that the researcher had couriered to me, although most of the time the words blurred before my eyes and I found myself staring distractedly out of the window. It wasn't that the highway scenery was particularly lovely at this time of year, but my stomach was in knots, knowing that I'd be spending more time than I'd like in the company of Max Gardiner. As if stage fright wasn't enough.

Of course, over the years, despite my better judgment, I've followed Max's career. Or rather, the decline of his career. I'll admit to more than one sleepless night trying to track down information about him on the Internet, fearing always that I'd find that he was sick or worse. I needed to convince myself that I'd done the right thing in leaving him. That it wasn't that I didn't love him enough.

At first there were the stories of Max with a new woman and I would hold my breath in case she might succeed where I'd failed. Inevitably, though, the breakup would be reported, and at longer and longer intervals another woman would take my place. I'd find myself hunting down the most recent photograph of Max, praying for evidence that he'd come to his senses and given up the crack cocaine. With the trained eye of someone who'd cared so much for him, I picked out more and more signs. I was deluding myself that his giving up was even a possibility. At first there was a slight slackness in his jaw, and then the tiredness and wariness in his eyes. He began to look haunted and hunted. And then he dropped out of sight altogether. I guess I could have asked Eddy, but I owed it to him to forget about Max. And that's probably why I still haven't yet told Eddy about seeing Max again; Eddy so wanted me to get over the heartache that he pulled me back from, the pit I was gladly falling into at a rate of several knots. But now, I need to take responsibility for myself. I don't want to use Eddy, and I need time to work out exactly how I feel about Max before I talk to him about all of this. It's just that, right now, do I need the memories?

I didn't turn tail and walk out of the house straight away. In a blinding flash, I understood the hints that had been coming my way from Eddy. I didn't say a word to Max. I walked up the endless stairs and called Eddy, not knowing or caring what time it was. He came to me. I couldn't talk, but he only needed to look at me to understand. Eddy held me in his arms for what seemed like forever, warming my icy body and cooling my febrile brain. In time, without saying anything, he left me to walk down those silent stairs. I recalled how many times he'd performed the same action before, but now I knew why. Eddy had been caring for Max, and protecting me too. He was gone for a long time, while I fought to push the thought of how Max had looked through me from my consciousness.

"He's okay, Carol."

"No, that's the last thing he is, Eddy."

"Well, he won't come to any harm."

"How can you say that? Look at what he's doing to himself. I should have seen it before. He's not the same person anymore."

"I wondered if you knew."

I laughed then and I guess Eddy saw something in my eyes that made him recoil. But it wasn't because of Eddy. At that moment, I was angry at Max, yes, at Eddy, too, but most of all at myself. How could I have been so fucking naïve? Because I was living the kind of life I'd only dreamed of before, I'd allowed myself to ignore all the shit that was going down around me. How could I pretend that I loved Max when I hadn't cared enough to understand why, or even see how he was destroying himself? I was supposed to be the woman he loved and I still couldn't protect him from himself. I wasn't enough for Max. That was the truth. Hot tears burned my eyes, threatening to spill. Eddy misunderstood the venom that was really directed at myself.

"How could I say anything, Carol? All I could do was watch. I tried to look after him. And you."

The tears fell in earnest then. "How come I didn't know?"

Eddy wasn't going to absolve me. He just shook his head. "Babe, I can't tell you how many times I've seen this happen before."

"And I guess I just didn't want to see."

"Carol, it's not your problem; it's his."

"So what am I supposed to do now?"

"You really want to know what I think?"

"I bloody well asked you, didn't I?"

"Get out, Carol. Pack your bags and go. Right now. There's nothing you can do here."

"And is that what you're going to do? Walk out and leave him?"

"No."

"So what makes you such a fucking Good Samaritan? You booking your place in heaven? What makes you think he'd want you around anyway? What you got that I don't have?"

He didn't answer at once. He did something I'd never have expected from Eddy. He opened my packet of cigarettes, lit one, and handed it to me. I took a deep drag. My hands were shaking.

"Carol, I'm only telling you to leave because I care about you more than I care about him. Max is a very special human being; I love his talent, his intelligence. Max is unique. It hurts me that he's destroying himself when he has so much to give. But it's you that I worry about. This thing with Max can consume everyone. He's selfish when he's smoking that shit. He doesn't want . . . can't think about anything but himself and the place where he's at. Why do you think you don't see the guys coming around any longer? They're burnt out, Carol. I'd hate to see him do the same thing to you. Besides, I think it would be easier for him. He knows I can deal with this crap. He doesn't know if you can."

I should have listened to Eddy then, but I didn't. It says a lot for him that he didn't walk away from both of us. No, Eddy stuck around and attempted, as much as any one human could, to help me and Max. *Me and Max*. It's been so long since it was me and Max that it's frightening how that combination of words can still affect me, especially now that I've got myself into the situation where, once again, there will be me and Max.

Not even watching *Pop Idol, Fame Academy,* and all those other talent programs had prepared me for what I found in Manchester. Auditions were taking place in a huge rehearsal studio, and even at seven-thirty in the morning there were queues stretching all the way around the building. I suddenly felt daunted by the task ahead. There would be auditions in five different locations across the country and we were supposed to end up with only a hundred candidates after the first rounds. That meant that we'd have to whittle this lot down to twenty. There must have been a couple of hundred of them at least. Even after all the other talent shows, you could still see excitement and expectation in the waiting faces. I guess the opportunities for fame, or infamy, are so few and far between that you have to grab them whenever they occur, even if the risk is short-term glory followed by a lifetime of obscurity.

Adrian came out to meet me. I wondered if he'd been worrying that I might not turn up. Him and me both. Had his researchers found out about my past? I couldn't tell, but it seemed as if he was as nervous as me. A muscle twitched above his right eye.

"Adrian, have you seen how many people there are out there? There must be hundreds."

"Don't worry, Carol. The researchers will weed out the vast majority before they get to you."

"How are they going to do that? Isn't it our job to be the judges?" Already, I was on the defensive about this program. I don't know why, but I still wasn't one hundred percent sure about Adrian's motives for doing the series. Perhaps because he kept springing these little surprises on me. I'm becoming so paranoid that I even wondered if Adrian had known about my relationship with Max all along. Had he thrown us together to make "good television"?

"We're only here for two days, Carol. There's no way in the world you guys could see all those people out there. The researchers will only get rid of the ones with no talent and no personality. Believe me, there are lots of those."

I looked out the window at the throng of desperate hopefuls and wondered what qualified the researchers to judge talent, but I decided not to take it any further. Adrian was right, it would be impossible to audition all of them.

Gary and Quentin were sitting drinking coffee, looking remarkably cozy together for two men from such opposite ends of the musical spectrum. Adrian left to check on the crew.

"Have you seen all those people out there?" I asked.

"Thank God we don't have to listen to all of them," Quentin laughed.

Gary joined in, "It's going to be bad enough as it is without having to deal with all them hopeless wannabes."

I was surprised. "But you don't know that they're hopeless," I objected.

"When you've been around as long as me, darling, you know how many self-obsessed, would-be stars with delusions of ability there are out there." I bristled at the "darling" and nearly remarked that I hadn't realized he was so self-aware, but I bit my tongue.

A researcher came to take us to makeup and Adrian popped in to give us the pep talk about being ourselves, ignoring the camera and mikes, and enjoying ourselves. I'd have been all right if he hadn't said all of that. I could feel the flutter of nerves beginning and my palms started to sweat. The makeup artist chattered away aimlessly, and I amazed myself by being able to respond with words of one syllable at regular intervals. I didn't trust myself with polysyllables. In the fifteen minutes or so that she took to do my face, I had time to reflect on the insanity and masochism that had brought me to this point. If there was any way that I could have just sunk through the floorboards or even tunneled my way out, I would have done it. I should have told them about the incident in the nursery nativity play when I disgraced myself on stage. I was so terrified of wetting myself again that I spent a good ten minutes in the bathroom, tapping the walls, searching for secret passages. All too soon, the researcher came to find me and she escorted me back to the rehearsal room. I loathed her for being relaxed enough to be able to talk. I opened my mouth several times like a goldfish, but no words came out.

I was so terrified that I hardly noticed when Max finally arrived, and I admit with some guilt that I remember little or nothing about the first couple of acts.

They might have been Justin Timberlake and Beyoncé
Knowles. I was so tense and nervous that I had to concentrate hard on not fainting or embarrassing myself.
I'm afraid I left the others to do all the work and make
the judgment calls. It was all very well Adrian telling
us to ignore the cameras, but there they were, with
their menacing, glinting red lights, looming large over
my shoulder or in my face. Even when they were concentrating on the poor bastards singing their hearts out,
you never knew when they might swing round to catch
you unawares.

It took about forty minutes for me to get agitated
enough to rise above my fear. I suppose my irritation
must have been growing steadily for me to explode the
way I did. We'd seen mainly men and I think they
were all mediocre, maybe worse, certainly unremark-
able. At least none of them had been good enough to
shake me out of my panic-induced stupor. And then a
girl came in. I'll admit she had long, long legs, barely
covered by the tightest, smallest hotpants I'd ever seen
and a constrictingT-shirt that stopped somewhat precariously above the midriff and did very little to cover
rather large breasts. She had dyed blond flowing hair
and wore bright, shiny lipstick. It was all so obvious,
but it certainly got her noticed. The problem was that
she could only sing half as well as Eddy's cat. I honestly thought the guys would have more sense than to
fall for her other assets but, to my astonishment, they
were voting for her to come back.

"You can't honestly be serious," I found myself saying, calmly but coldly. I was expecting Gary, at least, to
support me since I didn't have any great hopes of
Quentin or Max, who, most of the time, seemed to be
floating somewhere above Uranus. Gary astonished

me, though. He looked at me as if he didn't understand what I was talking about. "The girl's got potential."

"For what?" I could sense the camera whipping around to catch the scene that was developing but I was too annoyed to care. "She couldn't carry the tune if it was packed in her fake Gucci handbag. If she sang fifty notes, she might have got one of them in the right octave! How many guesses will it take for you to work out what exactly she was singing if using that word isn't against the Trades Description Act?"

Gary had the decency to look away from me. "She might need a bit of voice coaching; we can't expect these guys to be perfect."

"I'm not expecting perfection. Maybe just a tiny suggestion of ability would be useful."

What Gary said next really got to me. "What you got against the sista, Carol?"

He said it in a way that implied that I was only criticizing because I was jealous. I regret rising to the bait. "It's what you all would like to have against her that's worrying me." Fortunately, I think I said it in a steely whisper that would have been hard for the mikes to pick up. I needed to watch my temper. And I was going to have to watch Gary too. I'd made a serious miscalculation when I thought that he'd be an ally. In the end, I lost that particular argument, but I knew I was going to have to concentrate more carefully on each contestant if the other judges weren't to select their own personal harems. To be fair, I have to leave Max out of that statement. I can't say that he was susceptible to that girl's charms. It looked as if Max wasn't susceptible to anyone's charms. He was clearly living on another planet. And you know how dumb I am? Even though I was almost overcome with fear and excitement and tension, I couldn't stop myself from wondering what was going on in Max's head. Was it really possible that he didn't remember who I was? What we'd been to each other? I guess I wanted to hold on to the belief that I really had at one time meant something to him; otherwise, what was the point of all that hell that I had gone through? But if I had been significant in his life, how could he now look straight through me as if we'd never met? Anyway, I'm glad of that first run-in with the other judges. It left me too riled up to feel nervous any longer.

So the two days passed quicker than I expected. The worst part was deciding on the final twenty. I learned that I was on my own. Max was always going to be gently critical of the male auditionees. I sensed that deep down he saw them all as a threat. To what, though, was hard to imagine. I wondered if Max had agreed to appear on the program with the hope of reviving his career. That had gone way downhill, but he hadn't lost the voice, and whenever he gave advice, he would reinforce it with a quick few bars from one of his old hits. You know, it disturbed me that the sound of his voice could still, after all these years, make me instantly lustful. But I've always found exceptional talent incredibly erotic.

Quentin was mostly relatively quiet and that lulled us all into a false sense of security. I realize now that he is shrewd and experienced enough to bide his time, making sharp, cutting remarks when they make the most impact. For him, it isn't the talent that matters and he can be unnecessarily hurtful just to make himself look good. I understood that his sarcasm might easily be turned on me. I imagine that as a kid he probably tore the wings off flies and then drowned them in boiling water. This television business is far more complex than I'd imagined. Sure, I soon got used to the cameras and all the paraphernalia, but wading through the shark-infested waters of media politics is going to be far more perilous than I thought.

Gary is the one who puzzles me most. He's obviously bright, sharp, knowledgeable, and extremely talented. He can be amazingly charismatic too. You can see why he's got ahead in the media. But I think he might be utterly ruthless. He knows where he needs to lavish his charm, and it's certainly not in my direction. I found it hard to figure out why he would be so aggressive toward me when the camera was rolling and then so warm and friendly once we wrapped. I guess he's figured out where potential sparks might fly, and it's between me and him. I tell myself not to take it personally, but I constantly feel that I have to wear chain mail when I'm around him.

To add to the exhaustion of filming, I'm expected to call Eddy every day. It's not that I don't want to talk to him, but this is business. Eddy has to prepare behind-the-scenes reports that will go out when the series is aired. Of course, I'm the mole and I'm supposed to give him all the gossip. As soon as we finish the location stuff and we're back in London, then Eddy will be following us around and doing his own digging. Until then, I feel a bit like a guilty spy and I suspect my co-judges are a little wary around me.

What makes it all even worse is that every few days Patrick appears to take photos. I'm really not good at this kind of stuff and I know that when the posed group shots appear, I'm going to be the one with the crossed eyes or the fixed smile and cabbage on my teeth and I'll be described as "quirky" or "eccentric" or

some other subtle, insulting epithet. And Patrick's not
likely to tell me. He's not on my side either.

I can see why Patrick is so good at his job, though.
It's kind of creepy the way he seems to merge into the
background and the next thing you know, just as you're
doing something that's excruciatingly embarrassing,
he'll pop up with a flash. I don't know whether it's the
way he naturally is or the job that's made him like this,
but whichever way around, he makes my skin crawl. I
force myself to be pleasant with him particularly since
I'm using him to get evidence on Vince, but every time
I look at him, I picture a basking lizard.

On top of all of this, most of the time I find myself
in nonsmoking areas, and even though my nerves feel
as though they're being tightened till they're about to
snap, I can't even calm them with a cigarette. Smoking
alone in my hotel room doesn't even feel like much fun
anymore. Are the gods trying to tell me something?

My mood only began to lighten on our final night
in Manchester when we went to an old-fashioned blues
club that Gary knew. Max tagged along, amiable, but
distant. We persuaded a very reluctant Quentin to come
too—I guess this was our idea of a bonding session. We
were led to an anonymous-looking door with no sign
to indicate what was going down inside. The huge
room was packed, hot, smoky, and sweaty with the
aromatic smell of ganja in the air. Just the way I like it.
Max found some like-minded souls and joined them
over several rounds of overproof white rum at a table
in the corner. My feelings toward him had begun to
soften a little, though I stiffened involuntarily as I
watched him expertly roll a spliff and pass it round.

I felt it my duty to look after Quentin, so I got him
a couple of strong drinks and then led him on to the

dance floor. You don't have to twist my arm to groove, especially when they're spinning all that old-time stuff like Marley or Aswad or Burning Spear or Gregory Isaacs. Quentin was at first embarrassingly stiff and awkward. I kept my distance, trying to pretend that I wasn't with him. The room was so crowded, though, that he soon loosened up and surprised me with some bold moves as he got into the rhythm. I soon realized, with a shock, that I was actually enjoying myself.

I hardly noticed when Quentin staggered from the dance floor. A blues club is just like dancing around your own living room: you're completely anonymous. No one cares or even notices what you do. Everyone is lost in their own little cocoon of sound and rhythm and the pounding of the bass. I half came out of my trance when I felt an arm snake around my waist. It was like I'd been enjoying a dream and I didn't want to wake up, so I only half roused myself. I knew it was Gary. One arm around my waist, the other on my hip as he glued himself to me, hips rocking, knees bending, following my every movement instinctively, his crotch Blu-tacked to my backside. That's what I wanted from the music, the not-thinking-ness, losing myself, forgetting about my growing animosity toward Gary. I enjoyed the way we moved together. At that time, in that place, it felt right. We rocked in unison as one tune segued into the next, neither of us speaking, in fact, hardly moving, his body molded to mine. Pure delight in the sounds, the feelings, the soaring emotion of understanding and being one with the rhythm. When the music finally stopped, Gary brushed a fleeting kiss against the nape of my neck, said "Thank you," and disappeared to the other side of the room. It was such an old-fashioned and surprising gesture. As I looked over at him, he raised his glass to me questioningly and I nodded, accepting his offer of a drink.

I didn't make it to the bar, though, since Max surprised me by catching hold of my hand as I walked past and pulling me down to sit next to him.

"You been avoiding me, honey?" Question or statement? I couldn't help noticing the old endearment. Did he remember, or was that how he addressed every woman these days? I gazed into Max's eyes, which, suddenly, seemed clear and alive with a glint of humor. I didn't know what to say. He was still holding my hand and I suddenly wanted to pull away, frightened by his touch. He held firm.

"You think I don't notice how you is with them other guys? When my turn goin' come?" His lips were close to my ear, his alcohol-laden breath whispering along my neck. Beres Hammond was playing and allowing Max to hold me close would be like diving off a precipice, but I figured it would be safer than talking.

"How about now?" Max held my gaze for a subtle moment before standing, pulling me to him, and forcing a space for us through the crowd. We were much too close. Every nerve ending was screaming. I could feel a flutter of panic rising in my abdomen. The warmth of Max's body, the tightness of his arms around my waist, the musky fragrance of his skin, the rapid beating of his heart as he drew me nearer to him, the undeniable magnetism of his presence were taking me back into the past, to a place I knew I didn't want to revisit. Then Max was crooning, singing along to Beres, his deep bass voice echoing through my head, melting my resistance. I've always been a sucker for genius, and Max had lost none of his talent. I leaned into his body, completely under his spell, and if the music hadn't come to an end just then, God only knows what I might have done. Another public space, you notice. I breathed out, only now aware that I'd been holding my breath for several moments. At least now I could draw away from his body and feel safe. But Max held me close for a second too long and whispered in my ear, "Remember Martinique, honey?"

Exactly where I didn't want to go, but the heat of the club, the alcohol I'd drunk, and the heady, ganja-filled atmosphere took me back immediately.

We went straight after a tour, out of season, intending to be away from the reach of e-mails and cell phones. It was the rainy season, but worth it for the peace. A hotel right by Les Salines beach at the tip of the island. I knew I'd never before seen such tranquil beauty: pure white sand and lush green palms reaching out toward the transparent blue water. A picture postcard come to life. For the first two days at least I walked around in a trance, practicing school-girl French, eyes wide, unable to believe that I was really there. I know Max felt the same way because we'd only have to look at each other to collapse into fits of giggles, excited like children at a perpetual amusement park, with cotton candy thrown in free.

It was the hammock on the beach that was our downfall. With some difficulty I'd mastered the art of getting into it and felt sheer bliss lying there, swaying gently in the cool, early-evening breeze, gazing out at the azure blue sea. Through drowsy eyes I could just make out Max's head bobbing in the sea as he swam gracefully and effortlessly, pushing himself to the limit as was his habit. I watched him knowing that it would be a few days before he would relax enough to allow his body to drift in the warm currents, to literally go with the flow. The pale crimson of the sun reflected in the water and I thought of paradise as my eyes became as heavy as my relaxed body, as the rocking of the hammock lulled me toward sleep.

I screamed as I was startled by the icy wetness of Max's body, but I had to laugh at his attempt to join me in the hammock. He hitched one long, deeply tanned, muscular leg over the side, gripping the cord with both hands as I held on tightly, laughing at him. He ended up flat on his back in the warm sand. Completely illogically, he tried the other side. Same result. By now, I was convulsed. Too soon, because the next moment, Max had grabbed hold of me and we were both in the sand, both hysterical. By the time our laughter subsided, our bodies were hot, reacting to the fading sun and to each other. Max stood, grabbed my hand, and dragged me, resisting, to the water's edge. He picked me up as I screamed my protest and carried me into the sea. Now, I'm a woman who doesn't swim unless I have to. Hair. You know exactly what I mean; when I'd spent a fortune having my hair relaxed and styled especially for this trip, there was no way I was getting it wet. You can't expect a guy to understand that, but I thought Max had lived with me long enough to know better than to mess with my hair. So when he dumped me into the cool evening water, it was the shock that made me grab hold of his ankle and upend him. I was bedraggled, but fiery with righteous anger. We struggled for a while until I ran out of breath. I stood up, intending to surrender and make my way back towards the safety of the sand.

"*Dr. No*," Max said as I started to emerge from the waves.

"What?" I turned back to him.

"You remind me of Ursula Andress in *Dr. No*. Sexy as hell." I laughed at the idea that I could remind him of a blond, Swiss movie star. Max wasn't joking, though. He took my hand and pulled me to him. Standing chest deep in the clear water, he ran his hand across my scalp and grabbed my hair, pulling my head back as he lowered his lips to mine and kissed me roughly, bruising my lips as he forced them apart and thrust his tongue into my mouth, searching for something I couldn't fathom. His knee parted my legs urgently, roughly as he clutched me to him, pulling me down until we were lying together, floating in the water, my flesh holding on to the memory of sand warmth, shocked by the contrasting cool wetness of the sea. Then Max was diving under me, holding his breath while his slick fingers traced the outline of my melting flesh. I was disoriented, burning where his fingers touched, freezing the next moment, sensing his presence for one second, bemoaning his absence the next, flowing toward his touch, wanting, needing the heat from his body.

Then there was a sudden sensation of mild panic as we drifted away from the beach, out toward the open sea. Max was his confident self, but my senses were heightened by fear. Every pore of my body was open, alert, tingling, scared. I wanted to cry out to Max, but he had let go of me, diving beneath me, and before I could make a sound he was holding me again, his hard body pressed against mine, his fingers tracing the contour of my hip.

"Max," I gasped, trying to catch my breath, to still incipient panic.

"Carol?"

"I'm scared, Max. I've got to get back."

And Max was holding me as we kicked toward the shore. My feet touched the sand and I felt like an idiot. What the hell was I scared of? Max would never have put me in danger, would he? The relief made me shake and Max took me in his arms, rubbing my skin to warm me.

"I'm sorry, honey."

To this day, I'll never understand why, but I suddenly wanted Max more than I ever had before. I wrapped my arms around his neck, digging my fingers into his skin. I felt him wince, but I also felt the sudden rush of blood to his groin as his cock hardened against my stomach. Instantly, I was searing hot, frantic with the need for him. My lips found his as I raked my nails down his back, drawing blood. My nipples were turning to steel as his tongue plunged into my mouth finding a rhythm that echoed the grinding of his body against mine. His teeth nipped at my lips and then bit down hard making me moan with a mixture of pain and desire. I could feel his hand searching for the fastening to my bikini top and, frustrated by the delay, I pushed his fingers away and undid the clasp, pressing my naked breast against his chest, rubbing my nipples lasciviously against him. Tingling with desire for him, I grabbed his hands and pressed them against my heavy breasts, holding them there while he rubbed, pinched, and squeezed my erect nipples. The throbbing between my legs signaled a competing need, and I reluctantly took hold of his hand and gratefully directed it to my pussy. Holding his wrist, I rubbed myself against his hand, feeling the heat flowing from the center of my body, along the length of his fingers, up to my hardened nipples and down again, as if his hands were conducting the flow of electricity. Totally oblivious to anything around us, I had to take my pleasure right then, regardless of Max's needs. As it happened, they coincided with mine and I opened my eyes to see the look of triumph in his as he fully recognized the power he held over me.

It was a power that I was determined to experience. Under the lapping water, my hand reached for his trunks. Max gasped as my fingers slipped inside the waistband, teasing the wiry hairs that snaked down his belly. I tickled, caressed, traced a path downward and 'round, ignoring his thrusting cock, cupping the weight of his balls in my hand, squeezing gently until I heard his moan. This was Max, my lover, my love. I knew his body almost as well as I knew my own, but this feeling was new. Different. Another space. Another time.

I took a deep breath and, before he knew what to expect, I plunged my head into the water and took the hard but tender head of his cock between my lips, feeling the shudder of surprise ricochet through his body. Only a few seconds passed before the need for air, but enough to send a powerful message. I wrapped my fingers around him, appreciating the unaccustomed size of him.

"Carol, what you doing to me? I can't take much more, you know."

I didn't answer. There was no way I could explain the closeness, the intimacy I wanted, the desire to be one with Max, needing him to blot out the last residue of fear. A tingling ran the length of my body as I looked into his eyes. He took my hand and wrapped my fingers around his hard shaft. "Feel what you've done to me. You think you can handle it?" My pussy began to throb, clutching at his absent cock, recalling the feel of it, desperate to feel him inside me again. I wanted him right then. Couldn't wait.

"You ready, babe?"

"Mmm."

"I don't think so." Max shook his head as his fingers traveled between my thighs. "You're not wet enough."

"You're joking," I protested. "How can you tell?"

"Babe, I know you ain't ready for this." His smile, as he fondled his erection, was dangerous, igniting more fires in my abdomen. "I'll have to make you ready."

His long fingers were moving down my bikini pants, around the swell of my buttocks, between the warm softness of my pussy lips. I groaned as he parted them to gently push a finger inside me, moving slowly in and out, using the other hand to hold me as he murmured, "That's it, honey. Take it. Take what you want. I've got what you need. Just waiting for you, honey."

I could hear my breath, hoarse, rasping as I took my pleasure, moving against him, straining to feel his fingers deeper and deeper inside me. And then, suddenly, he pulled away, holding my body at arm's length, his eyes traveling the length of it, leaving me bereft as he searched for something. Then he must have found it, because all at once, he was frenzied, ripping my bikini pants away, lifting my legs, wrapping them around his hips as he found my opening, pushing gently at first, then harder as his breath grated, then thrusting deep, paining me with the strength of his rigid prick, clutching my buttocks, straining against me. This was pain and pleasure I'd never felt before, and I was still, desperate to hold on to that moment, not wanting to let it go. Then he was pulling out and I was fighting him, fearing any distance between us. Then we were moving together, buoyed by the water, swaying gently, exploring each other's depths, losing the urgency, enjoying the gentleness, the erotic stillness. We stopped moving. I looked down at where we were joined, savoring the beauty of his body, the manifestation of his desire for me.

The rain started then, soft, warm droplets at first. I moved against him, the need building, growing again, as I plunged my hips toward him, clutching, grasping, rising, falling, feeling the flutter, the crescendo, the flood, the bursting, wanting to hold on to the moment, fearing the storm. The rainfall became suddenly heavy, beating against my skin as he pounded into me. Overcome by helplessness as the ripples of pleasure joined and overflowed, I screamed Max's name and collapsed against him, languishing in the waves, both physical and metaphorical. Just as suddenly as it had started, the rain stopped and the weak sun reemerged.

It was a few moments before the rushing in my ears cleared and I recognized the sound of applause. I looked around and, in the dusk, made out several shadowy figures clapping enthusiastically. Max took a bow. I, the weak swimmer, swam as far as I could toward the horizon. Still, you can understand why, a few months later, we booked a cruise around the Caribbean islands.

I'd allowed myself to respond to Max too easily and I could tell, as he held my hips, bringing me closer and closer, that he wasn't unaffected either. I was slipping into a dangerous languor. I roused myself, shook my head to clear it, and forced my body away from his, hoping he hadn't noticed my state of arousal. I moved toward the bar and Max didn't try to hold me back. As I turned to look at his smiling face I saw something there that might have been regret before his eyes clouded over again.

Back in my hotel bed, I tossed restlessly for several hours, kept awake by roving thoughts and a raging fire between my thighs. Sometime in the early hours I remember picking up the phone, but then dropping it as if it burned. Who had I intended to call? I didn't want to grab the fleeting thought.

There was so much traveling. Manchester to Glasgow to Cardiff, seeing little or nothing of the cities on the way. Rehearsal room to hotel, to bar, back to hotel. No time, or inclination, for another blues club. I tried to keep my distance from Max, but it was probably unnecessary. There was no recurrence of the spark in his eye. It was like I'd imagined the way his body had felt against mine.

By last night my emotions were so strung out that I wanted to talk to Rob. I called Eddy instead. I didn't yet know Rob well enough to pour my heart out to him. Besides, how could I possibly talk to him about Max? I'd kept that part of my history under wraps for so long that I couldn't face any protracted explanation. No, Eddy was the only one I could trust.

Eddy was his usual, unfailingly sympathetic, supportive self. "Carol, what can I do? You want me to come up there? I can get in the car straight away. You shouldn't have to go through all this again. But remember that you got through it before. It's been a while since I saw Max, so I ain't saying he's still using, but be careful, babe. I don't know too many guys who manage to kick that shit. I know how you felt about Max and I can understand why." Eddy was silent for a few moments before asking the only question that needed to be answered.

"How you feel about him now, Carol?"

"To tell the truth, Eddy, I just don't know for sure. I always imagined that if I saw him again there would be nothing there. I wish I could say that's what happened. But he still has an effect on me. I don't know if it's love or lust. And I don't know if I want either anymore."

"You need to find out if you're still in love with him, Carol."

It was my turn to be silent. He was right, but I didn't want to explore that. Not with Eddy. I changed the subject and told him about Gary and my concerns.

"You got to remember that under all that front, he's just a boy. He's probably just as insecure as the rest of us."

"It doesn't show. So why did you ask him to look after me?"

"I honestly thought it would help, sugar. I should have known that the brotha would take it as you being weak and a prime target. I don't think you need to worry, though. From what you saying, you giving as good as you get. Just be gentle with him, girl. I know you with your sharp tongue and your evil eye. You could easily turn him to stone."

For some reason, I didn't tell Eddy about the blues dance. Gary hadn't mentioned it since and I felt a little weird about it, as if we shared a guilty secret.

"You think so?"

"I know so."

"I wish I had your confidence, Eddy. The trouble is, he seems to change tactics every day. I don't know what to expect from him. He always seems to come at me from out of left field."

"Girl, remember you don't need this program as much as Gary. He's got the most to lose. I know you can deal with him."

"You sound so serious I'm beginning to frighten myself," I laughed. I did feel better, though.

"Your friend Gabriela called me a few days ago, you know," Eddy said in a tone that I knew was meant to be casual but that he didn't quite pull off.

"I gave her your number. I hope you don't mind."

"No, I was just surprised."

"At what?"

"Nothing really."

"Tell me, Eddy."

"Honestly, it's nothing. Forget it. I met up with her for a drink the other evening."

"Just a drink?"

"Just a drink. I like her. She's spirited."

"And intelligent, and rich, and very beautiful. And married."

"She told me."

I was surprised. The idea that they had talked about it worried me for reasons that I couldn't articulate. I suppose it indicated a level of intimacy between them that I hadn't expected yet.

"What did she say about Pete?"

"Not much. But I get the impression that he isn't around a lot and probably doesn't figure too much in her life."

I didn't reply. I honestly didn't know what to say to Eddy. Or what he wanted to hear. That Gabby's marriage was dead? Was it? I truly didn't know. Sure, she'd always given the impression that Pete might be having affairs, but we didn't know for sure. She didn't seem too concerned at the idea that he was being unfaithful, but that might be just on the surface. Or was it just that it allowed her to justify her own infidelities? Suddenly I was being judgmental when I didn't want to be. It hurt a little to realize that my relationship with Gabby was, fundamentally, based on her listening to my adventures and escapades and problems while she kept her deepest feelings very much to herself. It occurred to me for the first time that there was a disparity in the level of trust between us. I'd trusted Gabby completely, while she obviously didn't reciprocate. I suppose I couldn't really blame her since this was the first time I was considering the nature of our relationship. Obviously, I'd been too absorbed in my own problems to ever turn any real attention to hers. Maybe I hadn't been a good friend to Gabby. I would have to make it up to her. I sighed loudly.

"What's wrong, sugar?"

"Nothing. I just don't really know how to be the best friend I can possibly be to you now, Eddy."

"You think I'm going to need a friend so bad?"

"I don't know. But I'll be here."

I made a mental note to invite Gabby 'round as soon as I possibly could. I thought we needed to talk.

"One thing, Carol."

"What?"

"Why didn't you tell me when you first saw Max again?"

I didn't have a good answer.

Chapter Eleven

God knows what made me do it, but I was missing home and my friends and the memory of the blues dance must have addled my brain. Maybe it was the ganja. In a slightly inebriated state, I decided it would be a good idea to have a party. In my tiny apartment! And I invited all these people. Why? My only defense is that it seemed like a reasonable idea at the time. Okay, I know it means letting my boss and his idiot secretary/lover into my home, but I was feeling drunkenly generous. I also foolishly thought that inviting everyone from *Soul Sensation* might mend some fences. Of course, I'd have to invite Max, but I very much doubted that he'd come. So I'd have to see Eddy and Gabby together, but Rob would be there too. All right, if I'd thought it through, I'd have seen the potential disasters. But I didn't. So shoot me!

The one sensible idea I had was to ask Gabby to help. I'm not the greatest cook in the world. In fact, I've only learned one dish and that's Chicken Adobo that a Filipino friend taught me years ago. It's delicious, but it is the *only* dish I can cook, so it's appetizer, main course, pudding, breakfast, lunch, and supper. Gabby offered to pay for caterers, but I was determined to do it all myself. Or rather, with Gabby. And Eddy.

I only got back from Cardiff in the very early hours of the morning, but I dragged myself to the supermarket to buy wine, gin, vodka, brandy, and rum—and that was just to get *me* through the day. Since Eddy was coming, I stretched to carrots, celery, red peppers, crème fraîche, and healthy shit like that. For the rest of us, I stocked up on chips, salted nuts, cheesy biscuits, and chocolates.

When I got back to the apartment, Gabby was waiting on the doorstep with what seemed like a truckload of groceries. We carried the bags up to my flat in relays, and I was impressed to find that Gabby had a plan. She'd written out a list of dishes to cook and she got straight down to it while I put on some music, poured myself a glass of wine, lit an illicit cigarette—I've almost decided to give up—and rested for a while, mesmerized by her organizational skills.

Funny, I'd never imagined Gabby as the mumsy, aproned, domestic type, but she seemed to settle into the role so comfortably that it seemed impolite to butt in where I wasn't needed. I watched in amazement as she sliced, chopped, diced, strained, simmered, stirred, and tasted.

I hadn't eaten for hours and was beginning to feel a little tipsy already. Probably not a bad thing since I had the courage to ask precisely what I wanted to know.

"So, Gabby, you invite Pete?"

"He's busy."

"You know, I realize that I haven't seen Pete in years."

"Really?"

"Come on, Gabby. You know I haven't."

"I suppose that's true."

"So why not? You never bring him anywhere with you."

Gabby took her time, stirring the pots, adding extra seasoning, a pinch of herbs or a dash of wine here and there, turning down the gas, assuring herself that all was well in that particular arena. It was like she was performing some sort of superstitious ritual.

She poured a glass of wine and sat on the stool opposite me. Gabby took one of my cigarettes, lit it, and inhaled deeply. I was shocked. I hadn't ever seen Gabby smoke before. I'd always been convinced that she cared too much about her appearance to risk damaging her flawless skin. She took a generous slug of wine.

"Peter's gone."

"What do you mean? Gone where? When?"

"He left. Oh, it must be approximately three months, six days and"—she looked at her watch—"thirty-six minutes ago."

"Gab, I had no idea."

"I didn't want to wallow. It's such an old, old story. It could have happened any time in the last four years or so. I knew there were other women."

"But you didn't seem to mind."

"Of course I minded." She sounded angry with me. "How do you think it makes me feel to know that my husband doesn't want me? Doesn't find me attractive, or desirable? That he's been looking for a younger, fresher model?"

"I don't believe it! You're so beautiful, Gabby. He'll never find anyone to come even close to you." I didn't have the words to express how shocked I felt.

I'd always thought of Gabby as the most beautiful woman I'd ever known. I'd envied every aspect of her life, including having a rich husband she could walk round on a leash and order to sit or fetch whenever she wanted. Guess I got that relationship all wrong.

"But he has. Found someone, I mean. I was so hurt. I loved Peter. I was devastated. I just had too much pride to admit it to anyone else, least of all to him. Girl, you know what it's like; you spend your whole time thinking you're being used. Wondering why he chose you. Waiting for the moment, the careless word, that's going to prove you right. You know one day they'll do something that will show you were justified in holding back that little bit of yourself." I could see the tears forming in Gabby's eyes and sensed that she was no stranger to them. She casually brushed them aside, not knowing how much they hurt me. This was the first time I'd ever seen Gabby cry with anything other than helpless laughter.

"I'm not justifying what Peter did, but I know there's a part of me that I never gave to him. Maybe that's what he's been looking for. Now he's found it in someone else."

I put my arms around her and hugged her tightly. I found myself reluctantly understanding that Eddy might be very good for her at this particular time in her life.

"Why didn't you tell me, Gabby?"

"A whole heap of things, I suppose. Pride. Not wanting to admit to myself that it was all over. That's probably why there have been these other guys. You know, Carol, nothing happened with any of them." Gabby laughed through her tears. "Girl, with your big foot you just jumped right into the wrong conclusion

and I let you." She sobered suddenly. "I needed the attention. I wanted to pretend that I didn't care what Peter
was up to. Then maybe I *really* wouldn't care."

I was stunned. I didn't know my friend as well as I
thought. "And you honestly believe there's no way
you two can work it out?"

In the background, Lauryn Hill was crooning, ap-
propriately enough, about someone killing her softly
with his song, and I wanted to beg her stop in case
my heart broke into a thousand pieces, and I didn't
want to draw Gabby's attention to her lament.

"Carol, it was all such a struggle in the first place.
His family never thought I fit in. They saw me as some
kind of gold digger. It was never like that, though.
Sure, it's been great having the nice house, car,
clothes, jewelry. But I never asked for any of those
things. It was always Peter wanting me to look right,
to not let him down." Suddenly, Gabby seemed so
vulnerable. I'd always thought of her as strong, invin-
cible. "The sickening thing is that it's all so *amicable*.
Peter's very generous. He's talking about a settlement
that's more than fair. He's got it all worked out. He
must have been thinking about it for a long time. He's
found a younger, more energetic model."

"Do you still love him?"

"I don't know. But one thing I'm sure of"—Gabby
lifted her head, deliberately relaxing her shoulders—"I
need a good time tonight. Let's get ready to party,
Carol." She stubbed out the cigarette. There was determination, but also a hint of uncertainty, in her voice. I
knew that Gabby would need to talk this out further,
but now wasn't the time. She was right, though—she
needed to party. I gave her a quick hug, filled her glass,
and left her to the cooking while I set about trying to

bring some order to the typhoon-hit area that was my apartment.

Eddy arrived not long after, bearing a crate of champagne to celebrate my new-found fame and fortune. I watched as Gabby flirted with him in a not-too-convincing fashion, and I kept out of their way as much as possible. I could see that, right now, Eddy was the best medicine I could prescribe.

By the time other people started to arrive, I'd managed to stow the worst of the debris inside cupboards, drawers, and under the bed. I'd drunk enough to be looking forward to the evening until Oliver, my boss, arrived first, just as I was retrieving a recalcitrant pair of knickers from under the sofa, down on all fours with my bum pointing skyward.

With him was his wife, Simone. I'd met her a couple of times before, but hadn't expected Oliver to bring her since he knew that Georgina was coming too. There were a few awkward moments until Eddy got to talking work with Oliver and Simone and I joined Gabby to help with the food. Simone is the last person you'd expect to be with a creep like Oliver. She's an elegant brunette, obviously intelligent, and once we'd got over the initial awkwardness, warm and funny. I wondered, for the millionth time, why Oliver is messing around with someone like Georgina.

The flow of guests soon became a deluge. It hadn't really registered that when I told Nicola about the party it went without saying that the rest of my family would turn up, too; Dad, Pauline, the kids, Aunt Bea, Vince, and Mom had all accepted virtual invitations. I was relying on Eddy to help me make sure that peace reigned since I could sense several potential flashpoints: Dad was talking to Vince, Georgina looking

daggers at Simone, and Mom covertly surveilling Pauline.
I wanted to leave, but it was my party and my apartment.
Where would I go? I spent the next half hour executing a
finely choreographed military maneuver, deftly guiding
potential foes out of each others' paths. In the end, my ef-
forts proved futile, so I decided to tackle the most likely
battleground first. As Pauline headed in her direction,
Mom pulled herself up to her full five-foot nine with her
nose in the air and a steely look in her narrowed eyes. She
didn't have a drink, so I poured her a generous shot of
rum punch and swallowed half a glass of champagne.

By the time I got to them, Pauline had already
taken charge. "Carol, your mother was just telling me
all the gossip about *Soul Sensation*. I hear say you was
calling her every day." I looked at Mom and raised one
eyebrow. She had the grace to look a little ashamed of
herself since I hadn't spoken to her once about the
show. I don't know what gossip she was passing on,
but it certainly didn't originate with me. I decided to
spare her.

"Well, it wouldn't be fair to keep my own mother
in the dark, would it?" I said. There was a half smile on
Pauline's face but she was too kindhearted to take advantage of the situation.

"You must be so proud, Josie."

"Yes, well, our side of the family have a lot of talent in it." Mom folded her arms beneath her bosom and
looked so smug that I wished I'd landed her in it after
all.

"You know I told Travis that Carol must get it from
you. I ain't seen any sign of talent in him, and Lord
knows I been searching like a starving man for a little
grain of corn." She burst into peals of laughter. I didn't
believe it for a second, but despite herself, Mom was

blushing with pleasure. I could safely leave these two. No matter how aloof Mom tried to remain, she wouldn't be able to resist Pauline with her lying self.

I wasn't feeling too kindly toward Oliver, though. He was standing a little too close to Georgina, and I didn't want to know what his hand was doing behind her back. She was looking up at him with an ecstatic expression that reminded me of a slug drowning in beer. I found Simone and led her over to them saying, "Have you met Oliver's *Personal* Assistant?" I stayed long enough to enjoy Oliver's growing discomfort. I could swear his beard was beginning to curl.

I looked around. Quentin and Gary had arrived along with Adrian and many of the team from *Soul Sensation*. I hadn't expected this many of them to turn up. The rooms were getting more and more packed. Adrian squeezed through and kissed me on the cheek, his lips a little too close to mine. "Great party, Carol. Good to see you again." I could smell the alcohol on his breath. I took a step back but his arm reached around me and I jumped half a mile when his hand rested on my butt. He leaned toward me.

"How's the star of the show, then?"

"Have we found one yet?"

His body was inching closer to mine and I was leaning as far away as I could without performing a backward somersault. I never was much of a gymnast, but at that moment I wished I'd concentrated harder in PE class.

"You know, Carol, I could make *you* the star." I was bending so far back to avoid his lips that it looked like we were performing a tango. He whispered in my ear, "We could work so well together." It was all I could do not to gag, but fortunately we were interrupted by the sudden silence in the room. I looked toward the focus of everyone's attention. Max had arrived. I should have known. Only he could have that effect, even after all this time. He looked straight at me and took a step in my direction, but his path was blocked by a crowd of people struggling to get near him. Leading the charge was my sister Nicola. *God help me*, I immediately thought. And he did, because Adrian suddenly let go of me, jigging up and down. "Got to pee." I pointed him toward the bathroom with a sense of relief.

I headed toward Dad and Vince, plastering a bright smile on my face.

"Vince, I'm so glad you could come. I feel honored. I expected you to be much too busy to turn up here. Especially on a Saturday night." I winked at him quite blatantly. "I thought you'd have much more exciting places to go."

I knew that he and Dad could sense the hostility in my voice, but Vince responded first. "Of course I'd come, Carol. You're my favorite future sister-in-law. Wouldn't miss it for the world." He bent over to kiss my cheek and I felt my skin crawl. I nearly recoiled, but Nicola was moving in our direction with Max in tow.

Her tone was reproachful and not a little hurt. "Sis, why you didn't tell me Max was coming? It's so wonderful to see him again. Mom's really happy." Just what I needed: my folks getting the wrong idea.

Max kissed me briefly on the lips and took hold of my hand. His eyes looked into mine and seemed remarkably focused. In fact, I felt a little honored—it was so unlike Max to turn up at any event before the early hours of the morning. There was a depth in his look that made me want to escape for air. Fortunately, Dad put a hand on his arm and the two men looked at each other for a moment before embracing. I felt tears rise to my eyes, so I took the opportunity to head for the kitchen and a refill.

That's where Eddy found me. The concern in his eyes made me head straight for his arms and he took hold of me in a warm embrace. "You okay, babe?" he asked in a tender way that made me want to weep. He lifted my chin and I looked into eyes that seemed so serious, so concerned. I nodded.

"I think so."

"I'm here if you need me." He stroked my hair. "You ain't goin' cry, are you?"

"No, but it is my party—"

"Babe, you're giving away your age now."

I laughed and reluctantly moved away from Eddy as Gabby came into the kitchen. She took my hand and pulled me into the living room. The lights were dimmed and the music turned up loud. Instinctive cowards that they are, most people shrank away from the center of the room. That wasn't going to stop Gabby; she maneuvered me onto the makeshift dance floor. When it comes to dancing, neither of us is particularly inhibited, and we put on quite a show until two by two, like animals entering the ark, the others began to join us. I even allowed Quentin a few minutes' bodily contact, a repeat of the blues session, which definitely seemed to perk up his spirits.

Inevitably it got to that time of night when a lot of people were hoping for an excuse to get closer to each other, so I put on some slow grooves. I watched in amusement as couples subtly paired off and eased themselves into the crush in order to feel flesh against flesh. It took finely timed ballet moves to avoid Quentin, who followed me hopefully.

From the shelter of the kitchen, I watched Vince and Nicola together. The way he held her and the expression on his face as he looked at her made me wonder if I'd misjudged him. You can usually tell by the way two people dance together whether or not they fit with each other, and I have to admit that they looked right. Then I reminded myself of the stories I'd heard and the photos I'd seen.

Next to them, Oliver and Georgina were locked in an obscene clinch. I couldn't see any sign of Simone. I was puzzled. Either Simone was incredibly tolerant or Oliver was amazingly stupid. I preferred the latter interpretation.

I did a double take when I saw my father leading my mother to the dance floor. From the way she walked I could tell that Mom wasn't one hundred percent sober, but as Dad took her in his arms, she struggled to maintain as much distance as possible given the crush around them. I stood stunned until I caught Pauline's eye and she winked at me, laughing gaily.

I was still shaking my head in disbelief when I felt an arm around my waist. "You can't be no wallflower at your own party," Max whispered as he urged me toward the other dancers. He took me in his arms and I fitted into a body that, despite the years, was molded to complement mine. Max held me tight as his hips swayed to the music and his hand cradled my head. "I've missed you, honey," he whispered.

A million volts of electricity shot through me and I must have stiffened. Max stopped moving. He looked into my eyes. "What, you thought I'd forgotten? Honey, I was never *that* far gone." He laughed softly.

I couldn't speak. This was the last thing I was expecting given that we'd spent several days together during which he'd virtually ignored me.

"Max, I—"

"Don't say nothing. Everything cool."

And then by some kind of petulant karma, Brian McKnight was on the stereo and, of all tracks, he had to be crooning "Shoulda, Woulda, Coulda" and Max was singing along in that voice that could always turn me to mush about how he'd made a mistake and knows it too late, but he "shoulda been a better man . . ." And my heart was about to rupture. *Why do this to me, Max? Why now?* I leaned my cheek against his chest and allowed myself to become absorbed in the music. I stayed that way for as long as I could, drifting, not wanting to think too much. But the feel of Max's familiar body against mine was stirring all kinds of half-forgotten, deeply buried sensations. I tried to resist, but I was being lulled into a hypnotic trance. I knew that it would be the easiest thing in the world to make love with Max. It might even be what I wanted. Max lifted my chin and gazed into my eyes. There was a question there. Something passed between us—I'm not sure what. Max brushed his lips gently against mine. I snuggled into his body, unsure of what was happening. There was no time to explore since I felt a tap on my shoulder.

"I been waiting a long time. Can I cut in?"

It was Rob. I hadn't seen him arrive and I felt a momentary irritation, first of all that he was so late, and that he then behaved as if I belonged to him. He'd brought me salmon pink roses, though, and one look at those big, brown, puppy-dog eyes made me forgive him. He bent to kiss me.

"I'm sorry I'm so late, honey. I had an emergency to take care of. I couldn't get out of it." There was too much noise for him to explain any further so Rob took me in his arms and held me close. I looked back at Max who smiled gently at me, then turned and left. For a long while, I allowed myself to think of nothing but the rhythm and the feel of the bass pounding to match the beat of my heart. I don't think I was even aware of Rob, just the sensation of heat as his thumb gently caressed my jawline, and then his fingers traced a lazy path along the length of my spine, urging my body nearer and nearer to his until we flowed together, just one body rocking to the rhythm. I could feel a longing deep inside me. Shit, I wanted closeness, warmth, intimacy. But with Rob? I was no longer sure.

All too soon the music stopped and I opened my eyes, blinking as I looked around. The first person who caught my eye was Nicola. I could have smacked her smug face. She looked half puzzled, half triumphant. I would have poked my tongue out at her, but she was talking to Mom and the way they were looking at me made it obvious that they'd been discussing me and Rob. Mom had that steely glare on her face that said, *I didn't bring up my pickney to behave like some brazen trollop,* and I knew that her loyalties would be with Max. In spite of my advancing years, I felt a flush rise to my face. I was ten years old again as I watched Mom head toward us like some battleship full steam ahead. I could only anticipate with horror what she might be about to say.

"Robert Elliott. What you think you playing at?

You too big to come say howdy to me? You just wait till I see you mother again." Her words were fierce, but a smile crept into her eyes. She'd never been able to resist his pitiful eye thing either. Rob stunned me by picking Mom up and spinning her round until she laughed and pummeled his back screaming, "Put me down right now, you big lump." I was stunned. No one behaved that way with Mom. His next words made me understand how he got away with it.

"Auntie Josie, you don't change. You're just as gorgeous and young as I remember."

"You too lie, boy. And I see for meself you can't keep your hand off my daughter." She giggled. I couldn't believe it. I wanted to tell Rob what a creep he was and that soft-soaping would never work with my mother, but one look at her face proved me wrong. She was lapping it up. The shock must have shown on my face because Nicola, hardly able to stifle her laughter, led me away to the kitchen where we both laughed hysterically.

"I've never seen anything like it," I gasped as soon as I could speak again. I peeked out the kitchen door. Rob had his arms around Mom's shoulders and she was absolutely engrossed in whatever he was saying.

"I can't believe it," Nicola said. "Just a few minutes ago Mom was going off the deep end about this 'rude bwoy' who was feeling up her daughter in front of everyone. Now look at her."

"It's amazing!"

Nicola was suddenly serious. "Actually, it's not that amazing, Sis. Don't you remember how Mom used to be with Dad? He'd tease her just like that, making her laugh when she didn't want to. Humoring her out of any bad mood."

We were both quiet for a while.

"You like him, though, don't you?"

"Nicola, you could have just put me off him. First he's all creepy with Mom, now you say he's like Dad was. That's not exactly sexy."

She laughed. "Remember, I saw you dancing together. You can't hide it from me." She was quiet for a moment, serious. "What about Max? Where does he fit in?"

"Can I phone a friend?"

"Be serious."

"I am serious, Nic. The truth is I just don't know. And I don't want to think about it all right now."

"You're lucky to have such a choice. You could bring either one of them to my wedding and I wouldn't be ashamed of you. Anyway, Sis, it's late. We're gonna have to go. I'll take Mom away and you can feel free to do a bit more research." She winked, kissed me, and walked out of the kitchen, gathering Vince, Aunt Bea, and Mom on her way.

I stayed in the kitchen for a while. I needed a breather. I could see my dad and Pauline making their way over to Rob. The whole family was obviously determined to evaluate him. It was good that my folks were so protective, but it felt a little oppressive too. It's not exactly flattering that my family is so desperate to get me paired off that they see any new man as a prospective candidate. I sighed and sat down at the kitchen table.

It wasn't long before Eddy and Gabby came in search of liquid refreshment. They'd worked up a sweat on the dance floor and were laughing together, obviously at ease with each other. I wondered when they'd got to know each other so well. Gabby looked so much happier than she had earlier, though, that I felt grateful to Eddy.

"Girl, what you doing hiding in here?" Gabby asked.

"Just had to get away from the matchmakers in there for a minute."

"He seems nice."

"Nice enough to charm my mother." I heard a slight sneer in my voice. Where was that coming from?

"What's wrong with that?" Gabby asked. "Seems like quite an asset to me. What you getting so picky about?"

I looked through the open door at Rob. Yes, why was I being picky? Tall, dark, and more handsome than I had any right to expect. Unattached. Intelligent. Funny. Considerate. What else could I ask for?

"You're right, Gabby. He's great. I do like him a lot."

"So is Max the problem?"

I looked at Eddy and saw the worry in his eyes.

"No, I don't think Max is a problem at all."

I got up and walked to Rob, ready to stake a little bit of a claim.

There was a glimmer of light in the sky by the time most folks drifted away. Eddy, Gabby, Rob, and I chatted easily, carrying out a postmortem while we cleared away the worst of the debris. Eventually, Eddy and Gabby left together, Eddy looking at me with a question in his eyes. I couldn't give an answer since I wasn't completely sure what he was asking.

It was odd that as soon as they left, I began to feel a little self-conscious with Rob. I suppose there had been so many expectations from so many people, plus the fact that we hadn't seen each other for a while, and I'd lost track of where I was with him. I'd been away and so much had happened since I last saw him that it was like we were back at square one. We circled each other as I busied myself putting things away unnecessarily. Anything to avoid the moment when we'd each have to read the subtle signals and hope we'd got them right.

To give Rob his due, he knew how to handle the situation. He walked over to me, took a dirty ashtray from my hand, put it on the table, and led me to the sofa. I was surprisingly sober and gratefully accepted the brandy that he poured, gulping it down. He didn't say anything, just sat down beside me and gently started to massage my shoulders, easing away the tension. When I started to relax, he followed his fingers with gentle kisses along the back of my neck, making me shiver suddenly. I wasn't cold, though. I was enjoying the feel of his lips against my responsive flesh.

I turned toward him, longing to feel his lips against mine. It had been a long time. I slipped my tongue into his mouth, wanting to taste the sweetness, to explore. I closed my eyes to shut out any distraction, needing only to concentrate on the emotions that Rob was bringing to life. I didn't want to think of anything or anyone else. He stopped, pulling away, trailing hot kisses down my neck, licking the hollow between my collar bones. My body arched toward him. He deftly unzipped my dress, easing it from my shoulders. Rob stopped then and leaned away from me, looking at my body with hunger in his eyes. His desire turned me on even more and I felt my stomach flip. My nipples hardened as if reaching out to him. He didn't let me down. In one fluid movement, he lifted my breast and began teasing it with his thumb and then squeezing it between thumb and finger until he heard the catch in my breath. He moved away from me, then picked up the glass of brandy and took a sip. He held the glass to my lips so that I could drink and then he put his finger in the glass. As if in slow motion, I watched as a drop of the golden liquid hung on his finger and then dropped slowly onto my nipple. Rob's lips followed quickly, and I gasped aloud as the alcohol burned only to be followed by the heat of his mouth as his lips enclosed me and his tongue flicked across my hard nipple. Over and over, brandy, hot tongue, cold air, brandy, warm lips, cold air until I didn't think I could take any more torture. So he moved to the other breast, repeating the pleasure and the agony.

He took another gulp of alcohol and kissed me, transferring the taste to my mouth as his fingers fluttered across my stomach. I took a deep breath. "Rob, I can't take much more," I whispered.

"I think you can," he laughed. "There's half a bottle left."

"That's not what I meant."

"I know," he said, his eyes darkening as his hand moved down, between my legs. I stiffened momentarily. I'd been expecting it, but even so, the force of the sensation shook me. Rob was still for a moment, and then he kissed me again, using the depth of the kiss as cover for what his fingers were doing under my dress. Stroking, probing, fluttering, caressing, rubbing, holding, anything that I didn't expect when I expected it least. Whatever he was going to do next, I wanted it more than anything.

Suddenly, Rob stood, taking my hand and pulling me toward him. With the other hand he grabbed hold of the brandy bottle and I just managed to pull my dress up as we headed toward my bedroom door.

"This time, we won't be interrupted," he murmured. Praise be to God, I thought.

I must have had my back turned to the bed as we opened the door; I was only aware of Rob's firm body pressed against mine as I clung to him. I fumbled for the light switch and remember being puzzled by Rob's sudden freeze. I turned and there, in my bed, was Oliver, pale, gangly, completely naked, and Georgina, barely covered by my duvet.

It's unbelievable how quickly passion can turn to icy rage. I could hear myself screaming at Oliver as he struggled to rouse himself from a drunken stupor, neither eye engaging with mine. I couldn't believe that they had done whatever they'd done in *my bed*. In fact, I didn't want to think about what they'd done. My fury grew as Oliver blinked at me, muttering, "What time is it?" oblivious to my rage. I leaped onto the bed, trying to drag him out while Rob attempted to restrain me. It took a few moments for Oliver to comprehend where he was, and with whom. A volley of expletives hit me as he understood the situation he found himself in. "Oh my god! Shit! Fucking hell! Where's Simone?" He was hopping around, trying to get back into his trousers and some semblance of dignity. I was cold with anger.

"I think your wife left some time ago. Now get that ugly bitch out of my bed."

To give him his dues, he tried. Georgina was out cold. A dead weight. The three of us together couldn't shift her. Rob managed to bundle Oliver out the door and into a taxi, but I was stuck with Georgina. Passion killer if ever there was one. There was no way that anything resembling sexual activity was going to happen between me and Rob now. We looked at each other and Rob smiled. "Third time lucky?" he said as he shrugged into his coat. He kissed me gently and let himself out. I could easily have strangled Georgina. As it was, I tossed fitfully on my lumpy sofa, trying not to think of what might have been with Rob and dimly aware that I'd been holding my breath and now felt a vague disappointment that Max had left so early, without putting up a fight.

Chapter Twelve

The night wasn't a total disaster in that both Oliver and Georgina now owe me. I'm beginning to understand the sense of power that Eddy must feel with all the secrets he's keeping to himself. I'm still determined to pry them out of him.

I waited until I heard the first groans before hustling Georgina into a cold shower. I lent her a particularly vile, lime-green plastic raincoat that I'd been too ashamed to donate to a charity shop and bundled her out the door before she'd fully come to. I wasn't running a Salvation Army hostel, and besides, I needed to occupy my bed. I used up the last of my energy stripping the sheets and remaking the bed, and then I fell into a deep stupor, only waking late in the afternoon.

I was still keyed up so I called Oliver, negotiating a conversation with Simone along the way. He sounded decidedly sheepish when he got on the line and I wasn't about to make it any easier for him. I was still seething.

"How dare you! You didn't even know where your wife was and yet you managed to find your way to my bedroom. I don't normally care what you do with that slut Georgina, but you did it in *my bed*, Oliver. I feel as if I need to delouse the mattress. How could you?"

"Carol, I'm sorry. Honestly, it was the first time."

"Don't bullshit me, Oliver. You're only making things a thousand times worse."

"Carol, I promise it won't happen again."

"You're damned right it won't. Get rid of her, Oliver. She's crap at her job, and the only reason you've kept her on is that you're screwing her. I'd like her gone before I get back. Then we can forget about it."

"Or else?"

"Don't even go there, Oliver." I slammed the phone down, incensed that he'd even ask if there was an alternative. Don't tell me this was *lurve*. Well, if he'd fallen for Georgina, then he could entertain her in his own time and at his own expense.

Rob called as soon as I hung up. He's almost too good to be true. He wanted to come round, but I needed time to recover and prepare myself for the week ahead. Besides, the moment had passed and I was too pissed with the whole of the male species.

I snacked on leftovers, filled my hot water bottle, made some hot chocolate, and went back to bed.

Today has to count as one of the worst days in recent history. I think, even two days later, I was still slightly hungover from the party, along with everyone else. Adrian was particularly snappish with me, and Gary and Quentin seemed to be moving in slow motion. My head was still foggy through lack of sleep and only Max, though he hardly looked at me, seemed relatively bright and chirpy, but that's only in comparison with the rest of us. We bickered throughout the morning, but in a half-hearted fashion, none of us having the energy for a real fight. Besides, not one of the singers managed to rouse more than desultory interest in any of us. By lunchtime, I was beginning to worry. This is London, my own manor. I *know* there's talent here. I couldn't really believe that my own folk would let us down like this, but it was beginning to look as if we'd struggle to choose even half of the twenty contestants we were looking for. I was, frankly, bored.

I should have made a sacrifice to the gods before I dared to think those thoughts. Halfway through the afternoon session I was nearly jolted out of my seat. Bursting into the room came the deepest, most soulful voice that I'd heard since joining the show, the kind of voice that makes you shiver in awe. A voice that makes your solar plexus contract. At last, I thought, this is exactly what we've been looking for. And more! The fog cleared in my head and the early mornings, long journeys, and bitter arguments suddenly seemed worthwhile. I looked up at this young man who was the answer to all our prayers . . . and shrank back into my seat, wanting to make myself as small and unobtrusive as possible. Even weeks later I couldn't fail to recognize the long, lean legs, the muscular chest, the beard, the braided hair, the fluttering in the pit of my stomach at the memory of his touch. The voice belonged to my anonymous encounter at Darryl's salon. His voice came to a spine-tingling halt on a note that was as pure as sunlight. His eyes traveled along the line of judges until they met mine. I couldn't hold his gaze and lowered my eyes, but too slowly to miss his lazy smile.

My brain turned to sludge. I was expecting one of the others to say something, anything, but for some reason, everyone was looking at me. I realized that they'd all done their bit; I hadn't heard a word, and they were waiting for me to speak. I coughed, playing for time.

"Well . . ." I realized that I didn't even know his name. I'd been given a list, and though I'd studied it carefully this morning, my mind was blank. I looked down at the names, trying desperately to work out which one he was but the letters were a jumble. And he was not helping either, just staring at me. I was the only female judge and I looked at the men; every single one of them seemed to be watching me with accusation in his eye. Nobody was going to rescue me.

"I don't know what to say . . . I'm totally speechless!"

"Is that a good or bad thing?" He was looking at me with such a confident smile that I was forced to pull myself together.

"Probably a good thing." I returned his smile as calmly as I could. "I'm only lost for words to express how great your performance was . . ." I blushed as he raised one eyebrow, teasing me. "You get my vote," I finished lamely.

What made the whole situation a hundred times worse was that it had to happen on the day when Eddy was shadowing me, hoping to get behind-the-scenes gossip for the magazine. If he only knew! I noticed that he was looking at me with a quizzical look. I scanned my notes, wanting to avoid any eye contact. I was still so stunned that Eddy would only have to ask and I'd blurt out the whole truth. I didn't dare look at him.

Calvin. That must be his name. Calvin Brown.

The rest of the morning passed in a dreamlike mist and I was praying that Eddy wouldn't hang around for the tea-break, or at least would have forgotten all about Calvin. Some hope! He obviously smelled a story. For a split second I contemplated revealing all and begging him for mercy, but then thought better of it. I wasn't sure he'd let the fact that we're friends stand in the way, and I didn't want to put our relationship to the test. Eddy is a journalist, after all. This was one occasion when I really was going to have to keep my mouth shut.

As soon as we broke, Eddy was by my side like a flea smelling blood. He took me by the elbow and led me to a quiet corner of the room.

"So, give!"

"What?"

"Don't play the innocent with me, Carol. What's with you and the young bro?"

"Which one?" I tried an innocent flutter of my lashes.

"Come on. You can't fool me. I'm Eddy, remember? You know, the one with the voice. It was like you been hit by a truck when you saw him."

"Oh, you mean Calvin Brown? Well, weren't you listening, Eddy? When last you hear a voice like that? Otis mixed with a little Marvin and a dash of Prince." It was true, but I was also hoping to divert Eddy's attention away from me and onto Calvin's more obvious abilities.

"And that's what made you lose your cool?" he persisted.

"The boy's a star." I felt the heat rising to my face as I recalled his hidden talents. I had to watch myself. Eddy can be like a yapping terrier who has sunk his teeth into your backside. I think I managed to shake him off, though.

And then Quentin thought it was his turn. "Carol.

Are you all right, my dear?" He took his solicitousness as an excuse to put his hand on my butt. "You looked a little unwell earlier on. You know, when that chap Calvin was singing." His hand was moving down, cupping my cheek. I tried to discreetly move away and I could see the amused look in Eddy's eye. I bumped into Adrian. He turned and zeroed in on Quentin's hand. Adrian's arms went round my waist and he was urging me closer to him. Then Adrian and Quentin were facing up to each other like two stags about to lock antlers and Eddy was almost choking with suppressed laughter. I prayed that he *would* choke and I managed to extricate myself from both men.

"I'm absolutely fine," I said. "I just need a breath of fresh air."

I walked outside and there was Max, sitting on a wall, smoking a cigarette. I was just about to turn and go back in when he must have heard my steps. He held his hand out to me and I sat down next to him.

Max was quiet for several seconds. For a brief time, we were almost companionable until he broke the silence.

"Did the brotha remind you of anyone?"

I hadn't wanted to admit it, but the depth of emotion, the longing, the *soul* that I'd heard in Calvin's voice was the same quality that had so moved me in Max. I could only nod, not daring to speak, not wanting to dredge up those memories in his presence.

"That brotha can sure sing! The way you looked at him reminded me of how it was with us. You remember that first gig you came to? Same way you looked at me." Max wasn't touching me, but the look in his eye felt like an embrace. The intensity was too much. I looked down.

"Max, I—"

"He's got his whole life ahead of him. Great things. Just like I had. And look what happened. Fucked it up, didn't I?" I couldn't reply.

Max stood up and looked at me for a while. Then he did something that was odd for him. He took my hand and kissed it gently. "I'm sorry, honey. The only woman . . ." he said, recalling the words from so long ago. He turned and walked away, humming an old Max Gardiner tune.

The rest of the day was fairly anticlimactic, which was just as well. I'm not sure I could have taken any more excitement. I suppose that's what got me into trouble in the first place: too much excitement! I think I coped pretty well under the circumstances, and I was in control of myself again by the time we had to announce to the waiting candidates which ones would be called back. Inevitably, it fell to me to tell Calvin. I expected him to be cool, but just like the rest of them, he whooped with pleasure. I was strangely touched. Underneath it all, he's like a little boy after all.

I couldn't wait to get home and call Gabby. I know I said I'd keep my mouth shut, but you can't expect me to keep this to myself after the day I had. I confessed everything.

"Girl, you one dark horse," Gabby laughed. "So Calvin was *that* good was he?"

"I ain't going into any detail."

"I'm talking 'bout his singing, girl. What *you* talking about?" she giggled.

"Gabby, be serious. What am I going to do?"

"I would tell you to lie back and enjoy it, but it seems like you prefer it out in the open. You really did that in a restaurant? A crowded restaurant. A crowded *West Indian* restaurant too! Here I am worrying that you not getting any and all the time you taking it any way and anywhere you can." Her voice was becoming incomprehensible with laughter.

"You're good. Carol?"

"Yes?" I snapped.

"You remember what else was on the menu?"

I laughed in spite of myself. In a way, it was a relief that Gabby wasn't taking it too seriously. All these weeks I've been looking back on the experience with a tingle of excitement, hugging my naughty secret to myself like a comfort blanket. I shouldn't let the awkwardness of my current position take away from the pleasurable sensations I've been reliving in my head. Especially when it seems like I might never have sex again!

"You don't understand, though, Gabby. I'm in a really difficult position now. I'm supposed to be an impartial judge. What would it look like if anyone ever found out?"

"How they goin' find out? You think he goin' tell everyone?"

"I don't know. I don't think so."

"Why would he tell anyone and risk people saying he only got this far because of you? You liked him, didn't you?"

"I didn't really have a chance to get to know him, but I suppose so."

"So why would he want to get you thrown off the show? I don't think you need to worry about him. And are you likely to tell anyone else?"

"No, definitely no."

"Then stop worrying, Carol. You're not *seeing* the boy. You didn't know he was going to enter the competition. I think you can be objective about his singing abilities. Forget about it, girl."

Easier said than done. But in the end, I think Gabby
is right. Regardless of everything else, Calvin Brown
has a huge talent, and with only one more day of auditions, I think he has a good chance of going all the
way—definitely no pun intended! Of course, nothing
is guaranteed, but I know in my heart that if it's just a
question of ability, then he deserves to win. And anyway, how would I explain quitting the show?

The hardest part of the show for us judges is over
now. It's been grueling traveling around the country and
having to disappoint so many people, Quentin among
them. I do hope he's got my gentle hints and stops following me around like one of Bo Peep's sheep. Despite
all the politics, the adrenaline, the arguments, the emotion, I think I've enjoyed the experience and I've certainly learned a lot. I can see why people get caught up
in the world of television.

I stayed behind after the final auditions today because I'd got to talking to Seamus, the video editor, at
lunch. I asked what would happen to all the material
that had been shot, and he offered to show me the editing process. He was working with Petra, one of the
producers, and I sat quietly, unobtrusively, at the back
of the editing suite. After I got over the shock of seeing
myself on the screen, I became absorbed in what they
were doing.

I was fascinated by how they could take an endless
stream of material and cut it together to make reasonable sense. Petra had obviously painstakingly studied
the piles of cassettes. She'd picked out the funniest, the
most dramatic, the most pathetic, the saddest, and
sometimes, the cruelest moments of the last six weeks.

I was certainly grateful for the way they cut my words together to make me seem eloquent, covering the cuts with shots of the others listening. I was amazed at how articulate I became and how intently everyone listened. I even started to believe the hype myself. After a couple of hours, I could see the first program taking shape and it was incredibly watchable, much more gripping than the reality. I appreciated the skill of these television folk, but I also began to feel a vague sense of disquiet. What I was watching on screen was slick, professional, and no one could claim that it wasn't accurate, but the emphasis had changed subtly. I couldn't sit still. I wanted to protest: *That's not how it was*. I got up to leave and bumped into Adrian. He looked surprised to see me.

"Carol? I thought you'd left with the others."

"Petra and Seamus let me sit in on the editing. Just wanted to understand how it all works."

"So what did you think? Petra's working on program one, isn't she?"

I told Adrian how impressed I was, but couldn't help expressing my concerns.

Adrian laughed. "Can you imagine anyone else wanting to sit through all those acts that you saw? That's what television's all about, Carol. Judicious editing."

I did wish that he didn't treat me like a complete idiot.

"I understand that. It's just that this program seems so different to how it really was."

"Yeah, look back on those days. Much of it was boring, tiring, or depressing. A lot of those auditions seemed endless. Remember the days when you guys wondered if you'd ever find ten, let alone a hundred acts with star quality? Think back to how frustrating it all was. Do you honestly think our audience wants to go through all that? Trust me, Carol. Years of experience. We know what we're doing." He hurried away.

I couldn't really argue with him. But I wasn't totally reassured.

It was late by the time I got home. I was exhausted and, not surprisingly, didn't feel like watching television. I ran a bath and had just undressed when the doorbell rang. I hauled on my robe and dashed to the intercom.

"It's Calvin."

"Who?" Playing for time again.

"You remember. Calvin Brown."

"What are you doing here, Calvin?"

"I need to talk to you and I can't really do it on your doorstep."

I thought I knew what this was going to be about and, no, I didn't want him talking about it on the doorstep. I buzzed him up. I debated trying to get into something less comfortable, but there wasn't time. I could hear his youthful footsteps bounding up the stairs.

There's something about the way the guy looks that I can't help responding to. As soon as I opened the door, the uncontrollable fluttering started in my stomach again. I think it might be his eyes; they're so inviting and so dangerous at the same time, slanting upward, saved from being sly by the long, thick lashes. Then again, it could be those oh-so-generous, warm, soft lips. You can't help imagining what he might do with them. I suddenly remembered that we hadn't even kissed. We'd been far too intimate for that! I had to push those kinds of thoughts out of my head because I was just standing there, lost in my baser emotions, while he stood on the other side of the door waiting for me to let him in.

I pulled the belt of my robe tighter, but that might have been a mistake; I could feel the rub of the fabric against my skin and knew that my nipples were clearly visible. I loosened the belt and felt a rush of embarrassment that the gesture might be misunderstood. Oh shit! I just opened the door wider and let him walk past me.

"Calvin, what are you doing here? I'm not sure this is such a good idea." I clutched the collar of my robe tight around my neck.

He stood a respectful distance away and I was grateful for that. He looked nervous and I realized that I'd spoken in my cold, hard-edged voice. He'd never heard it before and was obviously fazed by it. He didn't know how difficult this was for me.

"I couldn't believe it when I saw you. How could I have known that you'd be one of the judges? I didn't mean to upset you. I could tell how shocked you were. I was too."

His eyes looked at me in that Rob Elliott way that I can't resist. "Sit down, Calvin. D'you want a drink?" I knew I could use one. I needed a cigarette, too, but after all this time in no-smoking areas, I'd made the decision to finally give up. I regretted the impulse that had made me throw out all my emergency supplies.

I poured alcohol. Calvin was sitting on the sofa, and I placed myself directly opposite, as far away as I could get.

"I just wanted you to know how sorry I am to put you in this position. I'm not sure what to do about it."

"There's not much either of us can do about it now. But I do think it's best if we don't meet up like this, Calvin. Just think how it would look if anyone found out. You've got a lot of talent and you'll make it big just on the strength of that. You don't want anyone to think you did it any other way, do you? Anyway, I've got to be seen to be scrupulously fair. You might say whiter than white. Imagine how the others would feel if they thought there was something between us."

"I know. But I really do like you, Carol. And I don't want there to be any ill feeling between us." He looked at me and smiled. Suddenly, I wondered where the little boy had gone. As I looked at him, he let his eyes descend slowly, taking in the swell of my breasts and the curve of my thighs that the robe didn't cover no matter how hard I tried. His eyes locked with mine again and Calvin was all man.

"You sure are one sexy woman. And I still love the hair."

For heaven's sake! I've been frustrated for weeks, and now here's a young, rampant man offering satisfaction on a plate, with no likelihood of interruption this time. I could so easily fall under his spell and allow myself to be sweet-talked. I'd had a hard day and it sure felt good to know that this amazing young hunk desired me. I didn't want to insult him by denying the emotions he provoked, but I was the responsible adult—or so I told myself. I had to take control. I shook my head to clear it.

I forced a laugh. "Calvin, you need to go away and practice. And I don't mean the pick-up lines!"

"I'm serious, Carol."

"And so am I. I'll see you next week. No hard feelings?"

"I wouldn't say that . . ."

He moved toward me and I stood, trying to take a step back, to keep as far away from his magnetic charms as I could. But he was gaining ground, his heat coming closer and closer. In a couple of steps, he was looking down at me, his hand stroking my head. He lifted my chin and kissed me gently, his tongue exploring, probing. He certainly knew what he was doing. Where on earth did he learn his technique? Every man should enroll in that school. Involuntarily, my body was pressing itself against him and he was untying the belt of my robe, slipping his hand inside to cup my breast. "Mmm. I'd forgotten how good you feel."

He shouldn't have spoken. Something snapped in my head. What the hell was I doing? I pulled away, covering myself with the robe.

"Calvin, you haven't listened to a word I've been saying."

He looked abashed. "No, Miss."

"I'm not your teacher, you know."

"No, but I was hoping to show you my homework!"

We both laughed, and I pushed him out the door, leaning against it, asking myself what had got into me recently. Where were all these men coming from? And what signals was I sending out? I vaguely wondered how Calvin had got my address.

It's a lot easier now that the filming is all happening in London. The upside is that there's so much less traveling and no dull, faceless hotels. The downside is that I'm suddenly on everyone's most-wanted list. I come home to a full answering machine. Word has got around and they all want to know the gossip. I think a lot of folks get a kick out of being around someone who's nearly famous. I've even had calls from Marcel, the artist, and Stephen Saunders, the actor I met at that gallery opening. I suppose they think they really do know me. Or that I'm getting some!

It's all been so hectic that I haven't even had time to hook up with Rob. We've talked and I can just about squeeze in lunch on Saturday. That's the same day that Eddy has arranged for us to meet up at the lap-dancing club. Seems he's organized a surprise for Vince. And not so long ago I was moaning about my lack of social life!

It's been harder than I thought to whittle the hundred candidates down to just twenty. Part of the problem is that they have such different qualities and it's difficult to assess how they're likely to respond to voice coaches, dance tutors, stylists, the glare of publicity, and the adrenaline rush of live television. Come to think of it, I don't know how I'm going to respond, but I think I'm getting used to the cameras. I might even be starting to enjoy it all.

My one worry is that I can't work out what's going on with the other judges. I thought I had them all figured out, but the atmosphere has become quite tense and heated over the last few days. We've had the inevitable fights about the women, but I'd expected that and was able to stand my ground. Gary was his usual obnoxious, patronizing self. Quentin seemed to be sulking childishly. And Max? Max had, once again, disappeared to another place.

I began to question my sanity, though, because I knew that there were at least twelve auditionees whose talent shone through. I thought that agreeing on those would be plain sailing and that we'd have battles over the remaining eight.

We're all working to different agendas. Many of

the girls, usually the ones with the least talent, flirted outrageously with Gary, but I didn't expect him to respond by championing their cause. I was wrong.

Quentin was being Mr. Businessman, looking for the most commercial, the most malleable product. That and talent didn't always go together.

Max, I guess, felt threatened, resentful, or regretful at any sign of real talent. In those early auditions, he would offer gentle criticism and sensitive advice, but as the weeks passed, he has become less and less generous, with any unavoidable, complimentary remarks squeezed out of him through clenched teeth and usually with a sting of some kind in the tail. I really began to wonder whether I'd imagined those few times when I'd connected with him. Max now reminds me of the bitter, poisoned man I finally walked out on.

I should really have left the night I caught him smoking crack. That's what Eddy told me to do. He was willing to stay and make sure that Max came to no physical harm, but he urged me to go. Like some B-movie heroine, I was convinced that I could make Max change. Somehow, this must be my fault; maybe I hadn't shown him enough love; maybe I'd become too caught up in my career; maybe I'd neglected him. All that would change. My love and me were all that Max needed. I pushed Eddy away. This was *our* problem, Max's and mine, and we would deal with it together.

That night, I paced our bedroom in a state of shock, going over and over my time with Max, looking for where it had all started to go wrong, seeking out all the signs that I'd missed, desperate to find a key that I could turn to take us back to where we once were.

You know, of course, how naïve I was being. While
I wrestled with my thoughts, Max blissfully smoked the
night away, lost in some ecstatic space that didn't involve me. And that's how it was, night after night, except
that he now felt at liberty to smoke that shit in front of
me, lovingly explaining the process, caught up in the
intricacies. He was like a master *chocolatier*, deli-
cately manipulating the raw ingredients to create his
narcotic masterpiece.

It goes without saying that I couldn't get through to
Max. No one could. Max didn't want rescuing. He was
in love. With his pipe. I'd probably have stayed even
longer if Max hadn't offered his beloved pipe to me,
trying to turn me on to her. I was tempted. That's when
I swallowed my pride and rang Eddy, begging him to
come and take me away.

I wonder whether Max's variable personality is
down to some illegal substance or other. It's best if I
don't know. I really don't want to care.

Of course, I think I'm being impartial as a judge.
The others would say that I'm biased against the girls
and will always vote for the guys in preference. They
may be right, but that would only be because *someone*
has to do it. You can tell how bad things must be if I'm
championing the male sex!

Anyway, the last week has seen fairly heated arguments to put it mildly. For the first time, I think we forgot
about the cameras. Anger, jealously, self-righteousness,
and downright malice polluted the air and the jibes became more and more personal. Fascinating television.
I can't deny my own guilt. We've been working so
hard to get this far that the series has taken on an im-

portance that with hindsight will, I'm sure, seem un-justifiable. It was like we were all high on temporary power and we probably came close to doing physical damage, just to prove a point.

We managed it in the end. Thirteen girls and seven guys. I wouldn't have chosen all of them, but I owe it to my conscience not to hold that against them. The democratic process has worked as well as it could and now it will be up to others to make the final decision. I can't say that the series hasn't left me feeling bruised, but exhilarated too.

I was looking forward to seeing Rob again. It was as if I'd safely negotiated the crocodile-infested media river and needed to touch base with someone who was bound to be on my side. I'd been thinking too of Calvin, his presence in the final group making that unavoidable. The whole thing with him was so unrealistic, so juvenile. Max, too, though still utterly desirable, had to be history. Rob, however, meant grown-up sex, recognition of the fact that I wasn't a teenager anymore and was never likely to recapture those carefree days. He might even be the future. Maybe some kind of physical commitment to Rob would lay to rest all the childish longings that had rattled around my brain for the past few weeks. Not that it was going to happen straight away. Even feeling as horny as I was, I didn't see how Rob and I were going to get anything together between lunch and meeting up with Eddy and Dad to confront Vince. Unless I was going to seduce him in the restaurant. And you know what I'm like about these public spaces. When I walked into Wagamama, off Tottenham Court Road, I knew there wouldn't be any repetition of the encounter with Calvin. Those bare wooden tables and benches, shared with other diners, weren't conducive to any kind of under-the-counter activity.

I was relieved to find that a bit of spark was still there with Rob. Seeing Max and Calvin again hadn't diminished Rob's charms, although I pushed away a vague yearning for the *excitement* I'd felt with them both.

Rob seemed glad to see me and showed genuine interest in my time with *Soul Sensation*, asking a thousand questions. Thank God he wasn't one of those guys who can't deal with a woman's success. He commiserated with my feelings of disappointment in the judging process and wanted to hear more and more details of the behind-the-scenes activity.

"You should feel really proud of yourself if you've managed to find one real talent. So who is this person, the one who really stands out?"

"I can't tell you. This is all supposed to be really confidential."

"You mean you don't trust me."

"It's not that . . ."

He took hold of my hand across the table. "I'm not prying, Carol. You don't have to tell me anything you don't want to." He stared into my eyes and I wanted to look away. The conversation was heading down a path I was suddenly reluctant to take. "I've really missed you. I've been thinking a lot about us. I think this could be the start of something really serious."

Please! Oh God. Why did I think that? There was this unbelievably eligible man telling me that he has *feelings* for me, and that was my only response? What was wrong with me?

"You don't have to say anything, Carol. I know it's

early days, but I want you to know that you mean a lot to me already. It scares me how strongly I feel for you."

Scares me too! Most guys aren't so *out there* with their emotions. His words should have made my heart soar. Instead, I wanted to run away, maybe to the bathroom to throw up. What had happened to Rob in the days since I last saw him? It might sound perverse, but I don't want a guy to be overkeen. I prefer to keep him simmering for a while so that the sexual tension seethes. I want the whole business of "Does he really fancy me? Is it just lust? Can I live with lust? Is lust alone a sin? More lust please!" The minute they start getting serious too soon, I ask myself what's wrong with them. Guys shouldn't be too easy. I'm not saying that Rob isn't still desirable; if the opportunity presented itself, I might still go for it. But the edge was taken off my lust. I was surprised. I kind of thought that Rob was wise enough to choose his moment better. I thought he'd be the sort of guy to keep me on tenterhooks for much longer. I guess I was disappointed that the chase was over so early. He must have sensed my mood because he stopped pawing my hand and changed the subject.

"So you all think you've discovered the next Marvin Gaye?" What made him assume it was a guy? I got the feeling that he was genuinely interested, but I was suddenly overcome with all that I'd been through for the past couple of months. Not just Rob, but the whole thing with *Soul Sensation*, the rows with Gary, Max coming back into my life, Calvin's sudden reappearance, my worries about Nicola, concern for Gabby, and Eddy. Add all that together and what I wanted to do was to get out of there fast and be alone.

"I don't know if I'd go that far. Marvin was something else. But, yes, I think we might have found some-

one special. I can't say any more than that. You'll have
to watch the programs, like everyone else."

When Rob ordered sake with that suggestive lilt in
his voice, it was time to leave. I was being irrational, I
know. Rob hadn't done anything wrong. I was glad
when he got the bill, though. I refused his offer of a lift
home, preferring, for the moment, to battle it out on the
tube. Rob looked puzzled but there were no tear-filled
eyes. I was glad of that.

I soon regretted my impulsive decision. I'd forgotten what the subway was like on a Saturday afternoon.
Countless hot, sweaty bodies. Stacks of shopping bags.
Frayed tempers. Fortunately, I was so tired and caught
up in my own form of meditation that it all washed over
me. The walk from the station gave me time to ponder
what the hell I was doing with my life. It should be all
gravy; fame, fortune, fine man wanting to devote himself to me, and here I was looking the proverbial gift
horse in the mouth, or at least, turning down a ride
from that horse. What more did I want? Don't tell me
that Max had got to me? Or Calvin? I've always been a
sucker for real talent. Even though he would have been
way too old if he was alive, I fell in lust with Bob Marley after seeing a video of a live gig where he did all
those cool, sexy, subtle hip movements, his eyes fixed
to the ground, and then he looked up, straight at me
with those worldly, brown, suggestive eyes. Viagra on
legs. Okay, so it's not just talent. Physical magnetism
helps too. That's what both Max and his younger incarnation, Calvin, have in spades, but let's not go there.

If I analyze my problem, I think it's that I start to get
a bit claustrophobic when a relationship looks as if it

might be heading somewhere. That's probably Max's legacy. Maybe that's what's happening with Rob. He's perfect in so many ways and here I am behaving like a guy: commitment-phobic!

I called Nicola when I got home. I was thinking of what would be happening later tonight. I guess I felt a bit of a heel, deceiving her like this. Who did I think I was interfering in her life? She sounded down.

"What's up, Sis?"

"I suppose I'm getting last minute jitters, Carol. I know you're not a cheerleader for Vince, so I probably shouldn't be talking to you . . ."

"Girl, if you have worries, don't even think of not telling me. Nic, you're my sister. I love you and I'll do anything for you . . . I'd even get out the pom-poms and the rah-rah skirt."

At least she laughed.

"I don't know if I'm doing the right thing."

"Why?" I felt a glimmer of hope. The girl was coming to her senses at long last.

"Sometimes I wonder if we're too different. We don't always enjoy the same things. I used to think that space in a relationship was healthy, but I'm thinking maybe it just shows that we don't have enough in common. You see other couples who spend every spare minute with each other. We're not like that."

"You're right. Probably just prewedding nerves, Sis. Where's Vince tonight?" I felt bad asking since I was one hundred percent certain that he wouldn't have told Nicola where he was spending the evening.

Did I sense a moment's hesitation? Was she going to admit that she had no idea? I'd made a fatal mistake when I'd told Nicola my true feelings about Vince; there was no way she would confide in me.

"He's busy."

I don't know why, but I was filled with an over-whelming need to protect her. Irony of ironies, I found myself reassuring her, though I chose my words carefully. "Sis, I'm sure space *is* healthy. As long as you trust each other, that's all that matters." I kept my fingers crossed behind my back and prayed that lightning wouldn't strike me dead. The best option seemed to be to tell her what she wanted to hear. At least she sounded a bit more cheerful, for the moment.

"Thanks, Carol. I thought you were going to gloat and tell me to ditch Vince. I should have known that you'd be sensible. You're so much older and wiser!"

I wished that I'd followed my first instincts and told her what a two-timing, shiftless dickhead her fiancé was.

We were back at the same lap-dancing club. It didn't seem even half as glamorous when you're stone-cold sober. And certainly not when you're accompanied by your dad. Once again, we bypassed the queues. Eddy's got clout. He knows where all the skeletons are buried. He even got us into a private booth, one of those places designed for celebrities where you can see without being seen. Champagne was delivered—on the house, we were told. Must be more than a few skeletons buried under this dance floor. Dad looked completely bewildered and became even more ill at ease when Eddy disappeared "to make some last-minute arrangements." His eyes grew wider in panic when the lap dancer looked as if she was heading in our direction. I wondered whether he might not enjoy it if he wasn't there with his grown-up daughter. I certainly felt uncomfortable enough for the two of us. We avoided eye contact and sipped nervously at our drinks.

When Eddy finally returned, he had a sly smile on his face, winked at me, and whispered in Dad's ear. Thirty seconds later, the lights dimmed, a host of dancers carrying sparklers surrounded someone at the bar, and the DJ announced congratulations to Vince Daventry, who was celebrating his stag night. It was our cue to head for the bar as the circle of dancers parted to reveal Vince, a blond companion at his side. I don't know which one looked more dumbstruck. Vince was almost as white as she was and his eyes were wider than the Grand Canyon.

"Surprise!" Eddy shouted, slapping Vince's back a little harder than really necessary. "Couldn't let you go to the altar without a celebration."

"But . . . but . . ." Vince spluttered until he saw Dad.

"Vince, boy, you look shocked. You didn't guess?"

"Mr. Shaw . . . I mean, Travis, I . . ."

"Give him a chance to recover," Eddy said, leading Vince to our booth and giving me a knowing look.

I kept Dad busy on the dance floor. Over his shoulder I could see Eddy produce a brown envelope, about six by nine inches. Even in the dim light I could see the blood rush to Vince's face as he opened it and I experienced a certain grim satisfaction. I felt even better as I watched Vince's blond companion gather up her things and storm out of the club, face like thunder.

By the time we got back to the booth, Vince had a smile fixed on his face.

"It's a bit like *This Is Your Life,*" Eddy said, laughing. "Vince, you didn't have the faintest idea, did you? It took a lot of organizing. After all, you so busy these days that you don't have time to go out much, so it took a lot of effort to get you here." He punctuated each phrase with a playful punch on the arm, each of which made Eddy wince. "You not glad to see your future in-laws?"

"Yeah. Great to see you. Thanks for organizing this," Vince said through gritted teeth, giving Eddy a malicious look.

"Drink up, boy. Is your stag party. You don't look as if you enjoying yourself," Dad said. He sounded concerned.

"The night is young," Eddy commented. "Carol, you want to dance?"

I certainly wanted to find out what exactly Eddy had been up to, so I accepted readily.

"How did you know he'd turn up?"

"According to Patrick, he's become a regular. With that same woman."

"What did you do to him?" I asked as we hit the dance floor. "He looks as though he's just had a frontal lobotomy."

"I just showed him the evidence. Told him we'd be keeping tabs on him. I promised that we'd show those photos to your dad if I ever got the slightest smell that he was cheating on Nicola."

"So what did he say?"

"He tried to deny it all. Said these women were just friends. That may be so, I told him, but from now on you and the rest of the family is enough friends for him."

"He's sneaky, Eddy. What makes you think he'll be frightened by that?"

"I think he knows what your father's like when it comes to protecting his family. Even I wouldn't dare cross him." Eddy's expression was menacing at first, and then he looked into my eyes and smiled. I moved closer, wrapped my arms around his waist, and kissed his cheek.

"What's that for, sugar?"

"Just to say thank you."

He kissed the top of my head. There's something that makes me feel so secure about Eddy. Just the fact that he was holding me as we swayed to the music made me relax. It was like all the tension of the last few months drained out of me. I wanted to stay right there forever.

Trouble is, reality always invades and Eddy gently held me away from him and said, "Musical chairs time. I guess you'd like to dance with Vince now?" We walked back.

I know that my face was set like stone. "Dance, Vince?"

He looked a bit like a condemned man being led to the gas chamber. As I took his hand, I don't think my grip reassured him, not when I was digging my nails into his palm as hard as I could.

"Carol, you have to let me explain . . ." he started as soon as we were out of earshot of my father.

"Vince, you don't have to explain anything to me," I said sweetly.

"But I think you and Eddy got the wrong idea about me."

"Just like your ex-wife got the wrong idea?"

"She's a lying bitch—"

My heel on his instep stopped him in his tracks. "That's not a nice way to talk about a lady, Vince."

"We can't talk like this," he said, taking my arm and hobbling to the bar on the other side of the dance floor, far away from Dad and Eddy.

He got drinks, downed his in one, and ordered another. He had the grace to keep his head bowed, and it was difficult to make out what he was saying at first.

"I know what you think of me, Carol. Eddy made that clear. But you got the wrong impression. I know, I know—" He raised a hand to forestall my interruption. "Eddy showed me the photos. It looks bad. But it's not like anything happened with any of those girls. Sure, I like to party. I like to drink. I like to have a good time. God knows, I work hard enough to deserve it."

"So why can't you party with Nicola?"

"Carol, you know her. You think Nicola would enjoy a place like this? I'm not saying anything against her. I love your sister. Nic's idea of a night out is a good, home-cooked meal, then a video in front of the television. I ain't complaining; that's part of what I love about her."

"And it was the same thing with your first wife? You expect me to believe that?"

"No, it wasn't the same at all. I apologize for what I called her, but the truth is she has it in for me. I know the stories she and her friends have been spreading. I'm supposed to have had any number of affairs, but none of that is true. There was nobody else. We broke up because we grew apart. Nothing more sinister than that. I guess she was more hurt and angry than I thought. I might be guilty of not handling the breakup in a sensitive way, but nothing more than that."

I didn't know whether to believe him or not, but I was very reluctant to admit that I might be wrong. I'd spent so long despising him.

"Carol, you don't have to believe me, you know. Why don't you talk to Nic?" There was a triumphant expression on his face.

"What do you mean?"

"I don't hide anything from her. She knows that I go to clubs. She knows I like to enjoy myself. She knows where I am tonight. We trust each other. The same way I don't follow her when she goes out with you or any of her friends. We've got a grown-up relationship." I wondered whether that comment was aimed at me.

I was furiously trying to recall the conversation I'd had with Nicola. I'd asked her where Vince was. What had she said? I couldn't quite recall.

"If that's all true, Vince, why didn't Nicola tell me?"

"How much does Nicola tell you about our relationship? I know what you've said about me. Nicola says she doesn't even try to talk to you about us anymore. Whenever she even mentions my name she can see that cold look come over your face. After tonight, I know what she means. She's never been able to get through to you where I'm concerned. Don't get me wrong, Carol. She loves you to bits, but she says that I'm one area you two will never agree on. She was hurt at first, but I think she accepts it now."

I felt tears spring to my eyes. I was deeply upset at the idea that they'd talked about me like that. I was angry, but I wanted to cry because I knew that there was at least an element of truth in what he was saying. It's what Dad had been trying to tell me. I'd listened to gossip from near-strangers and I'd wanted to believe them rather than trusting my own sister's judgment. I recalled our earlier conversation. It hurt that I'd created such a barrier between us that Nicola couldn't turn to me when she needed to.

"Carol, I don't know what I've ever done to you to make you dislike me so much. I've tried to understand it. We've never really talked or taken the time to get to know each other. Couldn't we just call a temporary truce?" He held out his hand.

I looked at Vince. He didn't look evil anymore. Just a little tired and perhaps a little drunk. I wasn't going to apologize to him. I didn't want to just accept what he was saying without some kind of collaboration. But for now, I had to admit defeat in this particular skirmish.

I took his hand. "I'm not saying I'm convinced, Vince, but I'm willing to wave the white flag, for now."

"Thank God, my heart couldn't take being ambushed again like tonight."

I smiled. "But, Vince . . ."

"Yes?"

"If I ever find that you've cheated on my little sister, I'll personally track you down"—I held up my nails—"and I'll rip your balls out." He looked panic-stricken. "With my bare hands. And I'll enjoy every last minute of it."

Back in the office for a few hours today. Oliver was obviously calling my bluff because Georgina was still there. She was all smiles and kept out of my way as much as possible. I guess it's difficult to make small talk with someone who's seen you with your dress up around your waist and your panties off.

Oliver did his very best to pretend that nothing had happened. I did have a little sympathy for him; Oliver doesn't know what being normal means. Every time I looked at him I pitied his wife. Then again, she didn't have to work with him. I found out just what a lowlife he was when he didn't have the courage to talk to me man to man. Or creep to woman. He waited until the editorial meeting.

At least he didn't look at anyone directly. "Not long now till the launch of *Soul Sensation*. We all know how much coverage there's going to be in the tabloids. We'll look pretty silly if we're scooped by them when we've got our own mole." He laughed, but I didn't think it was much of a joke.

"The difficult thing," I said pointedly, "is knowing when to be discreet."

"Or knowing where your loyalties lie," Oliver responded. We stared at each other in a momentary stand-off. I'm glad to say that he broke off contact from his one eye first. At least the man had some shame.

"So, what are you saying, Oliver?" Eddy asked.

"I'm saying that we need some dirt. We all know what happened with *Pop Idol* and all those other programs. Everyone was fighting for a scoop. I don't want to be made to look an idiot."

I didn't make the obvious response. I was astounded that someone I'd found in my bed stark naked with his secretary could talk about being made to look like an idiot. I realized at that moment that this job was becoming oppressive, although I didn't want to think about the alternatives right now. I stood up.

"I think I need to declare a conflict of interest. Let the minutes show that I took no further part in this discussion." I walked out of the room and out of the office. I suppose I was angry, disappointed, apprehensive, and a little guilty about the secrets I was keeping to myself. It also upset me that what had started as an innocent, flirtatious, exciting, sexual encounter that hurt no one was threatening to become a bull's-eye for everyone to shoot at.

I took the afternoon off. I don't know why, but I risked turning up at Darryl's salon without an appointment. I guess news had reached him about my new status in life 'cos it suddenly wasn't a problem. Darryl saw to me himself and I had the works: wash, treatment, steam, conditioner. Okay, so Darryl didn't actually do the shampooing himself—I'm not Halle Berry, after all—but he did keep a watchful eye on what Franiq'ua was doing. My hair had become a precious commodity to the salon and, for once, like all them women with "good" hair, I enjoyed the attention.

We've just finished the last two days' filming. From now on, my contribution will be "live." It should all have been so easy, but I'd had to think long and hard about how I was going to handle the shoot. Adrian's "twist" for this reality series was that each of the judges would offer advice to the chosen finalists. It would be up to them whether they took the advice and when it comes to the first of the live programs in six weeks, we'll know whether they accepted or rejected our words of wisdom.

It sounds easy. I know that when I've sat at home watching these kinds of programs I've known exactly where each person was going wrong: too much makeup, crass choice of song, totally inappropriate image, over-confidence . . . I could go on. Now, when I had the chance to make my opinion count, I found myself almost frozen with fear. Sure these guys could reject my advice, but what if they took it and then didn't succeed? I'd feel the burden of that failure. I spent many a long hour and wakeful night considering what advice to give. And of course, the most thought went into what to say to Calvin.

I think all the judges realized that this, in essence, would be our make-or-break moment in the series. For the others, this could affect their future in the music business. For me, it was a question of my own integrity.

In the end, I think I was as honest and objective as anyone could be. If I seemed to be hypercritical, then it was genuinely because I believed that each of those finalists could benefit from the advice. With Calvin, though, even having searched long and hard for a flaw, there was little advice I could give. I truly believed that he was head and shoulders above the others.

Calvin's exquisite tones floated in the air, pitch-perfect, the surge of emotion moving the crew to rare silence.

"You obviously have a future in the industry, young man," Quentin started, his voice shattering the stillness. "Maybe a long future. But choose your material with care. Decide whether you're going to be a karaoke kid, mimicking the soul greats, or whether you're going to be an innovator. You're young. Choose the people around you wisely. Watch out for the ones who'll want to use you to further their own ends. Finally, get a good lawyer!" Quentin laughed to lighten the tone, but he surprised me. His advice was more valuable and more heartfelt than I would have expected. I thought I even heard a glimmer of emotion in his voice. Calvin's eyes were bright with excitement. He smiled and nodded his thanks.

I held my breath as we waited for Gary. His was supposed to be the voice of youth, the voice of the future. It was suddenly vitally important to me that he should be positive.

"Let's be honest, Calvin," Gary drawled, his words slow, trying to inject as much tension as he could. "I guess everyone, including you, has been thinking that you're the front-runner. Way out ahead of everyone else. Let's look at the evidence." There was a pause for dramatic effect. "You're a good-looking young man. You've got charisma. No one can deny that you've got a good voice. And I'm sure all the ladies will be wetting themselves . . ." He had the nerve to look straight at me. I put it down to my being the only female judge. I'd learned enough to know that the camera would have turned to me. I tried to look impassive, except for the slight, cynical raising of one eyebrow, though I was seething.

Gary continued, "And maybe I'm a little jealous . . ." We all chuckled dutifully. "But you've got a long way to go. I admit that you've got star quality. You haven't yet shown me that you've got the determination, though." Gary smiled in an almost avuncular way. He waited to let that sink in. As if he were Moses laying down the commandments. "First, I'd ditch the American homie look. Second, shave off that beard. Craig David's been there, done that. Third, change the name. Calvin Brown's not going to do much for anyone. Instantly forgettable. Fourth, forget about the Marvin imitation, or the Prince or Usher or even Justin Timberlake . . ." I could hear the collective intake of breath. "Decide who you are. I don't think there's room for any more cheap imitations."

There was silence. Gary had obviously chosen his

moment. Saving his best for last. He'd done enough to get himself talked about, column inches where it counted. I hardly dared look at Calvin, but the boy done good. He stood erect, looking straight at Gary, but emotionless. Then a slight smile crossed his face, as if to say, "I've got your measure, bro." I felt unreasonably proud of him.

Max started quietly. I had to strain to make out his words. "Remember, you only as good as your last performance. And there's always going to be someone coming up behind you wanting to pull you down." I wondered whether his words were addressed to Calvin or to himself. "Strive to be the best you can. Is easy to get overconfident. Maybe you need to show some humility." Harsh, I thought. But then, that said more about Max than it did about Calvin. "Whatever anyone says"—and he turned momentarily to Gary—"you have a righteous talent. Be careful of them people around you, bro. Watch yourself." Max turned toward me with a look that, to me, was unmistakable. I wanted to weep. But Max was being indiscreet enough for the both of us. How long would it be before the press started digging? "Find that one person you can trust, the one person who can save you from yourself."

Tears sprang to my eyes. But now it was my turn. I took a deep breath, swallowed hard, and forced myself to remain calm, to still the mixed emotions that were welling up inside me.

"Calvin, I'm not sure I can give you any better advice than you've heard already. What I will say, though, is that you've got the kind of talent that sends shivers down my spine. From the first moment that we heard your voice, I don't think any of us has forgotten who Calvin Brown is." I looked pointedly at Gary. "Sure, you're going to learn a lot from your vocal coach, your dance teacher, your stylist, your trainer, your therapist if you need one. They'll teach you how to perform all the tricks that you need to learn. But no one but you can build on that God-given talent. The only advice I can give you, Calvin, is to always continue to be you. Don't let them make you someone you're not. I think you owe that to yourself . . . And when you're looking for votes, choose a song that people know and recognize. That way, they'll remember you and vote for you! But at the same time, don't go singing 'bout no 'Puppy Love' or any of them Abba songs." The tension was eased by laughter.

Petra shouted, "That's a wrap, folks. Thank you all." Then I rushed to the bathroom and stayed there for quite a while. It's a good place not to think, even while the tears flowed. Eventually, I pulled myself together, repaired my makeup, and joined the others in the green room. I headed for Seamus, the video editor, the most friendly looking face in the room.

"Well done!" he whispered. "You were fantastic. So was Calvin. It'll make great television." I'm not sure that's what I wanted to hear. I needed a drink so I headed for the bar. I noticed that Adrian and Calvin were in a corner on their own, engrossed in conversation, an invisible *cordon sanitaire* around them. I didn't see any of the other finalists around and I was intrigued. At that moment, Gary approached. I didn't want a confrontation with him, but there was nowhere to escape to.

"Carol, that was quite a performance."

"I wasn't the one who was performing."

He laughed. "You take it all so seriously, don't you? It's all a game. All done for the cameras."

"Is that what you really believe, Gary? These kids

have been working their guts out. Putting their trust in us. Expecting us to be honest, to want to help them. And all you can do is play for the cameras?"

"You know it's really very sweet that you've got such pure motives, but do you really believe that's what this is all about? Look over there. Why do you think Adrian's cornered Calvin?" He obviously saw my confusion. "Don't be so naïve, darling. What do you think this series is all about? It's about the bucks. For all of us. That young guy is by far the best we've seen—"

"So why didn't you say so?"

He laughed. "Carol, we've got five live programs to go. Where's the excitement in telling the audience that he's going to win? The truth is, win or lose, he'll go a long way. You know that. I know that. Adrian knows that. And that's why he's getting in there. Trying to sign him up before the bidding war starts. As soon as the first show goes out, there'll be agents hammering at his door. If Adrian can do an exclusive deal now, then that's even more money for his company. Think of the agent's fees, income from record sales, concerts, merchandising, and that's all following on from the publicity the series will generate. I bet even *The Cream* is already calculating its profits."

"But that's not the way Adrian sold this to me."

"For God's sake, don't play the innocent. Did you expect him to tell you straight up? You know this business is all about the dough. Everyone's out for what they can get."

I was incensed. "So is that all we're here for? To help Adrian make money?"

"Not just Adrian. What about you?"

I glared at him, but his stare was steady. "Come on,

Carol. You were out for all you could get too. Snout in the trough just like the rest of us. What makes you think you're so bloody high and mighty?"

The hostility was back in his voice. I thought we'd got over whatever was bothering him. I couldn't argue with him, though. He was right. I felt my shoulders slump. I looked across at Adrian. I knew I was sending daggers in his direction. He suddenly looked up at Calvin, his face livid and contorted with anger. I don't know what Calvin had said to produce such a response, but he suddenly stood, looked in my direction, grinned, and strolled out of the room, confident, as if he didn't have a care in the world. I watched as Adrian struggled to compose himself and I strode over to him. I'm really not very good at choosing my moment.

"So what was that all about? Trying to squeeze the extra ounce of flesh?"

"Not now, Carol."

"You promised me that this was all about the talent—"

"Not now!"

"You said—"

"I know what I said." His voice had an unfamiliar chill that should have warned me.

"It's all about exploiting these young kids." I could have stopped there. Adrian's face was white with rage. "You lied to me, Adrian. In the end, it's all about the money, isn't it?"

"So what are you going to do about it, Carol?" His eyes burned with controlled fury. "Throw your thirty pieces of silver back in my face? Walk out on the series? You signed a contract, remember," he hissed. "We've got you by the short and curlies. Don't fuck with me, Carol."

I guess he must have spoken louder than he'd intended because there was a sudden silence in the room. Adrian looked around and then lowered his voice as the hubbub of conversation grew again.

"You've got a job to do. You had your own reasons for agreeing to do it. Now you need to make the best you can of it. Get on with mothering the talent." He sighed. "You don't have to worry about these kids. They're more streetwise than you think. Calvin Brown's already got people looking after his interests." I could hear the venom in his voice.

I walked out of the room. I couldn't bear the smug look on Gary's face as I passed him.

Eddy caught up with me across the road. He draped an arm across my shoulder and didn't say a word. I was too enraged to cry. I needed to talk, though, and as we walked I explained my dilemma.

"Babe, that's the way this industry is and maybe you've been too sheltered. You have to make the best you can of it. You could walk away, but what good would that do? I know you. You really believe in what you're doing. If some of these folks get recording contracts out of this, then you've achieved a lot. Even better if the right guy wins. Don't make any rash decision, Carol."

Eddy stopped and hugged me. I wanted to stay in his arms. I looked up at his concerned face. Gabby was certainly a very lucky woman.

Chapter Thirteen

I've calmed down over the last few weeks, mainly because life has more or less got back to normal. We've been doing quite a lot of prepublicity for the shows, mainly photo sessions, and it might freak me out if I have to do any more. I really do feel like a piece of meat when a photographer decides to arrange my limbs to best suit his agenda. It's a bit of a relief to get back to the old routine of the office. Eddy has been supportive and rational—a calming influence—and I think I've got life more into perspective. There's no sense in letting Adrian, Gary, or even Oliver and Georgina, for that matter, get under my skin. I've decided to remain aloof and rise above it all.

Funny how things seem to go like this, but now that my life's a lot less hectic, Rob's the one who is frantically busy. We speak regularly on the phone but seems like he's overwhelmed with work for a client. It really is true that absence makes the loins grow hotter. I can't wait to see him next week.

The first program goes out tomorrow night. I don't

know whether I'm looking forward to it or dreading it.
Those first auditions seem so long ago, almost another
life.

I want to hide in a dark cave. Never speak to anyone ever again. The phone's been ringing off the hook.
Everyone leaving awkward messages. Wanting to be
kind and supportive, but not really knowing what to
say.

I'm still not sure what's going on. I was in that
editing suite with Petra and Seamus. I thought I understood how the program was going to turn out. I wish
someone had had the decency to warn me.

I'd felt too nervous to watch with anyone else
around. I huddled under a duvet on the sofa, prepared
to pull the fabric up over my eyes as and when necessary, my heart thumping loudly, almost drowning out
the sound from the television. From the first five minutes, I had a vague sense that something was very different about the program, but I was fascinated by the
way it had been edited to show some performances in
the very best light, while almost dismissing others. It
was all a question of the weight given to some candidates, very much at the expense of others. I wondered
about how each of the judges reacted to each individ-
ual performance. It wasn't quite how I remembered
events, but at first I put that down to my erratic memory. And then, three quarters of the way through there
came a moment that will remain permanently imprinted
on my memory. What I remembered happening wasn't
exactly what I was seeing on the screen.

Calvin walked into the room, singing, looking
self-assured. Cocky, even. There was no disguising

the strength of his performance. Then there was silence. The camera lingered on my speechlessness, the blush that rose to my cheeks, my confusion, and then as I lifted my head the shot cut to Calvin staring at me with that confident grin on his face. I hardly heard my voice: "I'm only lost for words to express how brilliant your performance was. . . . You get my vote." Cut to Calvin's raised eyebrow, the startled expressions of the other judges. The implication was obvious. I felt a rush of intense anger, then shame. I wanted to scream. I wanted to cry. I wanted to tear Adrian limb from limb. "Don't fuck with me, Carol," he'd warned. This was Adrian's revenge. I hardly saw the rest of the program. The messages started almost immediately.

"Carol, is you mother. I know you there. Pick up the phone, girl."

"Sis, what the hell is going on? Call me."

"It's Gabby. I'm here if you need to talk. Don't let this get you down, sweetheart."

"Carol, it's Rob. I'm at home. Give me a call."

"It's me, Carol, Dad. Call you later."

"Is your mother. Again. I want to speak to you, child. You pick up this phone right now. Carol Shaw, if you ain't goin' talk to me on this ya phone, I will have to get you sister to give me a drive round to you place so you can explain yourself. All right, if that's how you want it . . ."

"Babe, I know you won't want to talk, but I'm in the car, on my way 'round to you now. I'm coming to get you. You have to get out of your apartment. Right now. I'll explain when I see you."

It was Eddy. I felt so humiliated that I didn't even want to see him. I didn't know if I could make him understand, if even he would believe me. *After all, everyone knows that the camera doesn't lie*, I thought bitterly. I couldn't make any sense of Eddy's message but, anyway, I could hardly move.

Within minutes, Eddy was at the door.

"Carol, pack enough clothes for a few days. You're coming to my place."

"Eddy, why? It wasn't as bad as that, was it?"

"I don't have time to explain. We've got to get going right now. Trust me."

I looked at Eddy and the grim determination I saw in his face made me act. We both tore around my bedroom snatching items of clothing and stuffing them into an overnight bag.

In the car, Eddy explained that he'd been tipped off that there would be a story I wouldn't like in the Sunday tabloids. It was only a matter of time before my apartment would be surrounded by journalists wanting to get their own angle and, if possible, an interview.

"What kind of story, Eddy?"

"I don't know exactly, babes."

"I don't understand. I haven't got any skeletons. I can't imagine what they could have."

"All I know is that it's got something to do with you and Calvin."

Eddy glanced at me and I thought I saw faint suspicion in his eyes. I might have imagined it. Maybe the program that had gone out tonight had made me oversensitive. There were only two other people who knew about that incident between me and Calvin: Gabby and Calvin himself. I can't imagine either of them giving that story to the papers. What would be in it for Gabby? Or for Calvin? My only worry was that Calvin might have talked to someone else. But even so, what could the papers make of that one incident? It would be my

word against his. I couldn't believe that they would go
big on that kind of gossip.

Before I knew it, we'd pulled up in front of Eddy's
block. I realized that he'd been staring at me for some
time and I couldn't work out what he was thinking. He
didn't ask me about Calvin. Instead, he handed me a
hat from the backseat. "Let's be ultra careful. Probably
best if nobody knows that you're here."

I pulled up the collar of my jacket, put on the hat,
and we walked, as unobtrusively as possible, to his
apartment. Once inside, Eddy sat me down, made me
herbal tea, offered brandy for shock, and put his arm
around me, massaging the muscles in my neck.

"Carol, you know you don't have to explain a thing
to me. I'm your friend and I'll do anything I can for
you. But if you want to talk, you know you can trust
me. I'll listen, sugar."

"I don't know what to say, Eddy. I don't understand what's going on. I watched that program tonight
and I can't explain what happened. Nothing was like it
really was. It's like they were setting me up for something and I can't figure out why. I was so shocked, and
then the phone just went mad with everyone calling . . ."
I couldn't say any more. The memory of those scenes on
the television brought a huge lump of embarrassment to
my throat, and all at once hot tears began to flow. Eddy
took one look at me, held me tightly to him, stroking
my hair and murmuring "Shh!" until I was all cried out.

"Don't worry, babe. We'll figure it out. I'll make
some calls. But you need to phone your family to let
them know you're okay; otherwise, they'll be going
crazy. It's best if you don't tell them where you are
'cos I wouldn't put it past some of those hacks to be
keeping an eye on your folks too."

He was right. I screwed up my courage and called Mom first. I was expecting her to be angry with me, but I managed to cut off her first words and explained as much as I could. I told her that there was a story to come in the papers the next day, that I didn't know what it would say, but I didn't believe that any of it would be true. Eddy whispered to me to warn her that the papers would be trying to get her to talk. I nearly cried again when Mom said that she knew I was "a good girl" since she'd brought me up as a God-fearing child and she would never believe that I'd done anything wrong.

"Hold your head high, child. Don't let them beat you down. I is proud of you and you know the whole of you family on you side."

And then tears did flow again when Mom asked, "You want me to call your sister . . . and your father? I know it not easy for you to talk, Carol." I knew how much it took for her to offer to contact Dad and, no, I really didn't want to talk any more. I wanted to be alone, to forget all about my life spinning out of control.

Eddy said he'd call Gabby and Rob and he'd also do a bit of probing through his contacts. "You need to get some sleep while you can."

"I don't think I'll ever sleep again."

Eddy ran a hot bath and made me some kind of herbal potion. Like a mother hen, he watched as I drank every drop, then wrapped me in his thick dressing gown and led me to bed. He stayed with me, stroking my forehead until I fell into a disturbed sleep. I woke frequently, but it seemed that each time Eddy was there, soothing me, holding me in his arms.

*   *   *

When I woke up this morning, all the papers were there, laid out on the bed. It was far, far worse than I could have imagined. How had this happened?

"I wish I could keep this from you, Carol, but it's best if you see it straight away. We need to work out what to do." I was glad that he'd used the word *we*. I wouldn't have been surprised if even Eddy had decided to abandon me.

On all the front pages there was a photograph of Calvin leaving my apartment, obviously late at night. Nearly all the papers had juxtaposed stills from *Soul Sensation* making it look as if Calvin and I were gazing adoringly at each other. The headlines were obvious and suggestive: "Soul Sensational Revelations," "Soul Mates?," "No Competition," "Body and Soul." One article was illustrated with the stills that Patrick had taken in the nightclub, stills that made me look like some kind of predatory sex fiend who was capable of leading a young man astray. I pointed them out to Eddy. He nodded grimly. He was ahead of me.

There's no denying that the story made compulsive reading, for me at least. There were no facts, just Calvin Brown photographed leaving my apartment, and a great deal of insinuation heaped on top. They obviously hadn't managed to talk to Calvin, but there were comments from rejected *Soul Sensation* candidates who claimed to have suspected a relationship between us and to know that's why they'd been denied their opportunity. Anonymous members of the production team were quoted as having noticed "something special," "snatched conversations," "suggestive glances." There was the hint that I'd vigorously supported Calvin, bullying the other judges. For me, the final straw was a quote from Adrian saying that he "could not imagine that there was any-

thing in this story" but promising "a full investigation." I laughed bitterly. I wouldn't be surprised if
Adrian was behind the story. It was fortuitously good
publicity for the series, and this could be his way of
getting his own back on both Calvin and me. Of
course, the broadsheets were above this level, but one
had managed to dig up the angle of my former relationship with Max. I knew that the other papers would,
even now, be searching for whatever dirt they could
find. Funnily enough, I found myself praying that they
wouldn't hurt Max by delving into his own particular
brand of shit.

"What do you want to do, sugar?"

"Apart from going to sleep forever, or strangling
Patrick, you mean? I don't know what I *can* do, Eddy.
I mean, they're not saying anything that I can deny.
Just innuendo. It's not as if I could sue them for loads
of cash. All they're saying is that Calvin was in my
flat. And that's true."

I waited, but Eddy didn't ask what Calvin had been
doing there. I felt ridiculously grateful.

"Eddy, I honestly don't believe that I've done anything wrong."

"Babe, I know you haven't."

"Calvin turned up at my flat wanting advice. We'd
met once before, but—"

"Sugar, you really don't have to explain."

"I want to, Eddy. He turned up out of the blue. I
told him that it wasn't a good idea for him to be there.
That's all that happened and he left. I don't even know
how he got my address. I don't understand the picture
of him leaving—"

"Sounds to me like you were set up." Eddy had a
hard look in his eye that scared me a little.

"But how? And who would do that to me? I haven't done anything that bad to anyone."

"This may sound like a strange thing to say, Carol, but it might not be anything personal. The music business is exactly that, a *business*, so you have to ask yourself who's going to benefit from all of this."

"Not me, for a start."

"I can't track Patrick down," Eddy said, speaking the name as if he were holding it between two fingers; something filthy that he was about to flush down the toilet. "But you know there was money in it for him. He couldn't have set this up on his own, though. Either he was part of it to begin with, or he was tipped off. So who gains from the publicity?"

"*Soul Sensation*."

"For one. And Calvin too."

"How can this be good for him? Just makes him look as if he cheated to get through."

"Babe, it's all publicity for him. By the time the public come to vote, whose name do you think is going to stick in their heads? There's a long way to go before the finals, but I bet you that while you're a judge nobody's going to want to kick him off the program. They're going to be waiting, praying for one of you to be caught."

I pondered that one. I know Eddy thinks I'm naïve about show business, but I don't believe that Calvin would have come up with something like this. I'm a reasonably good judge of character and Calvin seems genuine. I said as much to Eddy. "And besides, both he and I know that he has enough talent to go a long way without all of this crap. My money's on that bastard Adrian."

"You might be right. Anyway, nobody's talking.

That photo of Calvin was sent anonymously to all the tabloids with a note asking what he was doing leaving your apartment. My contacts are telling me that they don't know where the story originated. They may be lying, but I get the sense that it's true."

I thought for a moment. Maybe Eddy was right and this wasn't a personal attack against me; but whatever the reason, there was only one thing I could do. "I'm going to have to resign from the program."

"Why?"

"Eddy, you can't think I'd want to go on with it after all this and after the program last night."

"I watched that program. Remember I was there when some of it was recorded, and I know that's not exactly how it went down. I know you looked shocked when you saw Calvin, but you say you'd met him once before. I guess it's Adrian's way of making the program more interesting, I don't know. But you can't leave the show. That would be like admitting you have something to feel guilty about."

"But how can I go into that studio week after week and face all those people? You know they'll all be looking at me. Waiting for me to trip up."

"Well, you won't trip up. Carol, you know you've done nothing wrong. So you just have to go on being you. Don't let them turn you into something you're not."

"I wish I'd never got into this. I don't know what made me think I could handle it anyway. Foolish pride." The tears began once again, but this time it wasn't self-pity. I was just so angry with myself.

Eddy didn't move, didn't put a comforting arm around me. "Carol," he said in a voice that was sterner and harsher than I expected. "You can do it. You will do it." He stared at me, looking a bit like my old head-master.

The phone rang, rescuing me from that moment. It was Rob. He'd read the papers and wanted to see me, if I thought it would help. I looked up at Eddy who had his jacket on and was signaling that he was going out. I gave Rob Eddy's address.

It felt weird being with Rob in Eddy's apartment. I think that's what made me a bit out of step with him. It was good to see him. It would have been good to see anyone who was so absolutely convinced of my inno-cence.

"Carol, you don't have to say anything," were his first words. He took my hand in both of his. "I know is all lies. Nobody could believe any of that fuckery about you." The word made me laugh. It felt like the first time I'd laughed in years.

"Thanks, Rob."

"Nothing to thank me for, Carol."

He took me in his arms and just held me for a while. He lifted my chin and kissed me briefly. "I'd say sue the bastards if they'd actually made any real accusations. It's frustrating but it's best not to take it seriously. After all, it's going to raise your profile. There can't be many people who don't know who you are now. This could be great for your career in the end. Maybe you need a lawyer." He smiled at me, but it hit me that he was right. Perhaps a buffer between me and the press would be a good idea. It wasn't just a ques-tion of going into the studio each week; I imagined myself being hounded wherever I went.

It was as if Rob read my mind. "Carol, a lot of my

clients have been through this kind of thing. Believe
me, it will pass. Give it a couple of weeks and there'll
be another story around *Soul Sensation*. People have
short memories and they'll soon forget today's papers."

"So you're not offering your services?"

"Honey, I would, but mixing business and the hope
of some pleasure to come . . ."

The comment was crassly ill timed. Every now and
again, Rob and I seemed to be operating in parallel,
out-of-sync universes. I moved away and wandered
into the kitchen. I made coffee just to give myself
something to do. Rob chatted, filling the space with
idle trivia, and I was grateful. It covered the fact that I
couldn't listen to his words. My head was spinning
with the "what-ifs" and "maybes" and "if onlys" of a
still slightly guilty conscience.

It wasn't Rob's fault, but when he finally took me
in his arms again, kissed me deeply, and sighed how
much he'd missed me, squeezing my behind, pulling
me to him, I felt no reciprocal response.

"I'm sorry, Rob. Too much on my mind."

"No worries. I understand."

He stuck around for a while, but left as soon as it
seemed polite to do so.

So it was Eddy who was there for the next two days
whenever I needed him, cooking, brewing his concoc-
tions, and fending off unwanted calls. The few times I
snuck out of the flat I had to wear a wig that Eddy ac-
quired for me. Irony of ironies: Here I am with the
longed-for flowing, luxurious hair—and it's not mine.
It was easiest to stay holed up in the flat. I felt a bit like

an invalid, but relished being pampered, just like Eddy's cat. Eventually, I was bound to respond like a cat, relaxing at his touch, purring when he held me.

I was in bed, but wide awake last night when Eddy got back from the office. I didn't look at the clock, but only the occasional sound of a passing car crept through the silence. It must have been late. I heard him tiptoe into the bedroom.

"It's okay. I'm awake."

"Hey, babe. How you doing?"

"I'm all right."

He switched on the bedside light and examined my face carefully. "You sure?"

I nodded. And it was true. I really was getting over it, or getting accustomed to it. I'd had time to recover from the initial shock of seeing the papers and felt re-assured that they'd been unable to dig up any more crap to print. They'd been reduced to turning green— recycling the same stories. I was calmer than I would have believed possible. I even, momentarily, saw the funny side of the situation. There I'd been thinking that someone had tipped the papers off to the true na-ture of my encounter with Calvin when they obviously knew nothing at all about it. And yet they'd come close. If only they knew!

"So how are things in the office? Anyone notice that I wasn't there?"

"Girl, the phones are ringing red hot. Oliver is in his element. Of course, he's pissed at being scooped, but he's so happy with the extra publicity the mag's getting that I'm sure he'd pay you to stay away as long as the story runs. Even Georgina's having to do some work, so maybe this is all worth it for that alone."

I wasn't really worried about *The Cream*. I'd had time alone to think. Here I was in Eddy's apartment, rescued by him, with him trusting me completely, and yet I was keeping a secret from him. It didn't seem fair.

I waited until Eddy had showered and joined me in the bed. He coiled his body around mine, holding me comfortingly close.

"Eddy . . ."

"Mmm?"

"I have to tell you something."

"Babes, you don't have to tell me anything."

I turned around to look at him. "But I want to tell you, Eddy. About the time I met Calvin."

I found myself blushing and hoped that the light was too dim for him to notice. I took a deep breath and told him everything as fast as I could.

At first there was no change of expression on Eddy's face. And then he surprised me. Eddy began to laugh. A laugh that started deep in his belly and boomed around the room. He laughed until tears ran down his face. He laughed until he had to sit up, clutching his stomach in pain. Every time he looked at my shocked face, the laughter bubbled up again. Finally, he controlled himself enough to gasp, "That boy sure is talented. He deserve to win!" And that started him off again. In the end, I had to laugh, too, though perhaps not as heartily as Eddy. We clung to each other and what seemed like hours later, Eddy sobered up and looked at me seriously.

"Carol, I can't believe that you were so worried about telling me that. Girl, what's wrong with you? Is nothing to be ashamed of. So, you met a young man who was turned on by you. I can't blame him. He have good taste." I found myself blushing again. "The two of you made the best of an opportunity. You hurt anybody?" I shook my head. "You enjoyed it?" I nodded. Eddy leered at me. "Girl, you need more adventure!"

"You offering?"

"You better believe it." He smiled, but there was a serious look in his eye and I felt a flickering of nerves in the pit of my stomach. I don't know whether it was because I was in need of comforting or pure lust, but I moved closer to Eddy, easing my body against him, shivering at the intimate contact, the heat of his body enflaming my skin. I pressed my lips against his chest, nibbling at him, touching his flesh with the tip of my tongue, licking the tender skin between his collarbones until I felt him stiffen and pull away. He raised my head and looked into my eyes. I could see the question that his eyes were asking. This time, I understood it. At that precise moment I was one hundred percent intensely sure and I nodded, repeating the "yes" as my lips brushed his and my tongue forced him to open, allowing me to probe his mouth, tasting the sweetness there. His response was immediate as his tongue pressed against mine, forcing its way into my mouth. I closed my eyes, concentrating on the feelings swirling around my head. This was Eddy Stanton. My friend. I was in his bed. About to make love to him. Sober. Desperate. Praying that, this time, nothing would get in the way.

He rolled over until he was lying on top of me and he paused to look at me again. "Don't stop, Eddy. Please." At once, his kisses became harder, more insistent, and I was getting hotter. He raised up and I could feel his fingers caressing my skin like a whisper, so almost not there that my body involuntarily arched toward him in a prayer for more. I was clutching at him, my fingers raking his back. I know I must have caused him pain, but I couldn't stop, I wanted to feel him so badly. And then his lips were on my nipples, making me moan with delight as his tongue flicked across them. His hand slipped between my legs caressing me just where my body was crying out for him. I knew that his mere touch could bring me to climax and I didn't want that. I wanted to feel Eddy's cock inside me this time. I gritted my teeth. I needed to control my body. I gripped his hand tightly with my thighs, trapping it there, stopping any movement just for a while. Eddy must have known what was happening, because he stilled, just waiting for my signal. I could hear deep, harsh breathing and realized that it was coming from me. We stayed there, motionless, until the waves subsided a little and I could deal with the way he was making me feel. I pulled away from him for a second and then began to caress his nipples, gently scraping across them with my nails, pinching, squeezing, and licking until he lay back, surrendering himself to my touch.

I straddled him and sat back looking at him for a moment. Eddy sure was one sexy guy. Broad, muscular chest, thin waist, long, well-formed legs, and yes, an erection to die for. I couldn't wait any longer. I cupped my hands around his balls, watching as his penis nodded its appreciation. I held him for a while, teasing to see how long he could stay still, resisting my touch. Not long. Eddy groaned, took my hand in his, and moved it upward until I grasped his cock. Slowly, so slowly, he moved my fingers up and down the shaft, the hot, hard feel of it making my stomach flip. I was getting wetter. He was so rigid that I was desperate to feel him inside me. I tried to maneuver myself onto him, but Eddy laughed and pushed me away. "You're not ready for this, babe," he grinned, holding his cock and pointing it at me.

"I am, Eddy. Honestly. I swear to you. Truly. Cross my heart. I'm ready."

He laughed. "Babe, you don't know how ready I'm going to make you." His eyes narrowed.

Now he was on top of me again, sliding down my body, kissing and licking his way down my stomach, frustratingly missing the spot where all my emotions were suddenly concentrated, down my thighs, then up again, over and over, each time coming closer and closer to my clitoris. I wanted to scream at him, but he knew exactly what he was doing: bringing me near, so close, to climax and then moving away until the surge of feeling subsided, and then he'd start over until I was sure I couldn't stand any more, that I was going to die. I spread my legs farther and farther, reaching for him, begging him to make me come. His tongue touched my clitoris and I screamed as the fire surged through my body making it rise up. His tongue flittered fast from side to side; then he stopped. Waited. Then he nibbled and sucked until he heard my long, deep moan.

Then he was sitting astride my chest. "This what you want, babe?" I couldn't speak.

"See how hard you make me? All for you, Carol. Am I hard enough for you?"

"God, yes. Eddy. Don't make me wait." I took him in my hand, my thumb caressing the head of his penis, loving the feeling of how wet he was. Then I stopped for a moment to trace the vein that ran along the length of his cock. I smiled to myself. Giving him a taste of his medicine. Repeating the movements until I felt his shiver as he pulled away from me.

His hands were between my legs again, retaliating, his thumb rubbing my clit, one finger sliding inside me, making me gasp.

"Eddy, now!"

He looked deep into my eyes, then kissed me, smothering my cry as he drove his long, thick cock so deep inside me. We were still for a while, and then he moved, gently sliding the length of his prick out of my pussy, resting the head there, teasing me until I thrust against him, drawing him inside again. We were both moaning, muttering words like more, honey, sugar, deeper, fuck me, again, harder, don't stop, not knowing who was saying what, hearing sounds but not knowing whose they were. Then I was above him, astride him, his hands on my hips, moving me against him, feeling the rhythm, moving to the rhythm, with the rhythm, forgetting everything but the rhythm, the hard, hot, throbbing rhythm that was growing in my head, filling my head until it was about to erupt. And then he's screaming, "Now, Carol. Now!" and he's pounding his cock into me, his flesh into mine until I hear his deep growl and it's all I need. My thoughts, my feelings explode, mingling with his, and my body reaches an impossible peak and I'm still, drowning in ripples of sheer ecstasy that gradually subside, fading until I'm myself again. Me, being held in Eddy's arms. And it's where I've always belonged.

Chapter Fourteen

In the middle of the night I awoke, convinced that God was punishing me for what I'd just done: I'd had a stroke and couldn't move my legs. It took a while to work out that Eddy's cat was stretched across my calves, head curled into the bend of my knee. I was relieved, but slept fitfully after that, troubled by a vaguely guilty conscience.

I forced myself awake from disturbing dreams at around five o'clock. It was so still. The kind of silence that I'm not used to in my own neighborhood. I knew that the dreams that involved snakes, vertigo, scorpions, and running barefoot across broken glass were all to do with anxiety. I looked at Eddy, breathing deeply, sleeping peacefully with his arms stretched across my body. Why was I feeling so anxious? As my head began to clear, the name trickled into my consciousness: Gabriela. Shit! What the fuck did I think I was doing? I'd given Gabby the green light. I'd virtually pushed them together, and now here I was, in bed with her man. I felt the tears flood my eyes. How could I ex-

plain what I'd done? I know I'd been feeling incredibly stressed and vulnerable, but that was no excuse.
And I couldn't blame Eddy. I'd thrown myself, my
whole body, at him.

So I'm looking at Eddy's sleeping face wanting to
trace the shape of his eyebrow with my finger, longing
to stroke his cheek, his silky head, to kiss those warm
lips, to bury my head into his chest, and to feel the
strength of his arms protecting me. At the same time,
though, I know I mustn't. So I take this little bit of time
to learn his every feature, to shed the last of the tears I
intend to cry over what could have been. As the pale
sun begins to filter through the gaps in the drawn cur-
tains, I slip quietly from the bed, retrieve my clothes,
and dress before Eddy can wake. I have to go. It's
time. I leave the rest of my things. Later on there will
be time to clear away the debris. But not now. I take
one last look at dear, lovely, wonderful, beloved Eddy
and leave, gently closing the door behind me. Anyway,
I have to go home. I'm a big girl now and maybe it's
time I grow up. I take a taxi back to my flat.

There were only a couple of journalists hanging
around. They asked for comments in a desultory fashion as if they weren't really expecting me to respond. I
almost felt sorry for them; not much prospect of pro-
motion if they're given the graveyard shift on a story
that's rapidly being relegated to page nine or ten.

My apartment seems alien. I wandered around aimlessly for a while, feeling out of place, watching the orange light on my answering machine flashing furiously.
I pushed the button and listened again to my mother, my
sister, Patrick, Gary, Adrian, and then an endless array

of journalists, calling over and over, offering more and more ridiculous sums of money. I began to be impressed by myself, by how desperately they wanted to talk to me, but in the end, I got bored and switched the machine off. I didn't want to know if Eddy would call, so I unplugged the phone, scrabbled in my handbag for my cell, and switched it off too.

This has been my home, my retreat for three years now, and all at once, I feel out of place, edgy, restless. The phone has given strangers access to my space, allowing them to intrude. I got into the shower, hoping that the sting of the hot water would distract me. Instead, the prickle of the water on my sensitive skin only served to remind me of last night. Eddy was *so* good, I wasn't going to be able to forget for a long time. I shook my head, lathered shampoo onto my scalp, massaging, trying to physically draw thoughts of Eddy out of my head. I really need to think about what I'm going to do next. I can't run away forever. I'm going to have to face my family and on Saturday there's a live studio program. Eddy's right; I can't give whoever's behind this the satisfaction of seeing me walk away.

I dressed in clothes that would give me the most courage—short-skirted suit, linen shirt, and very high heels. If I couldn't talk my way out of trouble, I'd stomp on anyone who got in my way.

I had the upper hand. I hadn't bothered to return Adrian's calls, so when I arrived at the studio, ten minutes after the call time, an expression of relief flashed across his face before he managed to compose himself.

"Carol, sweetheart, I've been trying to talk to you.

Can't tell you how worried I've been, what with all this nonsense in the papers. I just wanted to offer all our support. How've you been coping? Must have been so awful—"

"Forget the bullshit, Adrian. Have you finished your 'internal investigation' yet? You haven't taken any evidence from me, so I'm not sure if I'm still wanted, but I know it must have been a very thorough investigation, nevertheless. I'm assuming that I've got your full confidence, Adrian; otherwise, I would have heard from you. But if you'd prefer me to leave . . ."

I let the words hang in the air. A challenge to him. He was going to look pretty stupid if I walked out now and talked to the press, but if I was going to stay, then there'd be no more of his evil machinations.

He had the sense to avoid my eyes and, instead, put his arm around my shoulders as we walked toward my dressing room. "You know I had to say that stuff for the papers. I never doubted you for one moment. Horrified that anyone would even suggest such a thing . . ." he burbled on.

It was a relief to be left alone for a while. I looked in the mirror and was surprised by the grim set of my jawline, the narrowing of my eyes, the slight flaring of my nostrils. No wonder Adrian was cowed. After the last few days, I'm surprised that I managed to summon up that kind of power. I'm not going to let it go. I won't let any of them think they can walk all over me, even if it means carrying a rabbit's foot, finding a four-leaf clover, tossing salt over my shoulder, and stuffing a horseshoe in my handbag. I'd talked to Mom, Dad, and Nicola, the people I care most about in the world, and I know they're on my side. I wanted to call Gabby, but I'm not sure that I have the right any longer. I'm going to have to fight to be the me I'd like to be. I don't know if it's a war I can win without Eddy, but I'm damned well going to try.

Somehow, I've managed to get through the last five weeks, mainly by being unbelievably selfish, concentrating on my own needs and nothing else. I've done whatever I needed to do to hold my own in the programs and have, therefore, won the reputation of being as hard as nails. It amuses me that the commentators haven't seen through Max's drug-induced self-doubt, Quentin's waiting-for-the-right-moment blandness, and Gary's thirty-second-sound-bite script. They're all looking out for Number One, yet I'm singled out for damnation: Caustic Carol, Cruel Carol, Shaw the Slayer. I tell it as I see it because I've learned that you have to be tough to survive at even the lowest levels in this industry. I won't take any more shit from anyone on that program.

So what I've needed over the weeks is to remain emotionless. I've talked to Rob, but have avoided seeing him. The truth is that there's no going back after Eddy. I've avoided Gabby, too, and I know she must be hurt, but if I'd had to face her, then I would have risked hurting her even more and I might have fallen apart myself. I've had to see Calvin, of course, watching as his confidence grew, week after week, as he negotiated the murky waters of the media sharks. He's more adept than I could have believed possible of someone of his age. There have been endless interviews in the papers with his mother, his sister, his former headmaster, his first girlfriend, all attesting to how innocent Calvin is, accompanied by the now-famous photograph of a younger Calvin looking sweet, guile-less, with a hint of moisture around his eyes. The kind of look that reminds me of how Rob Elliott was back in the day. And we all know what the implication is. Even I almost wondered how I could have taken advantage of such a sweet, innocent, young thing.

So I've relied heavily on my family. And each one of them has been there for me in a way that I'll never be able to repay. Dad and Pauline have welcomed me into their home whenever I've felt the need for shelter. Rosa and Jason are too young to understand the difference between good publicity and bad and are just thrilled to have a "mega-famous" sister. I suspect that the endless numbers of autographs they've asked me to sign have been sold off at school, generating enough profit to fund the new PlayStation games that seem to have appeared miraculously.

I've depended heavily on Mom and Nicola, in a way that I wish I could have avoided. But no matter how I might wish it otherwise, they know me better than anyone and are more willing to forgive my cruel outbursts of rage at the world.

And no, I'm not avoiding the subject of Eddy. I listened over and over to the messages he left. Pathetic as it might sound, I've saved them so I can hear his voice whenever I need to. The first messages sound cheerful enough, but surprised. Later, a suggestion of hurt. Then he becomes more insistent. And when he sounds frantic with worry, I pick up the phone and dial his number.

"Babe, what happened to you?" His relief is palpable and I feel like a wicked witch. "I was about to call the cops and then I rang Nicola. She told me she'd seen you."

"Yes, I'm okay, Eddy."

"So wha'appen, babe?" I could hear the smile forming in his voice and that almost destroyed me.

"I needed some time, Eddy. I had to get away. To think. Alone."

"And you couldn't tell me that? I didn't know what was going on, Carol. I was worried sick."

"Don't worry about me, Eddy. I can take care of myself."

I could hear the hurt in his silence and it echoed around in my brain.

"What did I do wrong? I thought I was pretty adventurous. I was just getting into my stride when I woke to find you gone. I did wonder if you still respec' me!"

Neither of us laughed. "Eddy, you know this isn't right."

"Why?"

Did I have to spell it out? I'd cheated on one best friend with another and I'd enjoyed every single passionate second of it. I couldn't let it happen again.

"I can't do it. Let's just leave it at that."

"Babe, we need to talk."

"Not now, Eddy. I've got too much on my mind with the studios and all that. It's just not the right time." The delaying tactic was obvious, but I played on the fact that Eddy cared enough about me to give me the space I needed.

"Okay. If that's what you want, I ain't going to put any pressure on you. I'll see you around." He put the phone down and I felt completely desolated, bereft.

Of course, I've seen Eddy around at the office. He's been coolly affectionate, hugging me in a way that, if only he knew, tortured my senses; kissing my cheek with warm lips that left a burning imprint and holding my hand in a way that might have been casual to him but made me want to throw him down on the floor and have my wicked way there and then. What a story that would have made for the Sunday papers! I've fought against it, but it's so hard not to respond to the mere sight of him. I have to blame this all on Calvin. I was coping reasonably well with my celibate lifestyle until he came along and reawakened forgotten desires. I number my problems from the moment I met him and he stirred those long-dormant emotions. All the same, I have to forgive him since the guy can certainly sing and the sound of his voice will always turn me to mush.

So I've managed to survive this far. Like Bobby Womack, I call myself a "Soul Survivor," and I use those words as a tantric chant whenever I find myself wavering. Tonight is the final and we're down to six contestants. I've had to accept the will of the public in voting for the two blond bimbos, neither of them truly blond and one of them not female. On balance, though, there is a core of true talent that might have gone unrecognized without the program. Maybe that's how I justify my involvement, but watch tonight and see if you can, hand on heart, disagree with me. I don't think you'll have any difficulty picking out my top three. I hold my head high and swear that I still think Calvin deserves to win. If you bear in mind the heartache he's unwittingly put me through, you know he must have a powerful talent for me to say that.

I'm feeling nervous for him, though, and also for me. It's down to the wire now and tonight's result is going to reflect not just on Calvin, but on me too. On whether all I've been through was worth it.

Chapter Fifteen

I think it's obvious which three I would have ditched immediately. And in a typical Cruel Carol way, I made that clear at the end of their performances. I just don't see the point of entering a competition that's to do with the legacy of the likes of Marvin Gaye, Sam Cooke, Otis Redding, Aretha Franklin, Gladys Knight, and Patti LaBelle if you can't sing. I think it's an insult to all they've achieved. But you might have got the idea from what I had to say. I was angry at the other judges for letting them get this far and I suppose all the tension of the last weeks came flooding out, and for that, I do apologize, but I still think I was right.

"If you even came here believing you had an ounce of talent, then the least you could do was work at it. You've had an opportunity that others would have killed for and you've wasted it. You thought that big breasts and a firm backside would see you through. That ain't the way this show works. I don't think the audience should give you the time of day."

"Let me check my notes. That was supposed to be Aretha's 'Natural Woman.' I suppose that was the genetically modified version. Have you ever *really* listened to that song? Do you know what Aretha was singing about? You need to age about thirty years before you dare try that song again."

"This could be the most depressing night of my life. For weeks you've been getting advice, coaching, and all the help you could possibly hope for. You've obviously chosen to ignore it. If you win tonight, then I'll stop believing that there's a God."

Maybe a bit harsh, but you must admit that they were truly dreadful. On the other hand, there was the handful of truly phenomenal performances. The sixteen-year-old I'd originally heard way back when on that tape in Adrian's office she sang her heart out and made mine almost stop with her version of Toni Braxton's "He Wasn't Man Enough." You wanted to ask how she could possibly understand the bitterness that went into the making of that song. I also held my breath as the forty-two-year-old father of four poured his whole being into "Dock of the Bay," tearing my heart apart as he captured the loneliness I felt.

And still, towering above the rest, there was Calvin. He'd decided to listen to our advice. He walked out onto the stage in a stylishly tailored, deceptively simple black suit, white shirt open at the neck. Gone was the beard. And there was nothing dodgy under it. Looking tall, slim, elegant, even more impossibly handsome and younger than his years, he took the microphone and looked up hesitantly at the camera, making us all feel for his youth, his vulnerability. He'd taken my words too much to heart, definitely choosing a song we'd all recognize. But Marvin Gaye's "Sexual Healing?" A bold, reckless choice, since no one, surely, could do justice to that song, could come close to the repressed sexuality of Marvin's performance.

I was wrong. He started softly, caressing each note, holding back, teasing, looking up at the camera under long, dark, innocent-looking lashes. And then, on the second verse, he took a step forward, stood tall and proud, spread one arm, and looked directly into the lens, eyes narrowed, growling a desperate need. My heart rose to my throat and I held my breath not wanting to hear what would come next. Suddenly, the sound came out in a whisper, gently stroking skin. The hairs on my arms stood on end as the sound grew, deeper, louder, higher and higher until he was screaming for release, and then he held the note, until everyone felt they couldn't take any more, and he let it go, releasing us all to whisper that last phrase, and he closed his eyes, bowing his head in surrender, vulnerable, offering himself up to his fate. His voice died and he opened his eyes, turned, looked straight into my eyes, and smiled that slow, sensuous, irresistible smile of his.

For several moments, there was not a sound, and then the tentative, embarrassed applause. It grew and exploded into thunder and everyone was on their feet, as if reaching out to Calvin to make him look at them until, finally, he turned to the audience as if coming out of a trance and mouthed "Thank you" before lowering his head in a not-quite bow.

Quentin first: "Truly stupendous, young man. Fine, fine performance. You deserve to go far." Applause.

Max: "Respect, brotha!" It wasn't just a phrase. You could tell he truly meant it.

Gary, as controlled as ever: "You took my advice, Calvin. You've worked hard and you deserve a long career in the business. There's stiff competition tonight so it's going to be tough." I found myself glaring at him, but then he redeemed himself. "But that was the finest performance I've seen. You're the best, bro."

And, as I'd known would happen, all eyes were on me. Everyone held their breath waiting for what I would say and what I would reveal of myself. Against all the instruction we'd been given, I stood, took a deep breath, walked toward him, and looked straight into Calvin's eyes.

"Calvin, believe me, I know how difficult the last few weeks must have been for you." There was nervous laughter from the audience, but I wouldn't let myself be distracted. I paused for just a moment. "This shit must have been so hard when all you wanted was to be judged on your talent alone. There have been any number of banana skins thrown in your path, but you've avoided them all. You know I've always believed in your talent since that first audition. But, all the same, I was very, very nervous when I realized what you'd chosen to sing. Marvin must be the hardest act to follow: devastatingly handsome, talented, and yes, sexy as hell." I waited for the laughter to die down. "But tonight your family must be very proud of you. You've lived up to the faith we've had in you," I hesitated. "The faith *I've* had in you. If the viewers decide to vote for you, I think you'll be a very, very worthy winner. You were simply incredible." I found myself choking back emotion, so I sat down, to a round of applause.

I was dancing on coals once the show went off the air. Calvin was clearly the front-runner, but you know

how often the talented black guy manages to get himself voted out first. Well, we had to wait two hours for
the result and I couldn't eat, just managed to force alcohol down my throat and chat idly with some of the
hundreds of people who turned up for the after-show
party.

In the end, the voting was closer than I would have
expected—viewers obviously taken in by the big tits.
Finally, in spite of the long, drawn-out announcement
that Adrian had ordered, Calvin triumphed. For a very
brief moment, I felt as if all was well in the world.

We'd done the job we'd been asked to do and,
oddly, I knew I'd miss both the highs and the lows of
the last months. I looked around. I wouldn't miss Adrian,
but I'd even developed a soft spot for Quentin. Gary?
Well, our paths would cross, I was sure, but I could
handle him now. And Max . . .

At that precise moment, he looked at me and
walked across the room toward me. There was obviously a great deal of interest in what might happen
since several pairs of eyes followed him. Max made
me nervous. His every move was so intense, focused,
unrelenting. He took me by the hand.

"Let's find somewhere quiet, honey."

We walked outside and I was glad to get away
from the feverish atmosphere, but afraid of what was
to come.

"Guess it's all over now." He entwined his fingers
with mine and then brought my hand to his lips. "I'm
going to miss being with you."

"Are you, Max?"

His eyes were clear, unshadowed. I think he was telling the truth. "I've never stopped thinking about you, Carol. But God knows I didn't have the right to try to find you. I hurt you bad."

"Max, you don't have to say anything. I think I understand."

"You know it was never anything to do with you. It was just all the shit—"

"It was also a long time ago, Max."

"And you don't feel anything for me now?" He moved closer to me and bent his head to kiss me. I couldn't help but respond. I think I'll always love Max, but in the cold light of evening, there was no passion. Tenderness, but no longing. Max pulled back, looked at me for a moment, and then held me close for a few seconds more.

"Too late, honey?"

I stared at him, pondering. I nodded. "Max, I'll always care about you."

"It helps to know that." He put his arm around me as we walked back into the party. I could see Eddy's anxious eyes waiting for our return. He looked relieved when I smiled at him.

I clearly remember the precise moment when all hell started to break loose. I was in a group that included Gary, Quentin, and Seamus, the editor, who was subtly making a not-so-coded apology to me about that first program, which I accepted knowing better than to blame the messenger. I appreciated the fact that he was making clear to the others what had been happening

behind the scenes. He was, after all, risking the wrath
of Adrian and, therefore, his job.

The next thing I remember, Eddy joined the group
and was chatting with Gary. Then Rob appeared from
nowhere, congratulating me on a job well done. I was
feeling curiously detached from him. Then Calvin, excited, overjoyed, exuberant, boyish, rushed over. "I was
going to introduce you guys, but you know each other
already!" He was smiling at me and Rob. I didn't know
what he was talking about and it must have shown.
"You know Rob," he repeated, "my lawyer!"

It all fell into place. Calvin knowing my address.
Photographer waiting. Story leaked to the press. I didn't
dare to look at Rob. Instead, I turned to Eddy. He looked
into my eyes and I could see understanding dawning
on his face. A barely perceptible nod before he took
Rob by the elbow and steered him away.

I hardly heard Calvin's heartfelt thanks, his promise that he'd never forget what I'd done for him, how
he swore he'd make me really proud of him, how Rob
had already got him a recording contract worth tons of
cash, how he owed it all to me and when could he see
me again? I didn't need to respond since flashbulbs
popped and he was soon surrounded by a crowd of
would-be hangers-on.

It was in a daze that I collected my coat and bag
and headed in the direction where I'd last seen Eddy
and Rob.

I walked around the corner and almost bumped into
them. Rob was lying in a gutter, exactly where he belonged. Eddy was walking away from him, toward me,
rubbing his knuckles. I ignored him and approached
Rob. He scrabbled to his feet, wiped his bruised lip,
and looked at me. I stared at the cut above his eye-

brow, the swollen, half-closed eye. I think he was feeling humiliated, because the tears welled into his one healthy eye. The pitiful look on his face brought back the tearful Rob Elliott that melted my heart all those years ago. I took a step forward, brought my arm up, and smacked his face as hard as I could. And then I walked away.

Chapter Sixteen

It's incredible the way all the papers were convinced of Calvin's talents all along, or so they're claiming now. He's the darling of the tabloids and you can't walk past any newspaper stand without seeing his face somewhere. I haven't avoided the articles. I feel genuinely proud of him, and he's been careful in all his interviews to put the record (almost) straight about the two of us. In fact, he waxes lyrical about how grateful he is for my support and the encouragement I gave. He calls me endlessly, wanting to carry on where we left off, not seeing the problem now that the show's over. He's sweet. I laugh gently at him. We won't meet up too often, though. Calvin can still send shivers down my spine and it's probably best to stay out of the way of temptation.

The publicity hasn't done me any harm and there have been one or two interesting job offers coming my way. I need a break from television for a while, though. I haven't yet made up my mind about the medium. It's dangerous in the wrong hands, and I don't know if I can handle it yet. It has taken too much out of me for now and I need to be sure that the results will justify all the heartache.

I don't know how much longer I'll be at *The Cream*. It's weird the way everyone treats me so differently. Oliver's almost subservient, and Georgina's forever offering me cups of coffee, cookies, cakes—I think if I allowed her, she'd be willing to wipe my arse. I don't understand this godlike status that an appearance on television confers on you. I can't say that I feel any more kindly toward Oliver or Georgina; though, to give them their due, they try to be a little discreet when they're around me. And Patrick? Well, Eddy's a true pal. He told me all about Patrick's role in the newspaper fiasco. It seems that Rob called Patrick to tip him off about Calvin's visit. He made a lot of money out of the story, but Eddy has him paying it back in ways that he could never have imagined in his worst nightmares. Every time Eddy has a story in the most dangerous parts of the country, the kind of place where, if you're not known, you're likely to get your equipment stolen at best and your head kicked in at worst, then he'll put in a special request for Patrick to accompany him. Of course, Eddy makes sure that he comes to no harm—I want the torture to go on for a very long time—but he lets him get to the point where he almost shits himself in panic.

According to what Rob told Eddy, he hadn't started out intending to screw me (metaphorically, at least). That's some comfort. I like to tell myself that he genuinely liked me or, at least, truly lusted after me. It's just that when I told him that I'd been chosen as a judge on *Soul Sensation* he saw his opportunity. To be as generous to him as I can, he was doing the best for

his client. It was Rob's idea that Calvin should enter
the competition. I think he intended to subtly influence
me in his direction until he realized that he really didn't
need to. I could have guessed that much, but I was puzzled by the salacious newspaper articles. Eddy says it
was, just as he thought, all about keeping Calvin in the
public eye. It was Rob who'd given Calvin my address
and suggested that he talk to me. It was just coinciden-
tal that the slant Adrian put on that first program helped
to spice up the story. I still feel hurt that Rob could use
me like that. Eddy keeps reminding me that there was
nothing personal in it. Nicola feels bad about bringing
the two of us together, but I remind her that I'm older
and wiser and should have known better than to trust
her judgment.

As for Eddy, I tell myself that one lesson I learned
in all of this is that I can get by without him. In the end,
I had to walk away from Eddy's comforting shoulder
and do it on my own. And I survived. I think our
friendship has too.

There was a bit of bridge building that needed to be
done. We'd skated around each other after that night
together, hesitating to touch any of those sensitive places
in each others' minds. I really didn't want to lose the
closeness that we'd had, so I suggested taking off work
today and taking a picnic to the coast. Eddy agreed,
as long as he brought the food. I don't know why he
doesn't trust my culinary skills! Well, actually, I do.
He keeps reminding me that he's braved the inside of
my fridge.

We took Eddy's Saab convertible. It was a glorious
end-of-summer day, pale blue sky, weak sun promising uncrowded beaches. I've driven with too many men
who roar away at traffic lights so you're pinned to the

back of the seat, fixed grin on your face, teeth ready to catch flies. Eddy's not like that. He's confident, self-assured, and he handles his car like it's an extension of his personality, forcefully but without aggression. As we headed south out of London, I felt the tension seeping out of my shoulders. We didn't talk much. I think we were both happy that we felt comfortable enough in each other's company not to have to speak. Until I saw the first signs for the Eastbourne seafront.

"First one to spot the sea gets a prize!"

Eddy won. "What's my prize?"

"I haven't decided yet. Depends on whether or not you're a good boy."

"Hey, you can't change the rules now. I won fair and square and I want my prize."

"Double or nothing?"

"Okay."

By now, he'd found a place to park on the almost empty beachfront. There was a slight chill in the salty air and the possibility of rain hung like a threat. I surreptitiously eased my feet out of my shoes and opened the car door.

"Right. Race you to the sea. Last one in is a jelly-fish."

I left him struggling with shoes and socks and I dashed from the car, sprinting to the beach, then trying to pick my way across hard, sharp pebbles. I made the mistake of looking back, wasting valuable seconds. Eddy was gaining on me, his long legs easily making up the ground between us. I was only going to win by guile.

"Eddy!" I screamed, pointing. "Did you put the emergency brake on?" As he looked round, I ran as fast as I could, but I still hadn't got far enough ahead. Just a few feet from the cold, foaming waves I felt myself being lifted into the air, over Eddy's shoulder as he strode into the water.

"Put me down, you cheat!" I screamed, laughing. "You're a bully. You can only win by cheating."

"Look who's talking. What about the emergency brake scam? Anyway, I want double the prize now."

"Cheats don't prosper," I giggled, still hanging upside down. "I'm not giving you any prize now. Just put me down."

"Okay." Eddy dumped me in the water. I grabbed hold of his leg and pulled him down to join me. We were both soaked, though giggling like children. Eddy stood, offering a hand and pulling me up. There was just about enough weak sun to dry us off. We trudged back to the car, got the picnic and blankets, and set off up the hill. I was out of breath by the time we got to the top but knew I'd never have made it if I hadn't given up smoking.

I sat down on the blanket while Eddy sorted out the food: jerk chicken, saltfish fritters, spinach patties, potato salad, coleslaw, and cans of Red Stripe beer. I ate until I could force no more into my stomach. "Eddy, you're quite a cook. I can't tell you how good that was."

"Any time, babes. You looking much better than you've looked for weeks."

"So what you complaining about now? I ain't had no bad hair days recently."

"You know that's not what I mean, Carol. You just look less tense, a lot happier than you have done. I know it's been hard. We were all beginning to worry about you."

"Who's 'we'?"

"Your folks, Nicola, Gabby, me . . . It's like you turned away from all of us."

"I just needed a bit of time out, Eddy."

"I guess. Rob must have really hurt you."

"Uh-huh. But it's not just about Rob, really." I looked away from him.

"We're not all like Rob, you know. We all love you, Carol, and want to help. But it's like you're pushing us away."

I looked into his concerned eyes. "Honestly, I'm not, Eddy. You're my friend."

I couldn't quite figure out his expression. As if he was looking for something in my eyes that he didn't find. I had to keep any emotion from my face. I couldn't let Eddy know how I was feeling about him. It wouldn't be fair. He had Gabby now, and I could only imagine how much she needed him. The best I could hope for was to get back to the relaxed friendship that we'd enjoyed before that perfect night together.

"You know what I need, Eddy?"

"What?"

"Cotton candy. We can't come to the seaside and not get cotton candy."

"You'll be sick!"

"Won't!"

"Bet you will!"

"Won't!"

"Okay. Race you to the pier, then."

"No, I beg you, Eddy. Let's just stroll to the pier."

Gathering up the picnic stuff, we walked arm in arm to the car, and then to the pier. Eddy managed to resist cotton candy, but we bought enough rock candy to stock a market stall. We went to the arcade and lost lots of cash on the half-dollar crane machines that used to be penny machines and soon will be five-dollar machines. I came *so* close to winning. A metaphor for my life. Eddy, however, managed to grab a hideous, fluorescent yellow furry animal with the crane. A gift from him that I'll probably always treasure. For this day, this moment, I felt truly carefree, happier than I could remember being for a long while.

We walked aimlessly, hand in hand along the shore, competing to see who could throw pebbles the farthest. This was how I loved the English seaside best. Dark skies lowering, wind rising, chill waves. So much more dramatic than summer lethargy and knotted handkerchiefs. I think we were content just being together, reestablishing the carefree, relaxed intimacy, not speaking, lost in our own thoughts, together. It was a special moment. And then lightning flashed, the wind lifted, and drops of rain began to fall, gently at first and then hard and fast so that by the time we reached the car, we were drenched.

We sat in the back and Eddy wrapped a blanket around me, along with his arms. I was shivering, but not just with the cold. I'd have preferred to put as much space as possible between us, but that's pretty impossible in the backseat of a car. I guess there was stuff that Eddy wanted to get off his chest too, 'cos he sure took the opportunity while I was trapped.

"Babes, I think we're cool now, but you left so suddenly and you never returned my calls. I felt bad. I didn't mean to take advantage of you, but I guess that's what I did. I apologize. The last thing I wanted to do was to hurt you any more."

"Eddy, you don't have to apologize. You didn't do

anything wrong. What happened was just as much my fault."

"Then why wouldn't you talk to me?" There was an angry edge to his voice that I regretted provoking. But at the same time, when we'd made love he hadn't been thinking about Gabby either. It wasn't entirely my fault, and although I wanted his friendship more than anything (well, almost anything), I wasn't about to take all the responsibility.

"I guess it was the wrong time, for both of us." What is it about us women that we have to cushion their hurt? It wasn't necessarily the wrong time for me at all. Well, okay, so there had been Rob, and Calvin, and Max, but I hadn't made any commitment to any of them.

I could hardly make out his face in the growing gloom. I think it was easier that way. "Eddy, I want to thank you."

"For what?"

"I've had such a good day."

"Me too, babe." We had a quick hug, which seemed to make everything all right again.

Eddy left me at my apartment, saying, "See you at the wedding." *Wedding?* Shit, I'd got so tied up in what was happening to me that I'd almost forgotten that my little sister was getting married on Saturday. It was late, but I had to call Nicola.

"Sis?"

"Carol?"

"How you doing? Nic, I'm so sorry I've been neglecting you. It's your wedding on Saturday."

"I know."

"But I'm not ready."

Nicola laughed. "It's all right, Sis. I'm ready."

"You sure? I haven't given you the pep talk yet."

"I think I can live without it. What you goin' tell me that I don' know already."

"You're my little sister. I certainly hope you don't already know everything I was thinking of telling you."

"Hey, girl. I'm not as young as you think."

"I know, Sis. Seriously, though, you happy?"

"Carol, I know you have your worries about Vince, but—"

"You don't have to explain anything to me. Nic, I know I've always treated you like you're a mindless idiot, but you don't have to tell me anything about Vince. I've no right to judge him. I've just been worried about you."

"I know, Carol. Just like Mom and Dad worry about us. I'm glad that you worry. That's what an older sister is for. But, honestly, I'm a big girl now."

"Believe me, Nicola, I know that. It's taken a bit of time to acknowledge that I don't always know best. Sis, it's your life and I'm sure you know what you're doing. I'm not going to worry any more. If you love him and you've chosen him, that's good enough for me. As long as you're happy."

"I am, Sis. At least I think I am. See you Saturday."

"See you, Nicola. Love you."

I put down the receiver. My little sister hadn't done so badly with her life after all. I suppose there was no reason for me not to believe what Vince had told me. He loved her and they'd worked out a way of living together that suited them both. More than I'd managed. But I'm going to pull myself out of this negative thinking. I've got through the last months. I can survive anything. Think happy thoughts, Carol! Be happy! And for God's sake, don't start with that New Age shit!

I had to make one more call, although I was reluctant. Why was I frightened? Gabby was my best friend. Correction: *is* my best friend. And I want her to be happy. God knows, she's been through so much and deserves better than the way Pete has treated her. She and Eddy are my closest friends, so it's no surprise that they would get on. I should congratulate myself on being such an excellent matchmaker. I'd been ignoring Gabby, so it was time to make amends. Besides, I was on a goodwill high and I knew that Gabby was sure to be awake at one o'clock in the morning. Another reason for hesitating was that I didn't know if she'd be alone.

I could tell immediately that there was more than a hint of frost in her voice. "Oh hi, Carol. Wasn't expecting it to be you."

No sense in trying to make any excuse, Gabby knows me too well. "I am really sorry, Gabby. I've been egotistical, inconsiderate, rude, self-centered, selfish, stupid, thoughtless, ungrateful, uncaring . . ."

"Well, you can stop when you get to V in the alphabet." But at least she laughed. "Seriously, though, girl, why you been ignoring me? You know how worried I been about you?"

"I know, Gabby. I guess I just needed some time away from everyone."

"And that includes me? That hurts, Carol."

"I didn't mean to hurt you. You know how much I love you."

"You had time for Eddy, though. You know, one of the reasons I've been upset with you is that I think I felt jealous of Eddy."

I laughed, but without much humor. "Funnily enough, I suppose I felt jealous too."

"Why?"

"I'm not sure, Gabby. I know I don't have any right to feel jealous. I feel bad because I know I should want the best for him. Just like I want the best for you. I surprised myself, you know. I didn't think I'd feel so upset. And I think I didn't want to admit to myself that I could be so selfish. I don't want to be such a horrible person."

"And you couldn't talk to me about it?"

"How could I talk to you, Gabby? You're the last person I wanted to know what I was thinking."

"I'm getting a bit lost here, Carol. Back up. You're saying that you're jealous because Eddy's got a new woman in his life?"

"Yes."

"So why you didn't want to talk to me about it? You've never had that kind of problem with me in the . . . Oh my God! . . . Carol, you don't think . . . You can't . . . ." Gabby couldn't continue. The laughter that had been bubbling up in her voice exploded and I had to hold the phone away from my ear as she screamed in hysterics. I could imagine her doubled up in pain as I heard the gasps as she fought for breath. I didn't understand what was so funny and half hoped that she'd choke. My right foot began to tap impatiently as I waited for her to control herself.

After what seemed like ten minutes at least, I heard Gabby take a deep breath. "Oh, Carol, thank you. I haven't laughed so much for a very long time. I should be angry with you, but I feel too sorry for you, poor cow that you are. All this time you thought that Eddy and I had got it on, didn't you?"

I couldn't see any way out of this one. "Well, yes. What else was I supposed to think? Eddy told me what he thinks of you—"

"Really? What did he say?"

I ignored that fishing expedition. "And you called me wanting to know all about him. Then you guys were spending so much time together. What else was I supposed to think?"

"You could have thought that we were just friends. Or you could have asked me. I'll admit that I was interested in Eddy at first. I was feeling so low after the breakup with Peter and he's just the kind of guy you need around at a time like that. Eddy knows how to look after a woman. He boosts my ego, makes me feel good. Yes, I enjoy his company, spending time with him. But that's as far as it goes."

"Oh yes?" I responded skeptically.

"Yes." Her response was firm. No trace of laughter now. "Is it so impossible for you to believe that Eddy might really like me—as a friend? Nothing else, Carol. Serve you right that you've been torturing yourself. The reason we've been spending so much time together is that I've been worried about you. I rang after the first program because you didn't talk about Max. And then there was Calvin. You wouldn't return my calls and the only way I could find out what's been going on was through Eddy. We've been together because he cares about you, too, and we've been trying to figure out the best way to help you get through all this shit. Anyway, Peter and I are, at least, talking again, so who knows what might happen?"

Did I suddenly feel like a turkey! "Gabby, I really am sorry. I've been so stupid. Of course Eddy would want you as a friend. You're a great friend. That's why I love you so much. You're an angel."

I was relieved to hear her laugh again. "I'm not *that* innocent, you know. If I'm truthful, I can't swear that I'd have turned Eddy down if he'd made a move. But he didn't. And you know why he didn't?"

"Why?"

"Cho, girl. You ain't got no brains? Figure it out."

Chapter Seventeen

The morning was chaotic. I arrived at Mom's house at the crack of dawn wishing that Nicola hadn't chosen an early autumn day to get married. Sure the sky had a romantic orange glow, but it was chilly and I would have done almost anything to be curled under the duvet. The house was already bustling, though, since I was the last to arrive. It was only six-thirty but Mom looked daggers at me. "What time of day you call this, child? I was just about to pick up the phone to ring you. And if I did find that you still in you bed . . ." Mom was wise enough to leave to my imagination what she would have done. I shivered.

"Come, eat you breakfast." Food was Mom's cure for everything, even lateness, and I was grateful for the plate of ackee and saltfish, boiled green bananas, and fried dumplings. She'd even made real hot chocolate. I realized that for as long as I could remember, this had been the "special occasion" breakfast—birthdays, anniversaries, Christmas. Nicola's wedding day certainly wouldn't have seemed right without this family ritual.

Okay, so Dad wasn't around, but you couldn't have everything.

"Where's Nic?" I asked, devouring the meal.

"Slow down, Carol. The food not goin' nowhere." I felt about six years old again. "Nicola sleeping, I hope. Let the child sleep. She goin' need it since this is probably the last good sleep she goin' get for a while." She laughed.

I nearly choked. Smut from my mother? And I think she even winked!

"When you finish, Bea in the living room with the others, waiting for you." Mom bustled away, leaving me alone in the kitchen.

I took time to savor the food and what would be the last few moments of peace in the day. I realized that I was feeling truly happy for my sister. All the activity going on around me, the controlled excitement that I sensed in my mother's every move, the hint of butterflies that I felt in my own stomach were all because we loved Nicola and wanted this day to be special, portentous with the hope that the rest of her life would be equally happy. I comforted myself with the thought that my previous dislike of her husband-to-be was only because I wanted the best for Nicola. I'd put all that behind me, accepting Vince's explanation of his behavior, and I was determined to make this day as perfect for Nicola as I possibly could. I was picturing a flower-filled church, the heady scent of white lilies, the buzzing of the congregation, a gasp as the bride enters in flowing white, her adoring fiancé, elegant in black awaiting his beloved, gazing adoringly . . .

"So, Sis, who's this mystery man you bringing to my wedding, then?" Nicola asked, pinching the last piece of dumpling from my plate.

Trust my sister to shatter the mood. I'd been feeling warm, fuzzy, thoughts about her and now she had to remind me of the promise I'd made. Of course, I'd forgotten that I'd told her I'd be bringing someone to the wedding. Her look was all innocence, but I guess she never believed me in the first place.

"The way you look this morning, I'd bet there ain't going to be no wedding today. Vince goin' take one look at you and run screaming in terror down the aisle."

She poked her tongue out at me. "Nah!"

"Nah! With wedding bells on."

"Girls! Behave yourselves!" Mom's reproach was automatic. "Nicola, sit down and let me get your breakfast. Carol, get yourself into the living room. Now! We ain't got time for no tomfoolery today." Nicola and I both looked shamefaced until Mom looked away, and then we poked our tongues out again. But I gave her a quick hug before surrendering myself to Aunt Bea.

I guess all the stress I've been through was positive in one way: I seem to have lost a pound or two and Aunt Bea was not happy at all. "I don't expect you girls to do this to me. I did leave a little room for you to put on a bit of flesh and you go and lose weight!" She had to do her best with safety pins and a few tacks here and there to stop my bridesmaid's dress looking like a shiny tent. I'm not claiming that I'm thin or anything like that, but the curves all seem to be in the right places now.

The ringing at the doorbell was constant as the cars turned up, flowers were delivered, and finally, Dad arrived. He looked so handsome in his dark suit, white shirt, and silvery gray tie. And I could see that Mom

appreciated his good looks because she suddenly became coy and girly. "Travis, you hungry? I have some
food in the kitchen if you want."

"Josie, you looking good yourself. You as beautiful as the first day I did see you." He said it in a matter-
of-fact way as he bent to kiss her cheek, but you could
see Mom blush with pleasure. Obviously, it takes your
daughter being publicly humiliated to bring about a
reconciliation. If only I'd known before!

The next hour was frantic as we rushed around lo-
cating the something old, new, borrowed, and blue and
answered panicky calls from distant relatives who
couldn't find the church. Before I was ready, the cars
were at the door and everything was quiet, the sudden
hush eerie. Mom and I both took time to be alone with
Nicola. I don't know what went on between the two of
them, but Mom came out of Nicola's room looking all
calm and serene.

It was my turn, and as we hugged I felt as if my
heart was going to swell up and burst through my chest
walls. This was my little sis. I'd looked after her since
the day she was born, and now I was letting her go. It
was okay for Mom and Dad; they'd prepared themselves for this day, but I hadn't given it a thought.
Tears welled in my eyes.

"Don't cry, Sis. Be happy for me."

"So what *you* crying for? I am happy, Sis." We
sniffed in unison for a while. "I want this to be the best
day of your life so far, Nicola. But I want it to get happier every day from now on. I goin' miss you."

"What you talking 'bout? I ain't goin' nowhere."

"It won't be the same."

"It'll be the same if we want it to be, Sis."

"Since when you get so wise?" We smiled at each

other. "You know I'll always be there for you, Nic. Anything at all. You just have to ask."

"Thanks, Carol. It'll be your turn very soon. I'm absolutely sure. I know I tease you about men, but I don't mean any of it. You know I think you're the best that any man could get. That's why I tried to fix you up with that bastard Rob. Sis, I'm so sorry. That was all my fault."

"Nicola, how many times you goin' tell me you sorry. This is the last time I'm going to say that it wasn't your fault at all. Let's not feel guilty about this one, Sis. That would be like taking some of the blame away from him. It was his fault and his fault alone. And I hope he rots in hell."

"Me, too, but I hope he suffers first." There was a brief pause as we both thought our own thoughts and mentally breathed a sigh of relief, consigning Rob to damnation.

"So what's got into Mom? Why was she all pink and flustered?"

"Dad arrived. But you'll never guess what she said. I could have died with embarrassment. Something about letting you sleep since you ain't goin' get no more sleep."

"No!"

"And have you seen the way she is around Dad? Girl, we have to keep an eye on them two—"

"Carol! Get your behind down here. This ain't the time for no chatting. Time don't wait on no man." Mom's voice interrupted any further discussion of her behavior and I gave Nicola another hug, making way for Dad.

When Dad and Nicola emerged from her room, the family trait emerged again. All our mouths fell open.

Dad could hardly take his eyes from Nicola and you
could see his chest visibly swelling with pride. In all
the bustle I hadn't had a chance to really look at Nicola.
Her white dress was simple, cut so that it hugged her
figure tightly. Long-sleeved, high-necked, trimmed with
randomly scattered seed pearls, it made her look de-
mure and yet sexy at the same time. And Nicola looked
more confident than I'd ever known her. My little sister was all grown up. Maybe it was about time that *I*
grew up. It was with visible emotion and great humility that Dad kissed Nicola's hand and joined it to
Mom's. Mother and daughter looked at each other for
a moment as if with mutual understanding, some eso-
teric knowledge that shut me out. I followed as the two
of them walked to the waiting car.

The vicar signaled to the organist. He began to play
the traditional "Here Comes the Bride," and as we
walked down the aisle, approaching Vince, I heard the
familiar words "Dearly Beloved, we are gathered to
celebrate this thing called . . . Life," and Prince began
to rock the church with "Let's Go Crazy." Nicola
looked back at me and winked. She was trying not to
laugh. This was her coded surprise for me. It took me
back to the days when we'd fought over who was
going to marry the "sex thimble." Everyone else was
taken aback, but even the most conservative were soon
tapping their feet. And then we were into the real meat
of the service and I found the tears returning when
Nicola said "I do" and all too soon they were pronounced husband and wife.

As the final photograph was being arranged, I felt
an arm slip around my waist and I looked up into Eddy's

beautiful eyes. I hadn't had time to seek him out in all the traditional wedding activity.

"How you doing, babe?"

"I'm fine, Eddy. Doesn't she look beautiful?"

Eddy glanced at Nicola. "Not as beautiful as you." There was a serious look in his eyes too. I felt the heat rise to my cheeks as his gaze lowered to the cleavage revealed by the tight satin. When he looked up again, I could see the uncertainty in his eyes. I needed to make my intentions clear. I reached up, held his face, and kissed him deeply. He looked surprised but recovered quickly.

"I've never been good at weddings, you know. We could just slip away," he whispered.

"Eddy!" I slapped his arm playfully. "This is my sister's wedding. How could you suggest such a thing?"

He looked at his watch. "In ten minutes?"

"No!"

"Twenty minutes?"

I laughed. "Eddy, stop it!"

"How long it goin' take for you to do what you have to do? Thirty minutes tops?"

"Eddy, you're not serious?"

"Well, not while your mother's watching us!" He took a step away from me and I immediately wanted to be back in his arms. But he was right, my mother was watching, keenly.

From then on, Eddy didn't leave my side. I wondered who had arranged the seating so that he was next to me at our table. I didn't need three guesses since Nicola kept winking at me in a highly theatrical way. Even when I had to do the round of family and friends, he was never far away, and whenever my gaze strayed back to him, I knew that he'd be looking in my direction. I felt a tremor of excitement each time I caught his eye.

Mom is trying to make us into one of those families that has traditions and so she'd agreed with Nicola that they'd open the dancing with "Red, Red Wine," the song that she and Dad had danced to on their wedding day all those years ago. It might seem an insensitive choice with Pauline there, but I know Mom didn't mean it like that. I think she just wanted Nicola and Vince to experience the intimacy and peace and joy that she and Dad had once shared. I got the feeling that not only had Mom and Dad reconciled, but earlier I'd even noticed her chatting easily with Pauline and petting the children. Even so, it would have been too much for her to dance with Dad, so I was thrilled when Dad came over and asked for the first dance. Swaying to the familiar rhythms with my father, I felt a deep sense of peace as I looked around at my family. It really did seem as if life was perfect. I giggled to myself as I noticed the number of elderly gentlemen competing to dance with my mother and Eddy gliding around the room with a tiny flower girl balanced precariously on his shoes. The thing was, he looked quite absorbed in her and that made my heart leap. I guess we're genetically predisposed to fancy guys who cherish children. Makes sense.

So Nicola danced with Vince, Eddy danced with maiden aunts, Nicola danced with Vince, I danced with uncles, Nicola danced with Vince, Eddy danced with eligible cousins, I danced with eligible cousins, Dad danced with Pauline, Nicola danced with Vince, Eddy danced with Mom and I longed to be in her place.

Then, finally, I was in Eddy's arms, slow dancing,

exactly what I'd longed for. His arms were strong, tight around me. I buried my head in his chest. Then, and this must be Eddy's doing, Calvin Brown was up on the makeshift stage and he was singing the most sensual song ever written: Marvin Gaye's "Let's Get It On." I was melting, my body molding to Eddy's.

"How did you manage to get him here, Eddy?"

"Oh, I just promised him I could arrange a date with you."

I pulled back from him, but he laughed.

"Seriously, I just called in a few favors. I wanted to make Nicola's wedding special."

I relaxed into his arms again, full of emotion for him. I guess he understood.

"Girl, the thirty minutes sure is up now."

I looked up at him. He looked serious. He bent down and kissed me gently on the lips. Now Eddy and I have kissed before, but maybe it was the occasion, the romance, the fairy-tale vibes being spread, but my world rocked. Something about the way he looked at me reminded me of what Gabby had said. I slowly began to put the clues together and wondered if I'd made one hundred and four out of two and two.

So Eddy was saying "All right, ten more minutes." And I was saying "Five." Then he was saying "Four," and I was begging "Now." Two and two really was one hundred and four. And then I looked around.

Mom was watching. Dad was watching. Aunt Bea was watching. Jason and Rosa were giggling behind their hands. I guess a hundred million relatives were hoping. Suddenly the focus of attention was on me and Eddy and everyone was smiling. Then Nicola chose that moment to throw her bouquet, directly at me. I don't need too many hints. That was our cue to leave.

I was in a kind of daze as we said our good-byes. It wasn't till I was hugging my baby sister that I noticed her new husband wasn't by her side. I didn't even think much of it as Nicola clung to me and whispered, "Go for it, Carol." I pretended not to know what she meant, but wished her a wonderful honeymoon and made her promise to call me as soon as she got back.

"I'll call, Sis, but the way things looking, you'll be too busy to talk to me." Her wink was beginning to look like some kind of medical problem. Eddy gave her a quick hug and took my arm as we went to retrieve my coat.

I suppose it was early. Maybe too early to be leaving a wedding. That's probably why Vince didn't expect anyone to come looking for coats. We were all taken by surprise. Quick-thinking Eddy managed to close the door behind us before anyone outside could get a glimpse of Vince and the blond bimbo who'd been looking after the coats.

They didn't have much to say for themselves. She just managed to retrieve her clothing and scuttle from the room before I lost it. It was the way Vince smiled at me that finally did it. I would have ripped his heart out if Eddy hadn't restrained me. And what made it worse was that I couldn't scream at him. Not at my sister's wedding. So I whispered, "You lying, good-for-nothing, low-down, cowardly, dirty dog." Well, actually, my language was a bit more colorful, but I'm in polite company now. I could feel the tremor rippling through Eddy's body as he held me back. I turned to look at him and saw his face, a granite mask. He let go of me and I stood motionless as every muscle in his body seemed to tense and solidify into iron. Vince took a step back as Eddy moved toward him. Eddy didn't touch him, but he didn't need to as Vince seemed to shrink in fear. I was terrified myself.

"I gave you one chance. I don't give nobody more than one chance. You hurt Nicola, you hurting my family, and I ain't goin' let that happen. You think about this, Vince. You think about this good. Either you decide to treat Nicola right or you take the earliest opportunity to just disappear out of her life. If you decide to stay and I hear say you do one thing to hurt her, then I promise you, I'll be coming after you." There was complete silence except for what I think was the sound of Vince's teeth chattering.

"And me too," I added feebly.

Chapter Eighteen

I was shaking all the way home. I'm not sure if it was shock or anger. I kept seeing, over and over, Vince's face as we walked into the cloakroom. I kept remembering, too, his protestations of innocence that night at the club. And gullible fool that I am, I'd allowed myself to believe him. I'm not sure whether I was more angry with Vince or with myself—again. In spite of my gut instincts and all the circumstantial evidence, I'd allowed myself to be conned.

"You okay, babe?" Eddy was looking at me with worry in his eyes. He managed to slip out of his jacket and wrap it round my shoulders, though I couldn't tell if I was cold. We got back to my apartment and Eddy held me close, stroking my hair, trying to calm me. I could tell by the set of his jaw that Eddy was furious too. In all the years I'd known him, I'd thought of him as a laid-back, mellow, gentle man, and yet, in just a week, I'd seen him roused to anger twice. And on both occasions it had involved me or a member of my family.

"You know, Eddy, I don't think we Shaws are any

good for you. You should run a mile when you see any of us coming." I tried to laugh, but it came out more like a sob. "What do you think will happen with Vince?"

"Well, whatever happens, Nicola is likely to get hurt. Maybe I shouldn't have told Vince to go. That probably should be Nicola's decision." The fierce look in his eye and the tight muscles reminded me of my father, so rarely roused to anger.

"But how could we tell her what happened, today of all days? Anyway, I've tried to warn her in the past, but she won't listen. She just thinks I've got something against her precious Vince and that I'm being unfair to him."

"All the same, I behaved like the sheriff in a low-budget Western." He mimicked the John Wayne walk. "Get out of town by sunset!" Eddy laughed and I could see the tension begin to seep from his body as he un-clenched his fists and relaxed his shoulders. I had to laugh too. He was right. The whole situation had been so B movie.

I poured us both a drink and sat on the sofa. Eddy joined me. "I guess the only good thing is that he knows we're watching him. One false step and I prom-ise I'll—"

"Eddy, don't say it. I really don't want today to end with anger. There's been enough of that for a while. We've done just about as much as we can for Nic. You know, Dad reminded me that she's an adult now. Vince told me that Nicola knows what he gets up to. I don't believe him, but maybe she knows more than we think. My little sister's not a child anymore, and I've got to remember that. One way or another, if she doesn't know what Vince is really like now, she'll find out soon enough. The only thing we can do is to be there for her when the time comes."

Eddy moved closer and kissed me gently on the cheek. "Since when you get so wise?" He smiled and just held me close for a while.

"Eddy?"

"Yeah, babe?"

"I've got to get out of this satin outfit and into something more comfortable."

"Sure thing."

I stood up and went into the bathroom, quickly unzipping my dress and slipping into my old, comfortable, pink bathrobe. I slipped into my bedroom and searched frantically for the thong that Gabby had bought me. This might be my only opportunity. When I got back, Eddy was draped across the sofa and he turned toward me, a look of disappointment in his eyes.

"Carol?"

"Yeah?"

"You know when you said something more comfortable . . ."

"Yes?"

"I thought you meant something more comfortable. Like a silk robe. Or a satin nightgown. Or stockings and suspenders."

"But I'm very comfortable in this," I teased.

"Come over here, babes. See if I can make you even more comfortable." Eddy held out his hand and I didn't hesitate for a moment. The desire in his eyes told me everything I needed to know and there was no reason to wait. Here was all the men I'd ever dreamed of wrapped up in one package.

Eddy pulled me down on top of him and kissed me hard, like this was something he couldn't wait for. I knew how he was feeling and I wasn't going to hold back. I wanted to lose myself in his arms and I pressed my body hard against his, struggling to get as close as I could. We kissed frantically and when we came up for air, he held me away from him.

"You sure, babe? You sure this is what you want? 'Cos you know I ain't goin' let you go again."

I looked into his eyes for a long while before answering, wanting to be certain of what I was seeing there. A hint of uncertainty, passion, concern, and something deeper than I'd ever seen in a man's eyes. I nodded. "I'm sure, Eddy. I want you more than anything else in the world."

He grinned, pushed me aside, and sprang up from the sofa.

"Eddy, where you going?" He didn't answer, but ran around the apartment like a whirling dervish, locking doors, unplugging every phone, switching off lights so that the room was lit only by the lamplight streaming through the windows. When he came back to me, he was laughing.

"Eddy, you going mad?"

"Babe, maybe I'm superstitious, but most times when we get this far, something gets in the way. This time, I ain't taking no chance." At that very moment his pager buzzed. He searched frantically for it and threw it across the room where it smashed into pieces. By now, we were doubled up with laughter.

We sobered up at the same moment, remembering where we'd got to. Eddy knelt down by the sofa. He took my face in both hands and kissed me oh so gently, brushing my lips with his tongue. I was honey, milk chocolate, marshmallow, treacle, syrup, molasses, everything sweet. I needed even more heat to melt me. I stood and started to loosen my dressing gown belt, but

Eddy held my hand away, wanting to do it himself. He pushed the gown off my shoulders and sat back on the sofa, just staring at my body, gasping at the sight of the thong. *Thank you, Gabby.* He didn't even have to touch me for the fire to start in my belly, tightening my stomach, making my nipples hard and my elbows tingle.

I didn't want to be apart from him. I bent down and knelt in front of him, his eyes following my every movement. I took his hand, kissed his fingers and placed them on my hip and then the same with the other hand. I moved nearer until I could straddle his knees. I kissed him again while I undid his tie and unbuttoned his shirt. Then I touched my lips to that tender spot under his chin and tickled it with my tongue. I ran my tongue along the length of his neck, wanting to taste the acrid saltiness of his skin. I heard a deep sigh, which encouraged me. I pulled his shirt out, needing his naked flesh against mine, and I touched his muscular, brown chest with my palms, just savoring the heat from his body that seemed to flow along my arms right down my spine. I wrapped my arms around him, clutching him tight, losing myself in the sensation of his bare skin surrounding mine. Then Eddy was kissing me again, his lips burning circles around my breasts, down my stomach, and I was pushed back onto the sofa, his fingers softly teasing my clitoris, making me shudder with excitement. I looked down and watched as he lifted his head, and then I saw the tip of his tongue headed for my clitoris. I tensed, just waiting to feel the touch. Sparks exploded and he was suddenly still, just the tip of his tongue resting there, motionless. I was frozen, not daring to move, frightened at the power of the growing sensation.

Then Eddy was above me, looking into my eyes.

He licked a finger and placed it on my lips. "I'm going to kiss you here." And his lips brushed mine, fleetingly. "And here." His finger touched my nipple and his lips followed. Then my stomach. My navel. My thighs. My calves. My feet. Then back up to my mound where he proceeded to finish what he'd started, licking, gently biting, sucking until I begged him to stop.

"Girl, I still haven't forgiven you for walking out on me last time. I'm going to make you pay." And he licked and stroked until I could bear it no longer and my body became rigid as I came in waves of pleasure, Eddy not stopping until he'd wrung the last drop of sweetness from me. He held me for a while then, unmoving, waiting, whispering arousing words in my ear.

"That's it, babe. Take it. I got even harder watching you come. I'm going to make you come again. Over and over. All night long. Babe, I've wanted you for so long. I ain't going to wait much longer. God, I'm so big and you're so wet. Let me feel how hot that pussy is. I want you so bad, Carol."

"And I want you, too, Eddy."

Before I knew what was happening, Eddy was behind me, his hard, heavy prick resting against my buttocks, his fingers fondling, squeezing my breasts; he was moving against me and the bubbles began in my vagina and then his fingers were there, teasing the mound of hair, slipping down and into my hot, slippery pussy fueling the fire and I was simmering as I felt his weight, and he was pushing my legs apart. My mouth was open and I was gasping. His finger was in my mouth and I could taste my own wetness as he slipped it in and out and I was sucking on it as the steam began to rise. Eddy lifted his hips and I was pushing myself upward to allow him entry. With one sharp thrust, he was inside me, moving in and out, 'round and 'round, rotating his hips, easing himself deeper as his finger rubbed my clitoris faster, ever faster and he was ramming his cock into me, no gentleness left as he fought to take everything I was offering. The froth of bubbles was rising faster, higher as I caught his rhythm, straining for release and I was hearing how hot my pussy was, how tight, how wet, feeling how big he was, how hard, how strong, and it was all for me. "All for you, Carol. Take it." And he was squeezing my nipples, thrusting deep, slow and I was on fire, bubbles effervescing, one strong, painful stroke and he was still, pressing deep against my womb and I was boiling over, melting into liquid, flowing into his body.

We lay for a while, wrapped in each other's arms. I watched as his eyelids began to droop. Eddy groaned as I took his nipple between my teeth, wanting to tease and arouse him again. This was going to be a long, slow night.

I lay back, happier than I could ever remember being. It was early in the morning. So eerily quiet, peaceful as if a spell had been cast over the whole of London so that nothing would disturb the moment. I turned to look at Eddy and all we could do was smile at each other. There was nothing more to say that our bodies hadn't already said. I didn't want to stop looking at his beautiful face, but eventually, I drifted into a blissful sleep.

I woke this morning with Eddy's body spooned around mine. I turned and smiled as he reached for me

in his sleep. I lay for the longest time just looking at
him, wondering how I'd managed to miss seeing what
I had. When Eddy woke, we kissed and just grinned at
each other for several minutes in that stupid way you
vow you'll never indulge in. I was thinking about all
that had happened yesterday and Eddy must have seen
the frown on my face.

"What is it, sugar?" He looked so concerned that
my heart ached.

"Eddy?"

"Yes, babe?"

"You know you told Vince that he was hurting
your family?"

"Yes."

"What did you mean?"

"You mean that after last night I have to explain
to you?"

"I just want to make sure."

"Okay. I want to make sure that you understand
too. Carol, I adore you, always have, from the moment
I met you. I've wanted you for so long. There's been
no one else for me. I've waited for you to feel the same
way. But there was Max—"

"Max isn't important, Eddy. There's a part of me
that will always care about him, but that doesn't matter."

"I know now, babe. But it took a long time for you
to get there. I guess I have *Soul Sensation* to thank for
that." He laughed. "You know, there were times when
I thought we'd finally got where I wanted to be, but I
was wrong."

"You should have told me how you felt."

"Is not just about how I felt. Is about how *you* feel
too, Carol. To put it bluntly, Carol. I love you. I've al-

ways loved you. I'll always love you. So your family is my family."

"Eddy, I love you too. I wish we hadn't wasted so much time."

"Shh! I don't plan to waste any more." Eddy kissed me again, just to prove what he'd been saying. Then he went on to prove what he'd said about wanting me, caressing my body, making me yearn for him again. But he stopped for a moment.

"You know I ain't joking, babe. Carol, I want you to marry me."

Of course, my mouth fell open. I could only stare at him.

"Babe, you need to get your mouth seen to. You goin' give me an answer?"

I leaped out of bed and ran around until I found my comfortable dressing gown. I got into it. Then I ran around some more collecting Eddy's clothes. I threw them at him.

"What the hell you doing, girl? You gone mad?"

"Get dressed, Eddy."

He looked at my face and then got up and struggled into his clothes. "Babe, what have I done now?"

When he was dressed, I pushed him toward the door. "Carol, just tell me. Did I say something wrong?"

I got him halfway out the door.

"Eddy Stanton, if I'm going to marry you, then there will be no more sex before marriage. What kind of girl you take me for?"

I slammed the door. But I'll always remember the smile on Eddy's face.

Don't miss Cydney Rax's next book in the
Love & Revenge series,

My Married Boyfriend

On sale wherever books and ebooks are sold
in September 2016!

1

The Sky Is Crying

Rashad Eason reached across the desk and handed the woman a fifteen-hundred-dollar cashier's check. She had pasty, pimpled white skin, a buzz haircut, and a thick mustache. She was very unattractive. To Rashad, she resembled a proud lesbian but that didn't matter. He had extensively researched Lily Tangaro online. He admired her track record and needed a competent person to do the job.

"You think you can get me everything I want?" he asked.

Lily examined the check, then reclined in her leather swivel chair. "You're serious about this, aren't you?" she said.

"More serious than a triple bypass."

"But it hasn't been that long since you physically separated from your wife."

"I know that. But if I don't do something fast, I may change my mind."

"I see." She paused. "We always recommend that the plaintiff think about the decision for six months."

"I can't wait that long. Thinking about this for six months would kill me."

She nodded and secured the retainer payment inside a classified file folder. "Sign these documents and we will get started on your case right away."

Rashad eagerly reviewed several papers that Lily gave to him. He took a blue pen and scribbled his name and the date. Then he stood and shook her hand.

"Thank you, Ms. Tangaro."

"Call me, Lily."

"Will do, Lily. And my son, Myles, really thanks you."

"Seriously? He's only six—"

"He's seven. Myles knows what's up. He's seen a lot, unfortunately. And this is why I gotta do this. It may be the only way I get to spend quality time with him. Plus, I don't want my son around his crazy mama any longer than he needs to be."

"Totally understandable. We'll be in touch."

"No doubt, Lily. I appreciate this."

Rashad drove away from his new attorney's office feeling more hopeful than he had in weeks.

It was a rainy Friday in Houston; the day after Thanksgiving. Rashad was lucky that Lily had agreed to meet him briefly in her office to sign his paperwork.

Light drops of water drizzled from the sky. Rainy days made Rashad feel depressed. But he had to shake it off and keep it moving. It was time to go see Myles. And spending time with his son was one of the few things he could be happy about these days.

When Rashad arrived at the designated pick-up spot, which was in front of Mama Flora's house, he let the car idle next to the curb. Technically, she could be considered his grandmother-in-law. Mama Flora was his wife's maternal grandmother, and the woman that raised Kiara. She was sensible and didn't stand for drama. Rashad and Kiara both agreed that exchanging Myles for visits at Flora's place would be the best option.

Rashad impatiently drummed his hands on the steering wheel. He listened to raindrops splatter on the ground. Minutes later, Kiara drove up and parked directly behind him. He observed her through the rearview mirror.

"Damn, I can barely see her but the woman still looks good," he admitted to himself. He hadn't laid eyes on Kiara in weeks. And after all they had been through, she still tugged at his heart.

He saw her mouth moving and assumed she was talking to their son. After a while, both Kiara and Myles emerged from the car. Wearing white gym shoes, the little boy ran behind the car then raced ahead of her. He fled into the street instead of staying on the sidewalk. Soon he tugged at his father's locked door handle and yelled.

"Hurry up, Daddy. I'm famished."

Rashad laughed and popped the locks. He got out of the car and scooped Myles off his feet and hugged him tight.

"Really Myles? You're famished? Where'd you learn that word?"

"The Food Network."

Rashad chuckled as he set him back down.

"Oh, so I don't get a 'hey, Daddy how you doing? I miss you. I love you, man'?"

"Hey, Daddy, I missed you. Can we go to Steak and Shake for dinner?"

"Myles," Kiara interrupted as she hurriedly approached them wearing a short, purple long-sleeve dress and four-inch wedge heel sandals. "I told you about running in the street. Are you crazy? Do you wanna get hit by a car? It's raining and that makes it harder for drivers to slow down in this weather."

Kiara eased up next to Myles. She thumped him on his forehead.

"Ouch, Mommy."

"Don't do that," Rashad scolded. "My little man misses me, that's all. It's been a minute."

"Whatever, Rashad," she spat at him. "None of that matters. He knows better than to do something reckless like running in the street. He doesn't listen."

"I do listen, Mommy." Myles mostly ignored his mother as he happily gave his father a few daps. The little boy always seemed calm and sure of himself when he was in Rashad's presence.

"You're a chip off the old block, son," his father said. He knew the danger of Myles not looking where he was going but Rashad didn't notice any cars coming down the street. He could tell how much his boy deeply missed him and that made him feel good.

"Damn, I've been dying to hang out with my little man. Has he gotten taller? What the hell you been feeding him?"

"That's a stupid question and you know how I feel about those."

"I was just joking, Kiara. Lighten up."

"Ain't got time for jokes."

Suddenly the air grew tense. Rashad felt himself getting agitated.

"Look, this is the holiday season. People are supposed to be merry. But you act like you on something. You been drinking? Can't you ever be happy and just chill?"

"Lord Jesus. More stupid ass questions. Don't start."

Kiara gave Rashad a sober look as she handed him Myles's backpack.

"Lucky for you, Mama Flora is away from her house right now. At the last second, she had something to take care of and she had to leave. So we both have to be mature enough to handle this without her."

"That's cool. I got no problem with that."

"Anyway, all his things are in there: two pair of pants, some shirts, underwear, pajamas, favorite electric toothbrush, all that."

"Hmm, seeing this makes me realize I gotta stock up on some stuff for him to keep at . . ."

He wanted to say he had to buy clothes for Myles to keep at his other place, a home he started sharing with his pregnant lover, Nicole Greene. Weeks ago, when his wife forced him to leave the house because she got sick of Rashad's lies, Nicole instantly suggested that he come stay with her. On that short of a notice, he had nowhere else to go. So he took her up on her offer. And now he was adjusting to his 'new normal.'

Rashad mentally switched gears as he gazed at Myles.

"Damn shame we couldn't eat turkey and dressing together, and watch the Lions and Cowboys game. That's what I did with my dad every Thanksgiving when he was still alive. I was *always* with my daddy on that holiday. Sitting up in that cold ass living room. Eating good food and talking smack. I wish we could have done that, Myles."

Rashad stared at his son but he was talking to Kiara.

"Um," she responded. "We had the whole day already planned so he wouldn't have had a chance to come by anyway. We went to the parade downtown. We ate a wonderful dinner. And then we drove down to see the Festival of Lights at Moody Gardens. Myles ended up having a *real* good time with us, didn't you?"

"Uh huh," he said.

"Cool," was Rashad's clipped response. "I'm glad for you."

He acted like he was unbothered. But Rashad hated that Kiara stopped him from spending time with his child two holidays in a row. *She* got to pick his costume and take Myles trick or treating. And *she* got to eat turkey with him too. What gave her the right? Just because she made him leave the house, does that mean she could enforce all her own rules as well?

Rashad fought to hide his anger as he leered at Kiara on the sly. She was holding one of those huge pink and black golf umbrellas in her hand. Even on a dreary looking afternoon, somehow this woman managed to appear elegant and beautiful. Her eyes were full of spunk and passion. It seemed she didn't have a care in the world.

And he hated it.

But at the same time, Rashad was strangely tempted to grab his wife in his arms, slap her one good time, kiss her, and tell her that they were both acting silly. He wished they could get their emotions in check, work things out, save the marriage. He really didn't want to file on her, but she was acting unreasonable. He wished she could get some sense into her stubborn head. Maybe she'd listen and let him come back home where he felt he belonged. But that scenario was a hopeless fairy tale. He knew Kiara was still pissed and he didn't want to risk getting swung at in public.

"All righty then," Rashad spoke up, anxious to leave. "Since I have less time than I originally thought, we need to make that move right now. I will have little man back here on Sunday night around eight."

"Eight?"

"Okay, then. Seven."

"Sunday *afternoon*, Rashad. I need him here by two so I can make sure he has time to take his bath, complete his homework, and eat dinner. Plus, if we decide to go check out that new Madagascar movie he's begged us to see, we will probably want him around noon."

We.

Rashad knew his wife was referring to her new man when she said "We."

"Back by *noon*? That means I won't even get to spend, hell, even a full twenty-four hours with him—"

"Sorry, but that's just how it is."

"You're not sorry, Kiara. You're selfish. I haven't seen my son in God knows how long. I have a right to be with the boy just like you do. And I will bring Myles back when I'm done with him."

"Wait one second here. I find it so strange that all of a sudden you are so desperate to spend time with him. You should have thought about how important he was back when you were sacrificing time with your son to go lie up and bump your nuts on that whore."

"W-what did you say?"

"You heard exactly what I said. If you hadn't done what you did, we wouldn't be out here on these streets doing this; exchanging a child like he's a drug or a piece of currency. Do you know how mad this makes me? I did everything and I mean *ev-e-ry*-thing I could to make you happy, but no, no, no. Nothing I did was good enough. You had to go get yourself a damned side piece. Her pussy must taste like Skittles."

"Kiara, you best better shut your mouth."

"So it's true? Her coochie taste like Gucci?"

"I'm warning you."

She was ready to attack him with more angry words, but she grew alarmed when she noticed a frozen smile gripping her son's face. He resembled a mannequin; he looked like he was scared something bad would happen if he moved an inch.

Kiara realized she'd gone too far. But she usually did when it came to Rashad. She hated that his whorish ways had destroyed their perfect family life. She hated that not only had he knocked up that heifer Nicole Greene, but he'd also been hiding a two-year-old daughter that he had with another woman who worked for her: Alexis McNeil, her own administrative assistant. Her hubby hiding baby mamas and side chicks that worked in her office was too much. Rashad made her look like a fool. The more Kiara thought about it, the crazier she felt in the head.

She reached and grabbed Myles's hand as if to snatch him back toward her car.

"What are you doing?" Rashad asked.

"Let me be clear. I don't know if we're ready for this informal custody sharing thing. I know it's the decent thing to do, but hell, I'm not feeling 'decent' right now. I think we need to take baby steps. So if you can't bring him back by noon, then he's going home with me right now. I'll let you have him in two weeks. For a full weekend. Promise."

"See, this is bullshit. I was supposed to get him last weekend, remember? You broke that so-called promise. Why you always got to be in control?"

They were still standing in the street next to Rashad's idling sedan.

"Why you always try to run shit like I'm your child? Or your employee. Huh? I'm a grown ass man." He stepped closer to her. "Who the hell put you in charge of me?"

Kiara snatched Myles's bony little arm and pulled so violently that he screamed, "Ouch! That hurts."

"Your crazy ass better let go of my son." Rashad grabbed Myles's other arm.

"Shut up! I don't like how you're talking to me."

"I don't like the fact that you fucked another nigga; now you pregnant. I guess we should go on the Maury show to find out who the real father is."

"What the hell? That's it. Forget this. Come on, Myles." She yanked him again.

"Mama, I want to stay with my daddy. I want my daddy." Myles inched closer to Rashad.

"I don't care what you want. He doesn't deserve you. We're leaving. Come on."

Raindrops poured from above as if the sky was crying. Kiara tried to hold her umbrella in one hand and drag away Myles with the other.

But the boy wrestled with her, pulling back from her, and tried to free himself.

"My arm. It hurts. It *hurts*. I don't like this. Let me gooo."

Kiara wouldn't release Myles, but Rashad did.

He'd been taught that real men don't cry. But right then, he was filled with uncontrollable rage and a lingering frustration that made his throat swell with pain. It wasn't fair that since Kiara banned him from their house he hadn't played with his son, hadn't looked him in his eyes, or helped him with his homework. He missed fixing Myles's breakfast and shooting hoops with him in their backyard. Little things meant a lot. And Rashad resented the legal system which granted numerous women so much power when it came to a man, his money, and his children.

He stared at his wife, almost in disbelief that feelings of pure hatred were boiling up in him and making him flush with so much anger that he started sweating.

"Mommy, I want to be with my daddy. Let me go."

"Stop all that yelling, Myles. I want you to come back home with me."

Several cars slowly drove past them, which infuriated Rashad. "Look at this shit. You got people staring at you like you're crazy."

"The hell with them. I'm not crazy. I'm just doing what I have to do to protect my son."

"He's my son, too, Kiara. I don't know why you seem to have forgotten that." If his wife wasn't pregnant there was no telling what Rashad would have done to her. He didn't want to fight, but her unpredictable reactions drove him to respond in ways that he hated.

"All I know is, it's damn near Christmas," he continued in a choked voice. "I wanted to take Myles shopping this weekend. I-I-I have all *kinds* of plans for him, don't you understand that?"

"I don't give a damn about your stupid plans," she retorted. "You better learn how to speak to me like you have some sense. You can't just say anything in front of a child."

Rashad felt like his wife was a hypocrite. She

clearly saw his sins but was blind to her own. But he counted to ten and calmly told her, "Kiara, I apologize if it seems like I was disrespecting you. But can we let go of this argument? Please. And let me give Myles the chance he deserves to hang out with his father . . . his *real* father."

"Oh hell no. I know you're not trying to throw shade at Eddison who's been nothing but remarkable to us. Plus, that boy's not stupid. He knows who his daddy is."

"Mommy, you're hurting me. Please let me gooo."

Kiara then realized she had Myles in a death grip. She felt his fragile bones between her fingers. She heard the hurt in his voice. She released him.

"Oh God. I'm sorry baby. I-I . . . please forgive me."

With tears in his eyes, he nodded and leaned on his father's stomach.

"Kiara," Rashad said in a gentle tone. "So you're going to let him be with me till Sunday night?"

She hesitated and reached in her purse. "Fine. I'll let him go with you since we went through all this trouble in the first place. We can negotiate a fair time for his drop off. But I want you to know that I bought him his own cell phone today. Whenever he's away from me, he must keep it on him at all times. And we taught him how to use it. In case of an emergency."

"You really don't trust me, do you?"

"No, I do not. But that's beside the point. I just want Myles to be okay. I just want him to be happy." Kiara's voice caught in her throat as she wiped tears from her eyes.

She kissed Myles's little cheeks and allowed a brave smile to brighten her face. "Bye baby. I love you."

"Love you, too, Mommy. Come on, Daddy. My stomach is growling. Can't you hear it?"

"That's a damned shame. We'll go eat right now, son."

Kiara swiftly turned around to leave. The street was slippery and wet. In her rush to get away, her feet got tangled together. The wedge heels were narrow and clumsy. Her right ankle twisted and gave in underneath her. Her umbrella plunked to the ground. She slipped on a pothole, and fell forward, but landed on her thigh. Her hand scraped the rugged, scraggly surface as she braced herself from injury.

"Ugh, ouch. Dammit."

She lay on her side feeling totally embarrassed and wincing. Rashad wanted to ask if she was all right, but he simply stared at her.

Rain water sprayed her hair and cheeks. Her hair became a matted mess.

"I can't believe this. Rashad! Can you help me up or are you just gonna stand there?"

He gaped at Kiara and wondered if she just got what she deserved.

She'd made life so difficult for him recently. Rashad knew she was now seeing that man from her job, Eddison Osborne, and Nicole told him that they'd had an affair.

Rashad could clearly see Kiara's tiny baby bump. He wondered if the baby was his, even though she'd told him that it was.

"Rashad, did you hear me? I need your help."

"Why should I?"

"Huh? I can't believe you said that!"

He had the eyes of a reptile; cold, curious, and calculating.

"I don't know whose baby you got inside of you."

"Rashad, oh my God. How can you go there?"

"Because *you* went there—with that other nigga!"

"Now is not the time. Help me up, please."

He stared down at her belly. And so did Myles.

Kiara felt completely humiliated. She never wanted their son to see her like this.

"Rashad, show your son how to treat a woman. *Show* your *son* how to *treat* a *woman*!"

Rashad looked skeptical and unmoving.

"Myles baby, please."

Myles raced to his mother and immediately grabbed her outstretched hand. His tongue stuck out of his mouth as he struggled to help Kiara. Rashad suddenly rushed to the other side of her and held out his hand too.

Wincing in pain, she got on her knees, and leaned on Rashad as he hoisted her to her feet.

"Thank you, baby." She ignored Rashad. "You are my precious son. You must always remember to be a gentleman, and help your mother. And always be good to a lady. Promise me."

"I promise, Mommy."

"Ha!" Rashad muttered.

"All right, okay. I can do this," she said to herself. "I can make it to the car."

"Bye-bye, Mommy. Don't forget to pick me up on Sunday."

"I can never forget anything that has to do with you."

She watched Myles excitedly race around to the other side of Rashad's sedan. He went and opened the passenger door for his son. Kiara waited until Myles was safely inside the car. She rubbed her hip and hobbled over to Rashad.

"You didn't act concerned about our unborn baby for one second."

"I don't know whose baby that is." He paused. "How many times did you fuck that dude?"

"How many times did you fuck both your baby mamas?"

"Oh, so you hooked up with him just to get revenge? Was his dick bigger than mine? I don't care how big it was, no man could ever love you like me!"

"Oh my God! Just be quiet with all that. I can't believe I used to love your pathetic ass. And you best believe that part of my life is gone. I'm moving on. And you're acting like a dick and trying to shame me in front of Myles is unforgivable. You'll never get this pussy again."

She turned away again, this time moving more slowly than the first time. Then she quietly limped away. Hair soaking wet, but head held high.

After Kiara slid into the vehicle, she slammed her door, revved the engine, and waved her middle finger at Rashad as she drove past him.

Eason v. Eason had officially started.